THE BELIEF OF CHRISTENDOM

D1150765

THE BELIEF OF CHRISTENDOM

A Commentary on the Nicene Creed

By

JOHN BURNABY

Fellow of Trinity College, Cambridge,
and Regius Professor Emeritus of Divinity

LONDON
NATIONAL SOCIETY
S·P·C·K

First published in 1959
Fifth impression (first paperback edition) 1974
Sixth Impression 1975
National Society and S.P.C.K.
Holy Trinity Church,
*Marylebone Road, London, NW*1 4*DU*

Printed in Great Britain by
Hollen Street Press Ltd at Slough

ISBN 0 281 02825 7

Contents

The Nicene Creed

I BELIEVE in one God the Father Almighty, Maker of heaven and earth, And of all things visible and invisible:

And in one Lord Jesus Christ, the only-begotten Son of God, Begotten of his Father before all worlds, God of God, Light of Light, Very God of very God, Begotten, not made, Being of one substance with the Father, By whom all things were made: Who for us men and for our salvation came down from heaven, And was incarnate by the Holy Ghost of the Virgin Mary, And was made man, And was crucified also for us under Pontius Pilate. He suffered and was buried, And the third day he rose again according to the Scriptures, And ascended into heaven, And sitteth on the right hand of the Father. And he shall come again with glory to judge both the quick and the dead: Whose kingdom shall have no end.

And I believe in the Holy Ghost, The Lord and giver of life, Who proceedeth from the Father and the Son, Who with the Father and the Son together is worshipped and glorified, Who spake by the Prophets. And I believe one Catholick and Apostolick Church. I acknowledge one Baptism for the remission of sins. And I look for the Resurrection of the dead, And the Life of the world to come. Amen.

Preface

THE course of lectures of which this book is composed was given for the Cambridge Divinity Faculty in the years 1956–7 and 1957–8. It was attended chiefly by Theological College students, for whom it was possible to assume at least an elementary knowledge of the Bible and the history of the Church. When, in the latter year, I was asked by the National Society to provide a book on the Creed suitable for school-teachers, I found myself unable to undertake more than a revision of the lectures which I had written —a revision which would so far as possible avoid technicalities, but would leave the general character of the treatment unaltered. How far the resulting commentary on the Creed can claim to be "popular", or to tell the ordinary reader the kind of thing he wants to know, I am unable to say: no doubt some parts of it are less "popular" than others. But I have tried to deal fairly with some of the chief difficulties which the ancient formulations of Christian dogma must raise for thinking people today. It seemed desirable to supplement the exposition of the Creed itself, clause by clause, by inserting here and there a consideration of some important points of doctrine to which the Creed does not explicitly refer.

I hope that I have made no bad mistakes in the field of history and scholarship: I should certainly not have avoided them but for the reliable guidance of Dr J. N. D. Kelly's *Early Christian Creeds*. It was a phrase of Dr Kelly's about the Nicene Creed—"one of the few threads by which the tattered fragments of the divided robe of Christendom are held together"—that suggested the title for my book.

I have to thank Messrs Duckworth for permission to use some material from my little book *Is the Bible inspired?* and Messrs Mowbray for permission to include part of a sermon published in *Good Friday at St Margaret's*. Other acknowledgements are made where they are called for in the notes.

Cambridge, October 1958.

INTRODUCTION

Origin and Use of the Creed

1. *Beginnings in the New Testament*

IN the tenth chapter of the Epistle to the Romans, St Paul is setting his Gospel of justification by faith against the Jewish principle that salvation is to be earned by doing what the Law commands. Christ, he says, is the end of the Law, so that righteousness may come to everyone that *believes*. The Apostle boldly appropriates to his purpose the passage of Deuteronomy[1] in which Israel is assured of the high privilege of knowing the Law of God; and he quotes: "The word is very nigh thee, in thy mouth and in thy heart." Deuteronomy continues: "that thou mayest do it". But it does not suit St Paul to finish his quotation; he simply comments upon "word", "mouth", and "heart". This word of which Moses spoke, "this is the word of the faith (the belief) which we preach: that if thou dost confess with thy mouth Jesus as Lord, and believest in thy heart that God raised him from the dead, thou shalt be saved".[2]

Here in shortest possible summary is the Christian Gospel according to St Paul. We must remember that it takes for granted, in those to whom it was addressed, the faith of the Old Testament. The preaching of the Apostles is the announcement to Israel that Jesus of Nazareth is the Messiah foretold by the prophets; and the claim is supported by the Apostolic witness to the fact of the resurrection of Jesus from the dead. Acceptance of the claim is the necessary condition of membership in the Christian Church, the community which is the heir of the promises made to Israel. So, for the convert from Judaism, the confession that Jesus is the Messiah is made, explicitly or implicitly, by his acceptance of baptism "in the name of Jesus".

This confession is the basis of the Christian Creed. It is probable enough that in the life of the early Church baptism was not the only occasion when a summary statement of faith was needed and used; and it may be possible to trace the influence of other occasions, such as common worship, exorcism, or confession under persecution, upon credal forms.[3] But we are justified in seeing the primary purpose of the Creed in the confession of faith which the candidate for baptism was required to make. In St Paul's Epistles the characteristic form is not "Jesus is the Messiah (the Christ)", but "Jesus is Lord"—a change of title which may be in part an adaptation to the understanding of Gentile converts: the Gentile Colossians, we read, "have received the Christ Jesus as the Lord".[4] But we cannot be sure that "Lord" is simply a translation of "Messiah" into the language of the non-Jewish world; for we find in the Acts St Peter in his Jerusalem sermon appealing to the Psalm-text "the Lord said unto my Lord", and concluding that Jesus is "both Lord and Christ", and again in the house of Cornelius (no stranger to the Jewish faith) telling "the good news of peace through Jesus Christ: he is Lord of all".[5]

Within the New Testament we can trace the extension of this primitive confession in two ways:

a. by an explicit statement of the facts about the Jesus who is Lord and Christ—that he died and rose again from the grave, as in St Paul's account in 1 Cor. 15 of the Gospel which he had preached; and by giving to these facts a more or less developed theological interpretation. Thus in the opening verses of the Epistle to the Romans, "the Gospel of God, promised aforetime through his prophets in the holy scriptures, concerns his son, who was born of the seed of David according to the flesh, and designated son of God in power according to the spirit of holiness by the resurrection from the dead, Jesus Christ our *Lord*".[6] Or again, more fully in Phil. 2: "Christ Jesus, who being in the form of God did not regard it as a prize to be on an equality with God, but emptied himself by taking the form of a slave, being made in the likeness of men; and being found in fashion as a man, he humbled himself, becoming obedient unto death, even the death of the cross. Wherefore also God hath highly exalted him, and given him the name which is above every name, that at the name of Jesus every knee shall bow . . . and every tongue shall confess that Jesus Christ is *Lord*."[7]

b. by an explicit statement of Jewish monotheism, the faith in the one God as the God who has raised his Son from the dead. This second development would naturally be made as the number of converts from heathenism increased, and especially after the Christian missionaries turned from the Synagogue, with its "God-fearing" fringe, to the purely pagan world; for that world needed more than a belief in or about Jesus. So when St Paul is warning against paganism in 1 Cor. 8, he will summarize Christian belief as in "one God the Father and one Lord Jesus Christ"; and his commonest epistolary greeting is "from God the Father and the Lord Jesus Christ".[8]

It is more difficult to find in the New Testament instances in which this summary is completed by the addition of belief in the Holy Spirit given to the Church. There are passages in the Epistles which indicate a trend toward Trinitarian conceptions. Beside the familiar "grace" in the last verse of 2 Cor., we can point to 1 Cor. 12.4ff., where the differing kinds of gifts, ministries, and workings of power in the Church are severally ascribed to the same Spirit, the same Lord, and the same God; and to the address of 1 Pet., made to those who are "elect according to the foreknow-ledge of God the Father, through sanctification of the Spirit, unto obedience and sprinkling of the blood of Jesus Christ". But none of these texts give, quite as clearly as those previously referred to, the appearance of formal confessions of faith. According to Matt. 28.19, the risen Christ charged his disciples to baptize all nations "in the name of the Father, and of the Son, and of the Holy Spirit". In Acts, baptism is always "in the name of Jesus", and St Paul's references seem to confirm the evidence of Acts in this respect.[9] This raises a doubt whether a charge to baptize in the Threefold Name can actually have been given before the Apostolic preaching began. But in any case we must see in the text of Matthew a crystallization of that Trinitarian faith, the elements at least of which are present elsewhere in the New Testament, and its intimate connection with the baptismal profession.

2. Creed and Catechism

In process of time the confession of the Threefold Name is further expanded. God the Father is named as the Almighty Creator; the place of Jesus in the Gospel of salvation is specified by the Christo-logical story of the birth, death, resurrection, and ascension; and in the third article the Church and its sacrament of initiation are included as the sphere of the Spirit's operation, the whole being completed by the profession of the Christian hope of everlasting life.

By the end of the second century, we find Christian writers making fairly frequent reference to a summary of this kind as the Church's "Rule". The earliest evidence for forms of baptismal liturgy, which may go back to this period, shows that the candidate for baptism is required to answer a series of questions, framed on the same pattern, with the word *Credo*, "I believe".[10] He must therefore have previously received such instruction as would enable him to know and understand the propositions to which at his baptism he would be called to assent—or (if we prefer so to put it) the unseen realities in which he would have to affirm his faith. It is not until much later that we have detailed accounts of this catechetical instruction, but it must have formed part of the preparation for baptism from very early times. In the fourth century, we know that it took the form of a systematic course of teaching on the Creed by the Bishop, who "delivered the faith" to his catechumens—as St Paul had done to the Corinthians in the fifties of the first century. The Creed itself was now called the *Symbolum*, a word which means "token" or "countersign": the possession and use of the Creed was the badge of membership of the Christian society. So the preparation for baptism led up to the ceremonies known as the Delivery and the Return of the Symbol, in which the Creed was solemnly presented by the Bishop to the candidates, and as solemnly repeated by them in his presence on the eve of their baptism.

3. *Credal Forms*

In the days before the establishment of Christianity by Constantine as the religion of the Empire, the local Churches, if not entirely isolated from one another, had to grow and live in a large measure of mutual independence. Naturally the form of the "Rule" and of the baptismal interrogations based upon it would vary. Even in one and the same Church there was for long no stress upon verbal fixity of formula, though in third-century Africa it was possible for a schismatic to claim that he baptized "with the same Symbol" as the Catholic[11]—which seems to imply at least a close similarity in the form of the baptismal questions and answers. But what is much more striking than the verbal variations is the substantial identity of the summary of belief, as it appears in the representatives of different and widely separated Churches in the second and third centuries—an identity of substance which enabled the defender of Catholic Christianity against heresy to appeal to the existence of a common Catholic "Rule" of faith.[12]

This anti-heretical motive might be expected to have influenced the development of credal forms from the first; for the Church had to face heresy (i.e. false teaching which claimed to be Christian) from New Testament times onwards. In the Epistle of St John, the confession that "Jesus Christ is come in the flesh"[13] is directed against those who because they held the flesh to be evil would not believe that Christ's human body was real; and similarly Ignatius, Bishop of Antioch at the beginning of the second century, finds it necessary in his attack on the same "Docetic" error to make repeated insertion of the word "truly" in his statement of faith about Christ's birth, death, and resurrection.[14] The surprising thing is that there is so little conclusive evidence in later times of this influence upon the formation of baptismal Creeds—until the day came when heresy became a concern of Emperors.

The primary purpose of the Creed was that those who entered the Christian Church should know what that Church stood for, and to what basic affirmations the member of the Church is committed. In the fourth century, however, the struggle with Arianism, by which the true Godhead of Christ was denied, led to the use of credal statements for the quite different purpose of controversy within the Church.

Hitherto there had been no universally fixed and acknowledged form of baptismal confession; and this fact made it possible for those who resisted or resented the measures taken against Arianism by the Council of Nicaea in the year 325 to assert the legitimacy of their position by the framing of successive statements of faith which took the form of a baptismal Creed and used much of the traditional credal language. These so-called "Creeds" of the fourth century were nothing more than instruments of controversy, called out by the imposition of the Nicene formula. But Nicaea itself had led the way. Instead of making a declaration in suitable terms that on this particular point of Christian belief the Arians were in error, the Council under imperial prompting had produced a "Creed" which purported to define the faith of the Church. This "Creed" ran as follows:

"We believe in one God, Father Almighty, Maker of all things visible and invisible;

And in one Lord Jesus Christ, the Son of God, begotten from the Father, Only-begotten, that is, from the substance of the Father, God from God, Light from Light, true God from true God, begotten not made, of one substance with the Father, through whom all things came into being, both things in heaven and things in the earth, who for the sake of us men and for the sake of our salvation

came down and was enfleshed, became man, suffered and rose again on the third day, ascended to the heavens, and is to come to judge the living and the dead;
And in the Holy Spirit."

We notice at once that in this formula the third article breaks off short without mention of much that regularly formed part of it in earlier summaries of the faith. It was clearly not adapted or intended to take the place of the ancient baptismal Creeds; and at first it retained its special character as a standard of orthodoxy for Bishops, who alone were required to give formal adherence to it. But as the "faith of Nicaea" it acquired a unique prestige, and no later formulary was ever held to supersede it. Nevertheless it was in fact supplemented and for practical purposes replaced by the so-called Creed of Constantinople, which is what we know as the "Nicene" Creed.[15] The origins of this formula and its connection with the Council of Constantinople in 381 are obscure. But it was accepted by the Council of Chalcedon in 451 as a fuller statement of the "faith of Nicaea"—which it does in effect maintain, while at the same time expanding the third article with the double purpose of safe-guarding the doctrine of the Holy Spirit and of assimilating the older statement to the typical baptismal Creed. In the East, after the Council of Chalcedon, it actually supplanted all local Creeds, and was introduced into the Eucharistic liturgy. The Western Church, however, retained the old Roman Creed (enlarged in time into our Apostles' Creed) for its original purpose as a baptismal confession; and centuries passed before the "Nicene" Creed everywhere found its place, in the West as in the East, in the central act of Christian worship.

4. Uses of the Creed

We have seen that originally and essentially the Christian Creed is the "form of sound words" in which the candidate for admission to the Church affirms his acceptance of the Christian faith—that faith by which the Church lives and which the Church exists to "deliver", to spread throughout the world and to hand on from one generation to another. This form of words provides (so to say) the syllabus of Christian *doctrine*, which expounds the faith so that its meaning and bearings can be understood. Different ways of expounding the faith will naturally and properly be used by different expositors. But if such liberty is exercised without due carefulness to preserve its integrity and balance, differences may lead to the dissemination by individual teachers of opinions which are found by the Church to endanger that integrity in one way or another; and such opinions when persisted in after their condemnation by the Church become "heresies". The menace of heresy compelled the Church in its first period of rapid expansion to formulate its doctrine with greater precision. It was no accident that the teaching which provoked the most violent reaction was one that touched the very heart of the faith—the place and person of Jesus Christ—and that the warding-off of this mortal danger left an indelible mark upon the Christian Creed itself. But the framing and use of Creeds to exclude heresy begins and ends with the fourth century. Thereafter, the Creed which had been designed and employed as a test of orthodoxy took its place in Christian worship as the collective confession by the Church of the Catholic faith. It became once more the Christian "symbol", the perpetual reminder, alike to the Church's members and to the world outside, of that for which and by which the Church stands and believes itself to have stood from the beginning.

At the same time, the Creed remains the programme and standard for all instruction in the faith. In the Church of the first days, as the New Testament makes us acquainted with it, we can distinguish (a) a definite and fairly uniform pattern of Apostolic *preaching*, traceable in the sermons recorded in the early chapters of the Acts, from (b) the detailed *teaching* given to converts, of which the greater part of the New Testament supplies examples.[16] "Teachers", we know, performed a distinct function in the service of the Church— a function which St Paul ranks after those of the Apostles and the Prophets;[17] but evidently there is much that we may properly count as "teaching" in his own Epistles. And the content of this teaching must have varied, not only with the particular interests and gifts of the individual expositor, but with the changing occasions and needs of the Church which he served. Paul and Apollos, Peter and "John", each had his own way of teaching; and the differences in setting forth all that Jesus himself began to do and to teach are not only differences between the first three Evangelists and the fourth. Similarly, in the world-wide Church both before and after Constantine, the instruction given to catechumens, while adhering to the outline of the baptismal Creed, will have varied, within limits not at all narrow, according to the theological and practical disposition of the catechizing Bishop. The general edification of the faithful by way of the Church sermon would of course be more varied still, since the Bible provided the preacher with an unlimited choice of texts upon which he could embroider very much as he liked. But even this embroidery would tend to follow that "pattern of teaching"[18] which had formed itself upon the Creed.

5. *Creed and Scripture*

The early Church regarded its Creed as a summary of the Biblical witness to the revelation of God. The terms and most of the phrases of the Creed were drawn from Scripture; and before the Council of Nicaea no one felt any necessity to defend the Scriptural character of the Creed. At Nicaea, the strongest objection to the introduction of the test-word proposed as necessary for the exclusion of Arian doctrine was that it was not Biblical but philosophical. After Nicaea, the defenders of the term *Homo-ousios* ("of one substance") had to argue as best they could that the meaning if not the letter of this test-word was to be found in Scripture; and those who drew up the Articles of Religion for the reformed Church of England in 1562 did not hesitate to assert that the Nicene no less than the Apostles' Creed "may be proved by most certain warrants of Holy Scripture".[19] For orthodox and heretic alike, the authority of Scripture was no more and no less absolute in the sixteenth century than it had been in the fourth. But the appeal to Scripture could settle controversy in the age of the Reformers as little as it had been able to do so in the age of the Fathers; for each side supported itself by the arbitrary selection of texts interpreted in accordance with its own doctrine.

Nevertheless, Scripture must remain the only available "control" for the exposition of the Christian Creed. It would be foolish at this time of day to suppose that the Christian faith can be interpreted without reference to its roots in the religion of Israel and the events which took place in Palestine in the first century A.D.—or that the ancient Creeds can properly be used as framework for a Gospel different from that which was preached by Christ and his Apostles. On the other hand, we can no longer use Scripture as the Fathers did, by appeal to an array of selected texts. We have to rely on our understanding of the Biblical message as a whole, and that understanding will not be static, "once-for-all", but progressive. Of any particular doctrine by which the Creed is expounded, we have always to ask whether it accords with what we apprehend as the central message of the Bible.

About that, we might claim a fair measure of agreement among Christian teachers at the present time to the following propositions:

(1) The Creator of the world is the living God who rules and is always active in the world he has made.

(2) God has made himself known in history by his dealing with a chosen people, as the God of righteousness and mercy—"a just God and a Saviour".

(3) Sinful men cannot satisfy the demands of God's righteousness, or save themselves from themselves.

(4) In the Cross and Resurrection of Christ, God has taken action to save mankind by delivering them from the power of sin.

(5) Salvation is realized in acceptance of the Saviour, who gives himself through his Spirit to the community of believers to be the transforming power of their life and the fulfilment of God's purpose for the world.

Our commentary on the Creed will therefore be in large measure a Scriptural commentary. But we shall use the text of Scripture not so much to "prove" the statements of the Creed as to draw out and illuminate the faith in God's revelation of himself of which Scripture is the record, and which the Creed is designed to affirm.

REFERENCES

1. Deut. 30.11ff.
2. Rom. 10.8f.
3. See O. Cullmann, *Early Christian Confessions*.
4. Col. 2.6.
5. Acts 2.34,36; 10.36; See further pp. 67f.
6. Rom. 1.1-4.
7. Phil. 2.6ff.
8. 1 Cor. 8.6; Rom. 1.7, etc.
9. Acts 2.38; 8.16; 10.48; 19.5; cf. Rom. 6.3; Gal. 3.27; 1 Cor. 1.13.
10. See J. N. D. Kelly, *Early Christian Creeds*, p. 46.
11. Cyprian, Ep. lxix. 7.
12. E.g. Irenaeus, *Adversus Haereses*, I.10f.
13. 1 John 4.2f.
14. Ignatius, *Ep. Ad Smyrnaeos*, 1f.; *Ad Trallianos*, 9.
15. See further pp. 70ff.
16. See C. H. Dodd, *The Apostolic Preaching and its Developments*.
17. 1 Cor. 12.28.
18. The phrase is St Paul's in Rom. 6.17.
19. Article VIII.

CHAPTER 1

I Believe

CREEDS are so called because they begin with the word *Credo*—
"I believe"; and the substance of the Creed is called "The
Faith". In what sense do we use these words? Let us first see how
they are used in the New Testament.

1. *New Testament Usage*

The Greek words translated "faith" and "believe" in our versions
(*pistis* and *pisteuein*) have the same root. In the Septuagint (the
Greek version of the Old Testament), the verb *pisteuein* translates
a Hebrew word which means to be assured, to have a sure trust.
So it was that Abraham "believed" God, trusted surely in God's
promise; and Isaiah tells Ahaz (with a play on the words) that
sureness of belief is the only surety: "if ye will not believe, ye shall
not be established".[1] Hebrew has no noun with the active sense of
belief or trust: the word translated "faith" in Hab. 2.4 means trust-
worthiness or steadfastness, and is commonly used of the "faithfulness" of God, his "truth" to himself. To believe God is to put trust
in his promises to Israel, his faithfulness to the Covenant.

In the New Testament, the characteristic sense of *pisteuein*
appears in St Mark's summary of the first preaching of Jesus. "The
time is fulfilled, and the kingdom of God is at hand: repent ye,
and believe in the Gospel."[2] The Gospel is the proclamation that
God in the coming of his Christ has fulfilled his promises, and men
are called to accept this good news of God with responding confidence and trust—to believe as Abraham believed. The faith for
which Jesus calls in those who are aware of their need of salvation
—for body and soul—is indeed more than the trust in God which
marks the devout Jew as such; yet it is not exactly (as is sometimes
said) a "personal relationship to Jesus himself": it is rather a recognition of the power of God present and working in him.

In the Acts and Epistles, to "believe" can stand both for the decision of a moment and for a lasting disposition—in scholastic terms,

both for an "act" and for a "habit". It can describe either (a) the initial response to the Apostolic preaching, the "turning to the Lord" which is conversion, or (b) the new relationship to God and Christ resulting from this acceptance of the Gospel.[3] Correspondingly the object of belief will be either (a) the Gospel itself, as in the text quoted from St Mark, or (b) God present in Christ to save. Thus the faith which is the mainspring of the Christian life is the faith of the forgiven sinner, the faith which "justifies" *because* it makes no claim but receives all as God's gracious gift; but this faith can only come from hearing and answering the call of the Word that is preached.[4] St Paul calls this act of believing acceptance "obedience to the Gospel": his apostleship is a commission to win the "obedience of faith among all the nations". God is glorified by men's "subjection in consent" to the Gospel of Christ.[5] This is because the Gospel message is itself a call, a summons to the acts of repentance and belief.[6]

The modern distinction between "believing in" as "personal self-committal", and "believing" or "believing that" as the act of mental assent to a credible proposition, is not to be found in the New Testament. "Believe in the Gospel" in Mark 1.15 is the literal translation of an unusual construction in the Greek, but it does not mean anything different from "believe the good news". Generally in the New Testament "believe in" translates a Greek phrase which means literally "believe into"—a construction which is not used either in classical Greek or in the language of the Septuagint. Its use in the New Testament is peculiarly Johannine: it occurs nearly forty times in the Gospel and Epistles of St John, and less than ten in the rest of the New Testament. Yet in the Fourth Gospel itself to "believe in" Christ is the same thing as to "believe that" he is sent by the Father.[7] To believe in or on Christ means to make the response of acceptance to Christ as the Word, the spokesman of God.

Such belief "in" Christ, which is at the same time obedience to the call of God, must be testified by the difference it makes to the whole life of the believer. In the Epistle of St James faith without works is the faith of demons, and is "dead".[8] The expression "living faith" does not occur in the New Testament, but it is what St Paul means by "faith working through love";[9] and in the eleventh chapter of the Epistle to the Hebrews faith is exhibited as the supreme power of action. Yet it is plain that there can be no "belief in" without "belief that". "Believe ye that I am able to do this?" Jesus asks the blind men.[10] "He that cometh to God must believe that he is."[11] There are of course "beliefs that" which can have little or no effect upon our actions—such as the belief that sailormen used to wear pigtails or that the planet Jupiter has eleven moons. But when a belief is of such a nature that it *ought* to affect our actions, and yet does not do so, others may reasonably infer that the belief is not vital, living. A living faith may sometimes fail to work, but not always.

2. *Faith in Catholic and Protestant doctrine*

a. The Catholic understanding of faith goes back to St Augustine, by whom the distinction between "believing" and "believing in" was clearly drawn. To believe *in* Christ, he says, is "in believing to love him, in believing to enter into him and become incorporate in his members": to believe *in* God is "in believing to cleave unto him, in order to work for good together with him who is the worker of all good".[12] Such "belief in" is a union of will and activity with the personal object of belief. But when Augustine comes to define formally what in any context it means to "believe", his definition is "to think affirmatively" (*cum assensione cogitare*).[13] So in traditional Catholic theology faith is treated as consisting primarily in assent. It is a *mental* act, but one which is not compelled—as we are compelled to assent to what cannot be disputed—but voluntary, an act of will. St Thomas Aquinas defines the "act" of faith as "an act of the mind giving its assent to divine truth at the command of the will, which is stirred by God through grace".[14] The act involves both the intellect and the will, and the "will to believe" is a moral decision: we remember St Paul's conception of faith as obedience to the Gospel. Faith as a "habit" or "virtue" is characterized by its act; and so St Thomas paraphrases the famous definition of faith in the Epistle to the Hebrews as "the habit of mind by which eternal life is initiated in us, causing the intellect to assent to things not evident".[15] More fully, the Vatican Council lays it down that faith is "a supernatural virtue by which, under the inspiration and assistance of God's grace, we believe that the things revealed by him are true, in deference not to the intrinsic truth of things perceived by the natural light of reason, but to the authority of God himself the Revealer, who can neither be deceived nor deceive".[16]

These Catholic definitions emphasize the function of the will in the act of faith, and its moral quality as submission to the Word of

God. But if we follow St Augustine and St Thomas in regarding the act of faith as a form of mental assent, we shall be disposed to follow them also in finding faith's immediate object in revealed truth in the form of statements or propositions. So our own seventeenth-century Bishop Pearson in his *Exposition of the Creed* defined faith in much the same way as the Vatican Council: "assent unto truths credible upon the testimony of God, delivered unto us in the writings of the Apostles and Prophets".[17]

b. The Council of Trent condemned the doctrine that faith is "nothing but trust in the divine mercy, forgiving our sins for Christ's sake"[18]—which was taken to be the teaching of the Reformers. In fact, Calvin's definition was more careful. Faith, he says, is "a sure and certain knowledge of the divine good-will towards us—which knowledge, founded upon the truth of the free promise given in Christ, is revealed to our minds and written in our hearts through the Holy Spirit".[19] It would be absurd to say that this makes faith "nothing but trust in the divine mercy". But modern Protestant theology is accustomed to insist that the content of the revelation which faith is called to accept is not a statement or statements but a Person—that in revelation God is making *himself* known, imparting himself. Accordingly, the Protestant tendency is to define faith in personal terms. For example, the Lutheran theologian Althaus calls faith "the reception by a person of personal and person-related truth ... whereby we come to know God in his self-disclosure".[20] Such a definition preserves the intellectual element which religious faith must share with all belief, while it maintains that the object of faith is God and not the propositions of any creed. So far as it goes, it could be accepted by a Catholic, with the reservation that the only knowledge of God normally possible to us in this life is the knowledge mediated in propositional terms which is given to us in the Church's teaching.

In any case it should be clear that even if faith is conceived as personal relationship rather than as mental assent, there can be no such relationship without the element of intellectual affirmation— "believing that . . .". Our personal knowledge of one another and trust in one another is not the same thing as an assent to propositions; but it certainly includes or implies a number of things which we believe on sufficient evidence *about* the person concerned. In the same way, when the Creeds profess "belief in" God, the Lord Jesus Christ, and the Holy Spirit, this "belief in" is grounded upon what are in effect statements about the divine Persons in whom belief is professed. The God in whom we believe is the Almighty Father and Creator; the Lord Jesus Christ is the Son of God of whom a whole series of theological and historical predicates are affirmed; and the Nicene Creed makes similar affirmations about the Holy Spirit. Moreover, in the third article of the Apostles' Creed, the phrase "I believe in" applies not only to the Holy Spirit, but to the Church, the Forgiveness of Sins, the Resurrection, and the Life Everlasting. In the original Greek of the Nicene Creed, the preposition "in" is extended to the Church only; but it is clear that the creed-makers did not use the prepositional phrase in the restricted sense of a personal relationship. The intention of both Creeds is to affirm, together with belief "in" the Holy Spirit, belief "that" the Spirit works through the Church and the Sacraments, and "that" there will be a Resurrection of the dead and a Life to come.

3. *Implications of Credal Profession*

The difference between Catholic and Protestant understandings of faith may be reducible to a difference of emphasis. But it remains true that the difference in emphasis results in a difference of attitude towards credal formulae.

If the direct object of faith or belief is the statement—the *credenda* or things to be believed—then, since the *credenda* are received as "revealed truths", the Creed becomes essentially sacrosanct and unalterable: its language has indeed the inadequacy which no human thought of God can overcome, but it is the best possible language. Doctrine will then be tied to the Creeds and other definitions of the Church, rather than to Scripture, and its function will be limited to expounding them as they stand. The necessary control of doctrine must be exercised by the authority of the Church.

On the other hand, if faith is to be regarded as primarily and essentially a moral and volitional act or habit, an acceptance of a personal relationship, its object will not be any Creed or collection of statements, but simply God himself as revealed in Christ. Then the Creed will be accepted in so far as its statements are felt to be a suitable expression of this faith in God. In principle there will be no reason why the living Church should not from time to time improve on any such expression of the faith—as indeed the Church may be held to have done in the fourth century, and as was attempted by the various reforming "Confessions" of the sixteenth and seventeenth. Some Protestant theologians look forward to this not merely as a theoretical possibility but as a thing to be desired and worked for: it is the business of doctrine in their view not merely to expound but to criticize the historic Creeds.

Most Anglicans, on the other hand, would hold that the ancient Creeds *ought* to be retained without alteration. But for those who take that position it remains possible to treat the Creeds in a variety of ways and degrees of respect. Thus:

(1) The Creeds may be regarded in much the same way as in official Roman doctrine, as having a permanent authority virtually equal to that of Scripture. So Article VIII asserts that not only the Apostles' Creed and the Nicene, but the Athanasian, "ought thoroughly to be received and believed: for they may be proved by most certain warrants of holy Scripture". In this case the result is likely to be a credal Fundamentalism all the more rigid because the Creed is taken to summarize the very heart and substance of the Biblical message. But it is not easy to attribute to the Creed an infallibility which is not allowed to the Scriptures on which it is based.

(2) The recitation of a Creed may be taken as implying no more than a general acceptance of the Christian revelation which it was built to enshrine. Weight will then be attached not so much to the wording of the Creed or to its particular statements taken separately as to its significance when regarded as a coherent whole. The retention of the ancient formula will mark the essential identity of the Church's faith from age to age. We may remember that the Nicene Creed in its original form began "We believe": it was not a baptismal confession for the individual, but a statement of corporate faith. So the individual who repeats it when he joins in the corporate worship of the Church may conscientiously intend to associate himself with the historic faith which it expresses, while aware of the imperfection of the form in which that faith came to be stated at a particular period of the Church's history.

(3) Some of the phrases of the Creed have (and have always been known to have) a symbolic character—e.g. "seated at the right hand of God". This symbolic character may be held to extend to the language of the Creed as a whole. It may be claimed that *all* language in which we speak of the nature and activity of God is inevitably anthropomorphic, as are the words "Father" and "Son", and that such language can never carry a literal meaning. Doctrine will then aim at the "translation" of credal symbols in such a way as to justify their continued use as expressions of the unchanging

faith. It is difficult, indeed, to see how this can apply to statements purporting to be historical, unless we admit that these statements, or some of them, are in fact not historical but mythical.[21] But this way out is likely to lead to the abandonment of the distinctive character of Christianity as faith in a God who has acted uniquely, once all, in a certain series of historical events.

(4) Finally, we may consider the attempts which have been made to interpret our Creed not as a belief about the nature of the universe and its history, but as an expression of the moral and religious attitude and intention of the Christian.

This way of thinking goes back to the man whose influence, for good or ill, upon the last hundred years of Protestant theology has been profound—the German Schleiermacher, for whom doctrines were "accounts of the Christian religious affections set forth in speech". "The description of human states of mind" (Schleier-macher declared) "is the fundamental dogmatic form: propositions of the second and third forms" (i.e. "propositions which assert attributes of God and qualities of the world") "are permissible only in so far as they can be developed out of propositions of the first form; for only on this condition can they be really authenticated as expressions of religious emotions."[22] This general tendency was encouraged by the Pragmatist movement in philosophy at the end of the nineteenth century, in which the most eminent figure was the American William James. The Pragmatists declared that "meaning depends on application", or in other words that all assertions claiming to be true must be tested by their *use*, and are true only so far as they work—like the hypotheses of the scientist.

In 1907 the French Catholic Modernist Le Roy published a book entitled *Dogme et Critique*, in which he tried to show that Christian dogma is primarily a rule of practical conduct. Thus "God is personal" *means* "behave in your relations with God as in your relations with a human person": "Jesus is risen from the dead" *means* "be with regard to him as you would have been before his death, as you are *vis-à-vis* a contemporary".

Very much the same position has recently been taken up by Professor Braithwaite of Cambridge, in a lecture setting forth *An Empiricist's view of the nature of Religious Belief.* "The meaning of any statement", he says, "is given by the way in which it is used"; and "the meaning of a religious assertion is given by its use in expressing the assertor's intention to follow a specified policy of behaviour"; such assertions "announce allegiance to a set of moral principles". The particular policy of behaviour or set of moral principles which the Christian announces his intention to follow is that which is governed by the New Testament concept of *Agapé*—Love. Braithwaite further admits that for Christians the intention to behave in this kind of way is associated with the thought of the Christian "story", i.e. with a definite set of empirical propositions the truth of which is subject to the same tests as are applicable to any other historical statements. By the Christian "story" he means roughly the "things concerning Jesus of Nazareth" of which the New Testament tells. But this "story" does not necessarily have to be believed to be true, in the sense that the events which it relates actually took place. Whether true or not, it is imaginatively associated with the Christian intention in such a way as to fortify the intention and assist its realization.

Professor Braithwaite is of course trying to reconcile his religion with the empiricist principles which he holds as a philosopher, and at the same time to meet the attack of contemporary linguistic philosophy upon all theology as being a set of statements to which no meaning can be attached, because no experience can either prove or disprove them. Now it is quite certain that most people who have professed the Christian faith in the past have supposed themselves to be making statements not about what they were trying to be or do but about what they believed to be the case quite apart from their own behaviour. No doubt, if we are honestly to profess the Christian faith, we must at least be intending to behave as Christians should. But it does not follow that the profession and the intention are the same thing—that the profession *means* the intention. The real objection to regarding Braithwaite's view of the nature of religious belief as legitimate, *when the belief concerned is the Christian,* is that the very essence of Christian faith is reliance not upon our own intentions but upon the grace of God which alone can give us the power to carry intention into action.

Accordingly, in our consideration of the Creed we shall be trying to understand what the Creed is saying, *not* (at least in the first instance) about the person who professes it—though doubtless a great deal about that person is implied—but about *God*. That does not mean that we can suppose the Creed to come nearer to the reality of God, to speak truth about God more perfectly, than the Scripture on which it is grounded. We have said that Christian doctrine must be controlled by Scripture, and that we can no longer treat the letter of Scripture as exempt from all error. We have to *search* the Scriptures in order to find the Word of God which speaks to us through them, in order to learn the meaning of the testimony which they bear to Christ who is that Word. We can only justify our retention of the Creed as our confession of faith if we can show that it is in essential harmony with what the Scriptures testify. The authors of Scripture were fallible men; but we believe that the Spirit of God was able to use what they were, in order to convey to us as to them things necessary for salvation. The Fathers of the Church, to whom we owe the formulation of our Creed, were certainly not less fallible. But unless we can believe that the same Spirit was able to use their imperfect understandings to give the Church a sufficient expression of its faith, the Creed must remain for us a document of historical theology—and nothing more. For our present purpose we shall take it for granted, without further argument, that it *is* something more than that.

REFERENCES

1. Gen. 15.6; Isa. 7.9.
2. Mark 1.15 (R.V.).
3. Cf. e.g. Acts 4.4; 8.12f., etc., with Rom. 15.13; 1 Pet. 2.7, etc.
4. Rom. 10.14.
5. Rom. 10.16; 1.5; 2 Cor. 9.13.
6. Mark 1.15; Acts 2.38; 3.19; 16.31.
7. e.g. John 11.42, 45.
8. Jas. 2.17,19.
9. Gal. 5.6.
10. Matt. 9.28.
11. Heb. 11.6.
12. Augustine, *Tractatus in Evangelium Joannis*, xxix.6; *Enarrationes in Psalmos*, lxxvii.8.
13. Augustine, *De Praedestinatione Sanctorum*, 5.
14. *Summa Theologica*, IIa IIae, q.2, a.9.
15. Ibid., q.4, a.1.
16. Denzinger-Bannwart, *Encheiridion Symbolorum*, 1789.
17. Pearson, *Exposition of the Creed* (ed. Burton, Oxford, 1847), Vol. I, p. 17.
18. Denzinger-Bannwart, op. cit., 822.
19. Calvin, *Institutio* III, c.2, §7.
20. P. Althaus, *Die Christliche Wahrheit*, p. 29.
21. See the discussion in *Kerygma and Myth* (S.P.C.K. 1953).
22. F. Schleiermacher, *The Christian Faith* (E.T. ed. H. R. Mackintosh and J. S. Stewart), §15 and §30.

CHAPTER 2

One God the Father

THE purpose of the Creed as a whole is to define the sense in which Christians understand the word "God"—in other words, to show what is involved in the claim that God has made himself known to men in Jesus Christ. Apart from the revelation in Christ, the word "God" is not meaningless. There were "gods many" in the world in which the Christian faith was first preached. But by itself the word "God" stands simply for the object of most (if not all) religious beliefs. In the western world of today, the use of the word has been deeply coloured by the long Christian tradition; but it is still possible to believe in God as a Being other than ourselves on whom the world in some sense depends, without accepting the Christian Creed.

1. *One God*

The Nicene Creed begins both its first and its second article with the words of St Paul in 1 Cor. 8.6: "one God the Father . . . and one Lord Jesus Christ". This is a universal feature of Eastern Creeds, though in the Creeds of the West, to which the Apostles' Creed belongs, the word "one" was not used. In St Paul's text, "one" is of course emphatic: he is opposing the Christian faith to all pagan beliefs in gods many and lords many. St Paul's words were adopted by the baptismal Creeds of Eastern Christendom before the Arian controversy had compelled the Church to work out a doctrine of God as Trinity in Unity; and even when that had been done, Eastern theologians continued to find the ground of the divine unity in the Person of the Father, from whom both Son and Spirit in different ways "proceed", derive their deity. Christians were held to maintain belief in one God not three, because the Godhead of Son and Spirit is the Godhead of the Father.

Historically, therefore, the Creed's opening words convey an assertion of Biblical monotheism against polytheism in all its forms. The assertion was necessary for the average Gentile convert; but it was in accord with the later developments of philosophical religion in the Graeco-Roman world. Platonist, Aristotelian, and Stoic could all claim that they believed in one God, though they had stripped their conception of deity of most of the personal characteristics which belonged to it in polytheism. Their God was the ultimate Unity by which the manifold appearances of the world are held together in an order, a Cosmos. Nowadays, polytheism may appear to be scarcely a live option. Either the existence or the personal nature of God may be doubted, but the word "God" in ordinary use has come to imply unity: to affirm that God is one may seem superfluous.

Yet the assertion of the unity of God remains significant and important as against all practical polytheism. There is practical polytheism not only in the worship of diverse material things, when men make money or pleasure or any other secular good the object of their idolatry, but also in all multiplication of "absolute" values as standing in their own right and deserving of independent pursuit. It is possible, for example, to think of Truth, Beauty, and Goodness in this way. No such value can for the Christian be absolute in the strict sense of the word. There are many good things, but all are subordinate, relative—in St Augustine's phrase, to be "referred" to God who is their Source. Nothing but the One God is to be *worshipped*.

2. *The Father*

The remaining statements of the Creed's first article—that the One God is Father, Almighty, and Creator—are all, as we shall see, anthropomorphic in their language: they take ideas derived from human experience and apply to God the words in which these human notions are expressed. They do not define the meaning of the word "God" in negative terms—"without body, parts, or passions", as the Anglican Article has it—terms chosen to indicate the "otherness" of God, his difference from ourselves. They use concepts with thoroughly positive content, with the meaning of which we are not unfamiliar and which are properly applicable to ourselves. The justification for this is two-fold: not only is it impossible for us to speak of God in any language but our human language, but it is also Christian doctrine (later to be considered) that man is made "in the image of God". There *is* a likeness between God and ourselves which is ground of the relationship between us and him. Still, when we try to say wherein this likeness consists, we can only use terms which describe our own human nature; and there will always be need to weigh and criticize such terms when we apply them to God.

The Creed does not proceed from the less plainly anthropomorphic expressions to the more so. It does not say: our God is the ultimate Cause, the source and origin of the world, who is also the Power that controls and disposes it, and whom yet we can call by the intimate human name of "father". It *begins* with this human name.

(1) The name *Father* is of course very widespread in primitive as well as higher religions in application to a divine being. It derives from the patriarchal organization of human society: the father is (a) the origin or author, and (b) the ruler of his family. In Homeric Greece Zeus is "father of gods and men". In later Greek religious thought, with its interest in cosmology—in the question, How came the world to be what it is?—the dominating element in the idea of the Father-God is *creation*. So in the most influential of Plato's writings, the *Timaeus*, God is "father and maker of the universe".[1] The Stoics, however, combined the idea of creative fatherhood with that of providential rule. Epictetus speaks of God as "our good king and true father", "our maker, father, and guardian".[2] It was the Stoic poet Aratus from whom St Paul quoted at Athens: "for we are also his offspring", and therefore the object of his concern and care.[3]

(2) On the other hand, the Old Testament *never* speaks of God's fatherhood in the sense of physical paternity, and very rarely connects that fatherhood with creation.[4] Jehovah is Father of Israel, and specially of Israel's anointed king.[5] But the fatherly relation of Jehovah whether to people or to king is not a natural fact, but an act of grace, of adoption, based on a free choice and taking effect in a Covenant. The purpose of a covenant, in the Bible, is to link together in friendly obligation two parties who are not naturally so linked: there could be no question of covenant between father and sons, who are such by nature.

Thus it is not the physical but the moral and personal aspects of fatherhood that are involved in the application of the word "father" to God in the Old Testament; and these aspects are those which are most prominent in Hebrew family ideals. The Hebrew father's relation to his children is one of (a) authority, claim to reverence and obedience, and (b) protecting love and care. The first has its expression in the Fifth Commandment, and its exposition in the third chapter of Ecclesiasticus; and it is applied to God in the text of Malachi: "If I be a father, where is mine honour?"[6] The second appears in such sayings as the claim of Job to have been "a father to the poor", and in the similar use in the Psalms in application to God: "a father to the fatherless", and "like as a father pitieth his own children".[7] But the great texts of the Old Testament about the fatherhood of God—the deeply moving language of the eleventh chapter of Hosea, and the appeal of Isa. 63.16: "Doubtless thou art our father, though Abraham be ignorant of us, and Israel acknowledge us not"—these great texts impress us with their rarity. The natural inference is that the Hebrew "fear" of God, the acute sense of his holiness and transcendence or "otherness", caused a shrinking from the use of so intimate a term as fatherhood. When it is used, there is a consciousness of metaphor; and it is very noticeable that the piety of the Psalms has not learnt to approach God as Father.

(3) In later Judaism, however, there is a change. The address of prayer to God as Father becomes habitual, as in the prayer of Ecclus. 23; and the fatherhood of God is a familiar theme for the teaching of the Rabbis. But still God is Father, not as Creator or as universal Father of men, but as God and Father of his people Israel. The name keeps its connection with the Covenant-relationship, felt by the individual Israelite as his peculiar privilege. And as the cleavage within the nation between the "righteous" and the "wicked" makes itself felt, there is a tendency to restrict that privilege, the true sonship to God, to the righteous who are the true Israel. In the Book of Wisdom, the "ungodly" hate and persecute the righteous man because he "calleth himself the child of the Lord", and "maketh his boast that God is his father".[8] That "he is not a Jew, which is one outwardly", was a belief that might well have been held by Saul the Pharisee.[9]

(4) We come then to the teaching of Jesus. In his recorded sayings the word "father" is used almost always of God: yet his teaching is entirely in line with the Old Testament conceptions of human fatherhood—authority and protecting love. The Fifth Commandment is recalled and reasserted, and the father's claim to respect and obedience is assumed in the parable of the Two Sons; and on the other side we have the great *a fortiori* argument from the human father's care for his children ("How much more shall your heavenly father . . .?"), and the profoundly suggestive parable of the Prodigal

Son, of which the central theme is the father's limitless, incorrigible generosity. The teaching is summed up in the Lord's Prayer, where the Father in heaven is (a) to be honoured and obeyed, (b) to be trusted in all his children's needs, (c) ready to forgive. The twin parables of the Lost Sheep and the Lost Coin express, in condemnation of Pharisaic exclusiveness, the character of the God who goes out to seek the lost—the initiative of God's fatherly love which is admitted to have been a neglected theme in Rabbinic teaching.[10]

But here the lost are the "lost sheep of the house of Israel". Did Jesus teach the *universal* Fatherhood of God, as a truth implicit in his creatorship? As we have already seen, there is little if any trace of this either in the Old Testament or in the Rabbis. The question turns on the interpretation of the great passage in the Sermon on the Mount on the love of enemies as the "imitation of God". God sends his sun and rain upon the just and unjust alike, and is good to the unthankful and the evil: by doing likewise men may *become* sons of their Father in heaven.[11] It seems best to understand this in connection with Jesus's preaching of the Kingdom, the sovereignty of God. God *is* King, as the Old Testament proclaims, King by right of all mankind: "his kingdom ruleth over all"; yet its realization is future, for men must acknowledge their allegiance, must enter into it: "Unto me every knee *shall* bow."[12] Jesus tells men to look forward and pray for the *coming* of God's Kingdom. So God wills to be Father of all men, i.e. to know and be known of all as Father; but men must "remember themselves",[13] "come to themselves" like the Prodigal Son, and recognize what sonship means.

(5) In the Epistles of the New Testament, the most striking fact for our present purpose is the absence of all express teaching about God as Father of *men*, and the almost exclusive appropriation of the Father-name to formulae of salutation, blessing, and confession—in all of which it is constantly linked with the name of Jesus Christ: "God our Father and the Lord Jesus Christ", "the God and Father of our Lord Jesus Christ".[14] That we may address God in prayer as Father is no matter of course. Christians can pray "*Abba*, Father", as Christ himself prayed, *because* Christ has won for them the "adoption of sons".[15] Thus for St Paul Fatherhood and Sonship are strictly Christological terms: the divine fatherhood is by no means a commonplace—it has been *revealed* in Christ. *It is as the Father of Jesus Christ that God has made himself known.*

(6) And this is the constant theme of the Fourth Gospel. "No man hath seen God . . . the only-begotten Son . . . hath declared him."

The completeness of union between the Son and the Father who has "sent" him rests upon the Father's love for the Son and the Son's perfect obedience to the Father's will. Because the Son "does nothing of himself", he manifests the "name", the essential reality, of the Father. The claim of the Jews to have God for their father is disproved by their rejection of the Son. The only way to "know" the Father is to recognize his words and works, his active presence in the Son.[16] As the Epistle says, only by confessing the Son can men "have" the Father, i.e. be really themselves children of God.[17] It has often been noted that in all the Johannine sayings of Christ before the Passion God is either "the Father" or "my Father": only the risen Christ will speak to his disciples of "your Father".[18]

"No man knoweth the Son, but the Father; neither knoweth any man the Father, save the Son, and he to whomsoever the Son will reveal him."[19] That saying reads like a piece of pure "Johannine" writing. As belonging to the tradition common to the First and Third Gospels, it proves at least how deep were the roots of Johannine Christology. But we can go further. The main Synoptic tradition from Mark onwards grounds the Messiahship of Jesus upon his consciousness of *unique* Sonship to God. In the great Messianic crises of the story—Baptism and Temptation, Peter's confession and Transfiguration, Gethsemane and Trial—it is as *the* Son of God that he knows himself and is entitled.

> "Thou art my beloved Son"—
> "If thou be the Son of God"—
> "Thou art the Christ, the Son of the living God"—
> "This is my beloved Son"—
> "Abba, Father, not what I will . . ."—
> "Art thou the Christ, the Son of the Blessed One?"—
> "Truly this man was Son of God"—[20]

"Abba" on the lips of Jesus is the familiar address of the child, the "Daddy" which the affectionate son will not abandon when he grows up. *The Father whom Jesus preaches is the Father whom he knows as his own.*

3. God the Father in the Creed

We should therefore expect that when Christian baptism was first administered in the name of Father, Son, and Spirit, the terms Father and Son would be understood as strictly correlative, as in the text of St John's Epistle: "our fellowship is with the Father and with his Son Jesus Christ".[21] Yet we find that the first article of the Creed was not so interpreted by writers of the second century, by whom (partly perhaps under the influence of non-Christian religious associations) "Father" was always taken to mean "Father of all things" in the Platonic sense. In its earliest form in the West, the article consisted simply of "I believe in God the Father Almighty"; and it is probable that the clause "Maker of heaven and earth" was added at a time when "Father" was beginning to be referred (with greater faithfulness to the New Testament) to Christ and not to creation. At all events, this latter became the invariable sense of Patristic exegesis from the fourth century onwards; and our own Bishop Pearson *On the Creed* follows the Patristic tradition.[22]

The Father in whom we believe is the Father of Jesus Christ, to whom we are able to address our prayers in the words which he taught to his disciples, because we have learnt from him what it means to be the child of God. When we confess our belief in one God the Father, we are confessing our belief that God who sent his only-begotten Son to redeem us has thereby given to believers the right to call themselves God's children, to pray and to live as Christ prayed and lived.

Note. Before we pass to the other terms of the Creed's first article, it is well to remember that our Creed, though framed like every Christian Creed on the Trinitarian pattern, neither contains nor implies a doctrine of the Trinity. The changes and additions which were made in it during the fourth century were designed to establish the deity of Christ and of the Holy Spirit in the face of heresy. But by the end of that century theologians had only begun to occupy themselves with appropriate means by which to express belief in the Three-in-Oneness of God. Words were needed to convey the distinction between the divine Persons within the Trinity, as well as words which should hold of the one Godhead which is equally present in all the Persons; and the words "Almighty" and "Creator" were seen to belong to the second class and not to the first. For both denote relations of God to the world, to that which is not God, and neither is applicable to a relation or distinction within the Godhead.

So when the Creed says that God the Father is the omnipotent Creator it is not saying what is exclusively true of the First Person of the Trinity. "The Father is almighty, the Son almighty, and the

Holy Ghost almighty", as the Athanasian Creed says; and creation is the work of the Tri-Une God. When we come at the end of our exposition of the Creed to consider the doctrine of the Trinity, we shall see in what sense particular relations of God to the world are "appropriate" to our thoughts of one or other of the divine Persons. But we need not regret that the Creed as we have it is not concerned with such subtleties.

REFERENCES

1. *Timaeus*, 29 E.
2. *Discourses*, I.6 and 9.
3. Acts 17.28.
4. Perhaps only Isa. 64.8 and Mal. 2.10.
5. Ex. 4.22; 2 Sam. 7.14; Ps. 89.26f.
6. Mal. 1.6.
7. Job 29.16; Ps. 103.13; 68.5.
8. Wis. 2.13ff.
9. Rom. 2.28.
10. Mark 7.10ff.; Matt. 21.28ff.; 7.11; Luke 15.
11. Matt. 5.44ff.
12. Ps. 103.19; Isa. 45.23; cf. Ps. 22.27f.
13. Ps. 22.27.
14. Rom. 1.7 etc.; 2 Cor. 1.3.
15. Gal. 4.6; Rom. 8.15.
16. John 1.18; 5.19ff.; 17,25f.; 8.41f.; 14.8ff.
17. 1 John 2.23.
18. John 20.17.
19. Matt. 11.27 and Luke 10.22.
20. Mark 1.11; Matt. 4.3; 16.16; 17.5; Mark 14.36,61; 15.39.
21. 1 John 1.3.
22. See Kelly, *Early Christian Creeds*, pp. 134ff., 372ff.

CHAPTER 3

Almighty

IT is this single word in our Creed which more than anything else in it is used by the unbeliever to justify his unbelief, and troubles from time to time the faith of the believer. The old dilemma is continually posed: If God at all resembles a good father, if God is good, then he cannot be almighty in a world that contains so much evil; if he is almighty, then he cannot be good. But a Being who is either not almighty or not good is not what we call God; therefore there is no God.

This makes it all the more important that we should enquire what this word actually meant and what it did not mean for those who first made use of it in the Creed, what the Bible teaches about the divine control of the world and its course, and what kind of power the Christian must ascribe to God.

1. *The Meaning of "Almighty"*

The word "almighty" in the Creed translates the Greek *panto-crator* and the Latin *omnipotens*. The Greek word is very rare outside the Bible. It never occurs in prose except in late inscriptions as an epithet of deities such as Hermes or Isis. In the Septuagint, the Greek translation of the Old Testament, it stands in the great majority of cases for *Sabaoth* in the divine title "Lord of Hosts". Jehovah Sabaoth seems originally to have meant the God of the armies of Israel, but later was taken as referring to the "heavenly hosts", the armies of angels. In the prophets, the title expresses simply the superhuman might and majesty of Jehovah. *Omnipotens* similarly is a divine epithet in Latin poetry; but the poets apply it indifferently to Jupiter, Neptune, Juno, and even Fortuna. It is not a word of prose, still less of philosophy. Neither the Greek word nor the Latin convey the strict notion of "omnipotence" as commonly understood, viz. power to do anything, or even power to do whatever is willed. They are adjectives of "glorification", which in the mouth of the suppliant or worshipper express little more than the contrast between human weakness and divine strength.

2. *The Sovereignty of God*

In the New Testament, *pantocrator* is almost confined to the Apocalypse, where the prophetic title of Jehovah is closely linked with the thought of God's sovereignty. "The Lord God omnipotent reigneth." The Lord of Hosts is "he that sitteth upon the throne".[1] The central idea of Biblical religion is not of "omnipotence" as an attribute of God, but of his sovereignty, his rule in action. The kingdom of God is his rule, the government which he exercises in the world. For the prophets, the rule of God means that the history of mankind, the process of events which is apparently determined by human actions, good and bad, is in reality controlled throughout by the will and purpose of God.

The existence of this control is not evident: it is a matter of faith. There are times when such faith is difficult, when God seems to have let things go their own way, when the powers of evil seem to be dominant. But there are also "occasions" (*kairoi*), turning-points, crises in history, when the mighty act of God is clearly recognizable. The greatest and most momentous of these *kairoi* are in the Old Testament the deliverance of Israel from Egyptian bondage, and in the New the resurrection of Christ—which fittingly takes place at the time of Passover.

3. *The Purpose of God*

If the will of God controls history, to what purpose is his will directed? There are two possible answers, which are not mutually exclusive.

a. The purpose may be, as in human government, to maintain order, to hold the Cosmos together, to ensure that Chaos never returns, that wickedness which is essentially *dis*order never succeeds in establishing itself. This could be the meaning of *pantocrator*, and in this sense the credal use of the word has sometimes been interpreted, e.g. by Gregory of Nyssa in the fourth century. "We understand by this word", he says, "that God holds together all things in being . . . that all things may remain in being, grasped by the embracing power of God." As the word "physician" implies the existence of sick people, so the word "almighty" implies the existence of "a creation which needs a power to contain it and preserve it in being".[2] In this sense God's rule would be comparable to the rule of law in any form, or to the activity of an engineer in

charge of a machine which will go on working so long as he is
there to check and remedy faults as they occur. That the power of
God does in fact control the world in this way is indeed part of the
faith of the Bible. For the Old Testament prophets, the order of
the world culminates in a moral order which is maintained by the
righteousness of God, whose inviolable law ensures that unrighteousness cannot triumph.

b. But the purpose of God in the Bible means more than this. It
means that the process of history as a whole is being guided by God
to an *end*: that God's rule is not satisfied by maintaining an existent but precarious order. The prophets look forward to a realization
of God's rule in the future, which will consist in the visible establishment of his reign on earth, when all men will acknowledge his
sovereignty because there will no longer be anything to suggest a
doubt of its reality. When the great prophetic line came to an end,
and the prophetic hope faded, its place was taken by the visionary
constructions of the apocalyptic writers, who were persuaded by the
evil days in which they lived that *this* world is inevitably doomed
to destruction because of men's sins, but yet believed that God's
kingdom will be set up in a new world—the "Age that is coming"
—and so his purpose will be finally fulfilled. The purpose of history
in this case is not contained in history, but the whole time-process
is moving to an End outside itself.

New Testament eschatology—its belief about the End—differs
from both the prophetic and the apocalyptic. In it, the End is not,
or is not only, a state of things in the future which may or may not
presuppose the winding-up of history as we know it. The manifestation of God's kingdom is not postponed to a later time or to the
end of time; it is an End which has drawn near in the coming of
Christ, who is himself the fulfilment of God's purposes. So the
Christian Gospel is not in its essence a prediction of things to come:
it is the proclamation of One who *has* come. The Eternal has entered
into time, and though time goes on and its continuance may be
long or short, it can never be the same as before.

4. *The Manner of God's Rule*

We still ask: *How* is God's control of the world and its history
exercised? Is the world any nearer now to acknowledging his sovereignty than it was when Christ came? The phrasing of the Lord's
Prayer clearly implies that God's Kingdom is not yet fully come,

that his will is not yet done on earth "as it is in heaven". To say, then, that the sole cause of all that happens is the will of God would be to obscure the ultimate difference between good and evil, and to make our own sense of responsibility illusory; for no decisions of our own could be held to make any difference to the course of events. But if men are real actors in history, able by their own action to influence its course, to *change* the state of things, that can only be because it is the will of God that they should have the power to do so. Men *can* be "workers together with God",[3] real contributors to the fulfilment of his purposes; or they *can* work against the purposes of God. And since it is plain that some men do so work against God, we are bound to think of the effective operation of the will of God in the world in terms of a *conflict*.

And this brings us back to the name "Lord of Hosts". What are the "hosts of God" in this war? We have no reason to deny the existence of the "heavenly hosts" who were altogether real for the writers of the Bible—though we cannot (as things are) know anything about their share in the struggle. But something we do know of how God wins his victories in history—through the endurance and the sufferings of his faithful soldiers and servants, who know at the same time that whatever power they have comes from the presence in them of the Spirit which *is* the power of God.

4. *The Power of God*

What then is the nature of this power?

a. The Biblical symbols of warfare and victory inevitably suggest the meeting of physical force with physical force. On the human level, warfare means that conflicting purposes have proved irreconcilable, and that nothing remains but for each of the opposing sides to try to break the other. All such warfare is destructive, and the side that can command the greater forces of destruction wins.

b. But we also speak of a warfare of *ideas*, in which victory goes to the idea that prevails. This warfare can of course be carried on by the use of material force, oppression, and persecution. But it need not be: it can confine itself to the appeal to reason and the method of persuasion. Then the more "powerful" idea wins acceptance instead of the weaker: it takes the place of the other in men's minds. There is no destruction, for the object has been not to destroy but to convert: if truth has the victory, that is because it has been freely accepted by those who once opposed it, or because the oppos-

ing idea has lost its power to propagate itself. The case is the same
in the warfare of good and evil. Where good and evil wills are
confronted, the object of the evil will is in general not to change the
good will but to dominate it, to make and keep it powerless. Its
natural instrument is therefore the use of force. Here again, the
good will *may* use the same instrument, as in the maintenance of
law and order: the malefactor must be forcibly deprived of his
power to do violence. But the purpose of the good will, because it
wills good, is not to crush or imprison the evil will but to convert
it, to make it good. In short, the good will seeks to *give* itself, to
impart itself to its adversary. And that can never be done by force;
for (as St Augustine says) no one can be compelled to will.

c. The power which belongs to a personal agent is in itself morally
neutral: it is simply ability to carry out whatever is willed. Power
in the service of goodness is power ethically directed. It cannot be
power to do *anything*, for goodness can only will to do good. When
we say that the power of God is the power of love, we mean that
his power to do what he wills is always the power to give himself;
for goodness doing good is goodness giving itself, and that is the
meaning of God's love.

Love as we know it is certainly powerful; but it is not omnipotent:
it does not always win, for it is often rejected. Yet we can feel certain that no *other* power can overcome the evil in the world: the
constraint of law can check but never cure it, the advance of knowledge can serve the evil will as well as the good. To assert the omnipotence of God is to assert that self-giving goodness cannot be de-
feated in the long run. And that is, manifestly, an act of faith.
Appearances are strong against it, but "nevertheless"—we believe.
The Christian's right to declare his faith in God's omnipotence
rests heavily upon his assurance that the Christ in whom God's
gift of himself to the world was rejected has risen from the dead
and given his Spirit to believers.

5. *Omnipotence and Miracle*

The miracle of the Resurrection was the "sign" to its Apostolic
witnesses that Jesus the Crucified was Lord and Christ. Thus it
remains the "sign" that the power of God, which is the power of
love, is unconquerable.

But miracles generally have been treated as *proofs* of God's
activity, on the ground that they could not have any other cause;

and to doubt the fact of the miracle has been taken to be a denial
of God's omnipotence. This clearly assumes a quite different notion
of divine power from that which we have been considering. It is
important, therefore, to distinguish the common meaning of the
word "miracle" in modern speech from that which it bears in the
Bible.

a. The modern usage of the word is connected with the modern
conception of the natural order and its uniformity or subjection to
law. A miracle is a breach of the natural order—an event which can
never be accounted for as an instance of the working of a general
law or combination of laws. It is assumed that we already know
enough of Nature's laws to be able to say that if certain events took
place the principle of the uniformity of nature was violated. In
view of the continuing progress of natural science and the startling
acceleration of that progress, this is certainly a large assumption.
But it is plain that *some* alleged miracles could only be explained
as having taken place in accordance with the regular order of nature
by an upheaval of accepted knowledge such as few scientists will
regard as at all probable: they will feel it much easier to disbelieve
the fact alleged on the ground that the evidence for it is insufficient.
On the other hand it is equally clear that many if not all of the
"miracles" alleged to have taken place cannot in the present state
of our knowledge be certainly known to have been miraculous—
if they really occurred. For example, the healing "miracles" recorded to have been wrought by Jesus may be accepted as historical
because they are no longer regarded as miracles—viz. breaches of
the order of nature.

But if there are laws of nature, for the Christian they are God's
laws. Nature's uniformity is a fitting expression of the unity and
constancy of the Creator. Why then should God interfere with the
order which he has himself imposed upon the world he has made—
an order which (as far as we can see) has in no way been changed
by the sin of man? It is this question which makes the religiously-
minded scientist reluctant to believe in the occurrence of miracles—
in the sense in which he supposes them to be asserted. He finds the
order itself much more marvellous, much more worthy of God,
than any breach of it.

b. The Biblical writers know nothing of natural law in the modern
sense, though they know the difference between the ordinary and
the extraordinary, between what may be expected to happen and
what may not. But they do know of "signs and wonders". We

must note, however, that, e.g., the signs and wonders of the Exodus
would lose none of their significance if the plagues of Egypt and
the crossing of the Red Sea were naturally explicable: indeed we
can trace in Ex. 14 a "miraculous" and a "non-miraculous" account
of the crossing which have been woven together. We must note
also that it is not supposed that all wonders are the work of God:
the Egyptians and the false Christs foretold in Mark 13 can perform them. "Miraculous" occurrences are therefore no proof in
themselves that God is at work. The wonders of which God *is* the
author are "signs"—significant events. The sign is necessarily a
wonder, a striking event, for otherwise it would not attract attention—it would not "signify". But what it signifies is not that God
can break his own laws: a natural event like the return of Israel
from Babylonian captivity is no less a sign than the deliverance
from Egypt. What it signifies is that the God of nature is not
indifferent to the affairs of men, that he is a present help in trouble,
and that in this particular emergency he is acting in accordance
with his unchanging goodness and mercy. The Bible miracle, then,
is not an event which creates faith;[4] it is an event which challenges
and invites faith.

c. We agree nowadays with Francis Bacon that God has not
wrought miracles (in the modern sense of the word) to convert the
atheist. They cannot do so, for the atheist will refuse to accept them
as miraculous; and Jesus himself refused to give a sign to unbelief
—except when it prayed for help to believe.[5]

We believe with the Biblical writers that the mighty works of
God are to be discerned in history, that God not only can but does
act in and upon the world creatively, making a difference. But we
do not believe *in* miracles. We do not believe in Christ *because* he
was born of a virgin or because his body was raised from the tomb.
If we believe these things, and if we believe that they were in fact
miracles in the modern sense—breaches of the natural order never to
be naturally explained—it will not (or should not) be because we
believe in the omnipotence of God. It will be because we find it
fitting that God's redemption of the world should have been
wrought not through the natural order but in spite of it. It is not
necessarily a proof of unbelief or human pride of knowledge if
others find it *more* fitting that the natural order of the world, which
God created and saw that it was good, should be capable of acting
as instrument of his redemptive purpose, in spite of the sin and
unbelief of man.[6]

REFERENCES

1. Rev. 19.6; 11.15ff.; 4.8ff.
2. Gregory of Nyssa, *Against Eunomius*, II.11.
3. 1 Cor. 3.9.
4. As the Archbishop says in Shaw's *St Joan*.
5. Mark 9.24ff.
6. The last section of this chapter repeats, sometimes in the same words, what I have said about miracles in the last chapter of my little book *Is the Bible inspired?*

CHAPTER 4

Maker of heaven and earth, And of all things visible and invisible

WE have observed that the Creed does not say of our God *first* that he is the maker of all things, *then* that he controls all that he has made, and *lastly* that we may trust his control because he is the Father of Jesus Christ and therefore our Father.

The belief that the whole world and all that is therein is the creation of the one God who is the God of Israel—this belief which is proclaimed on the first page of the Old Testament as we have it belongs historically not to the infancy but to the maturity of Hebrew religion. The prophets had first to recognize that the sphere of Jehovah's sovereignty cannot be limited to Israel, that "his kingdom ruleth over *all*";[1] and only then were they led to see this universal rule of God as grounded in the right of the Creator to govern his creation. "The Lord reigneth", *because* that over which he reigns derives its very existence from him. And so the creation itself is represented as an act of God's sovereign will. The creative word of God is *command*: "God said, Let there be light, and there was light."[2]

This Biblical belief in God as Creator is not the outcome of any logical or intellectual necessity to postulate a First Cause for the existence of things. Philosophers like Aristotle may argue that there could be no motion or change without an unchanging Mover. But in the Bible we are not led to believe in a Creator because we need to account for the world's being there. Christian belief begins with the acknowledgment of God's sovereignty, his right to command because he is righteous, his lordship over ourselves and over the world of which we are a part; and it proceeds to the confession that we owe obedience to God because we are debtors to him in all things, because we owe our very being to his will. "It is he that hath made us, and we are his."[3]

1. *Elements of Biblical doctrine*

The doctrine of creation in the Bible contains two elements, which together express the complete and absolute dependence of the world upon God. Not only has God brought the world into being by an act of his will: his presence and power sustain in being the order which he has created. Neither the origin of the world nor its continued existence from one moment to another are to be conceived apart from the divine operation.

a. *In the beginning.* Neither the Bible nor Christian doctrine as such is concerned with the solution of the philosophical puzzle, How is time related to eternity? The puzzle was set by the Greeks. Plato had laid down a hard-and-fast division between the Changing and the Changeless, and claimed that what does not change and is therefore unaffected by time has a superior reality to that which is always in process of change. He believed that though our bodies change and decay, our reasonable souls can be in touch with the world of eternal reality, and thereby share in its immortal changelessness. He did not realize that our thinking itself is limited and conditioned by the fact of our existence in time. Thus it is impossible for us to think of a beginning of time without asking what was there "before" time began—which is to push time back into eternity; yet it is no easier for us to think of a temporal process that had no beginning. We can see, however, that both time and space are conditions of the world's existence. If the world had a beginning, it was not *in* time: there was no time "before" the world began. A witty theologian whom St Augustine quotes in his *Confessions* (without approving the witticism), in answer to the question, What was God doing before he created the world?—said, "He was getting ready a hell for the inquisitive." St Augustine's own answer was a serious one: that time, without which there can be no "before" or "after", was created *with* the world.[4]

If the existence of the world is an existence in time, it would in any case be nonsense to speak of the world as "co-eternal" with God. But Christian thinkers have often insisted that we must hold to belief in a real *beginning* of the world, in order to avoid the idea that the world is necessary to God, that he needs a world in order to be God. It is urged that the creation of the world is an act of God's outgoing love, and therefore must be entirely free: nothing can have "obliged" God to create. He could have done without a world if he had so willed. But it is not really possible to think of God's freedom as though it were, like our own, an ability to choose between alternative courses of action. God's willing must be wholly determined by his being: what he wills, he wills because of what he is. "The world is what it is because God is what he is."[5] The Christian God *is* the Creator of this world; and a God who had not willed to be its Creator would not be the God in whom Christians believe.

However, the first words of the Bible—"In the beginning"—decide no question either of science or of philosophy. The phrase is *imaginative*, introducing a *myth*—a poetic tale suggestive of truth; and the story of creation could be told in no other terms but mythical. What it conveys is that the world has its source, its origin, in the act of God; what it excludes is the thought of the world either as existing "on its own", or as in any sense to be identified with God. And because everything in the world has its beginning from God, everything is bounded, limited by that beginning: it is the essence of creatureliness to be finite.

b. *Continuance.* The Bible teaches that the dependence of the world upon God is not only a matter of origin, of once-for-all coming into being. When we read in the second chapter of Genesis that "God ended his work which he had made", we are hearing the natural conclusion of the myth. That the world depends on God not only for its existence but for its sustenance is the common belief of the writers of the Old Testament. "In his hand are all the corners of the earth, and the strength of the hills is his also." "Thou hast made heaven . . . the earth . . . the seas and all that is in them, and thou preservest them all." It is the "breath", the spirit of God, which both made and continually "renews" the being of creation.[6] So the New Testament, which in one place speaks of Christ as the Word "through whom all things were made", in another says that "by him all things are held together", and in another that he "upholds all things by the word of his power".[7] As the first creative act of God called the world "out of nothing", so his sustaining act keeps it from relapsing into the nothing, the "not-being" from which it came. But the acts which we so distinguish are not to be separated. God's creative power is constantly active. To the charge of violating the Sabbath day on which God "rested from his works", Jesus answers: "My Father worketh hitherto, and I work."[8] God's world is still in the making.

2. *God the only Creator*

These two aspects of God's creative activity mark the difference between it and all human making. The difference is emphasized in the Hebrew language by the use of a word for God's creating which is not used of human activity. The modern usage whereby we speak freely of creation and creative power as the highest capacity of human nature is a departure from the Biblical reserve.

a. Man is indeed a maker: he has power to bring new good into being; but this power is always dependent upon what is already given. Man can only use what is at his disposal by adapting it for some new purpose. In Aristotelian terms, he can only give new "form" to an existing "matter"—whether the matter be what we call material or spiritual. That God's creation is of matter as well as form is expressed in the traditional phrase "creation *ex nihilo*"— "out of nothing". So, while the maxim "Nothing comes out of nothing" is true enough for our human experience, for our faith it is equally true that "Everything comes out of nothing".[9]

b. Again, all human making ends in the production of something which can exist afterwards apart from its maker. The finished work of artist, craftsman, poet, or thinker does not depend upon the continued existence of the producer for its own continuance. But the world depends on God for its maintenance not less than for its origination. Here the nearest but still imperfect analogy is that of parenthood; but the world unlike the human child never "grows up" into adult independence.

It follows that the act of God in creating can never be described in human terms: it is strictly inconceivable and ineffable. We are led into error whenever we try to think of God's creative "work" in terms of the things we make ourselves—the machine, the picture, the poem—just as we are led into error when we try to think of God's power in human terms; though there may, as we shall see later, be a *likeness* between God the Creator and man his creature even in respect of the creativity which belongs to God alone.

3. *Implications of the Christian doctrine of Creation*

a. "God saw everything that he had made, and behold it was very good."[10] There are bad things, but the badness of a bad thing cannot be the work of God. The Creed's statement forbids us to think of any created thing as evil in itself, "by nature". For the early

Church, this was the bulwark against Gnosticism, the various forms of would-be Christian theosophy which under the impact of both Greek and Oriental thought ascribed the origin of evil to material existence as such, and sought salvation in escape from it. For St Paul, the things that are seen are temporal and the things that are not seen are eternal; but St Paul would never have said that the things that are seen are evil because they are temporal.[11] It follows that it cannot be the aim of the human spirit to escape from the body by flight, through contempt of the "flesh". The way to union with God is not by any attempt to shake off the conditions of our bodily nature. St Augustine in his maturity denounced the Neo-platonist maxim—"Flee from all things bodily"[12]—which as a young man he had embraced. Similarly, the goodness of God's creation forbids us to see anything evil in finitude, in the limitations of our existence and our powers. It is not finitude but our resentment of finitude that leads to sin.

b. The essential goodness of the world in its finite condition implies that God's own goodness is reflected in his creation. "The heavens declare the glory of God."[13] So the world, inanimate as well as animate, claims from us a share in the reverence which we owe to its Maker. "The invisible things of him, his eternal power and divinity, are to be perceived by our minds through the things that are made."[14] And this is the justification not only of the artist and poet but of the scientist: both the beauty and the order of the world are a disclosure to us of the eternal glory of God, and thus a call to worship. It is also the justification of the philosopher; for the very existence of the world as we find it is a challenge to the understanding. The philosopher tries to "see life steadily and see it whole"—to grasp the meaning of the world in which we live. God cannot be read out of the world, for he is not contained in it. But he has not left himself "without witness" in his creation.

In this connection the artist-analogy is not without use. When St John writes: "In the beginning was the Word. . . . All things were made through him": he clearly has the creative word of the first verses of Genesis in mind.[15] But for his Greek-thinking readers, this *logos* would mean not so much the utterance of God as the thought of God, "the meaning, plan, or purpose of the universe"[16] in the mind of its Maker. Taking these two ideas, Hebrew and Greek, together, we are naturally led to think of the created universe as the voluntary and purposeful expression of the divine Mind. Now we see in a work of art the "self-expression" of the artist, and we think of the artist as "giving himself" to us in picture or symphony. Yet the really great artist is never "expressing himself"—perhaps it is just as well that a Perugino or even a Beethoven did not do that —but expressing a vision which has been given to him: it is the artist's vision of something quite other than himself which is present in his work and conveyed to us through it. But God, in creating the world "out of nothing", could express nothing but himself: thus it is God and only God who can truly be self-expressed in his creation.

Of course this raises great difficulties, for to our minds the world we know is by no means wholly good; and we cannot say that the evil in it as well as the good expresses the mind of God. We cannot be satisfied by the aesthetic justification of evil as providing the necessary shadows in the picture. It is only faith in God's *victory* over evil, a victory so complete that evil is converted into good, that makes it possible for us to believe in the goodness of this world's Creator. And that comes only through the revelation in Christ, where the worst thing that ever happened is transformed into the best.

4. *The Purpose of Creation*

a. The difficulties raised for our belief in a good Creator by the evils of the world are unnecessarily exaggerated by certain assumptions which we sometimes make without considering whether they are required by our Christian faith. In the first chapter of Genesis it is the making of this earth and the provision for life upon it which leads up to and is crowned by the creation of man. With our immensely wider horizons, we easily read the story as though the whole structure of the universe had no other purpose but the production of the human species and that all things in it had been made for the use of man. And we may slip from there into the further assumption that the "use" of man can only mean his happiness or even his material comfort.

Now the human species does appear to be the species most highly organized and adapted for life on this planet—as indeed the Biblical story of creation implies. Man has "all things in subjection under his feet . . . sheep and oxen and the beasts of the field". Yet the Psalmist can still exclaim: "What is man, that thou art mindful of him?" And the Book of Job enforces the counsel of humility from the sheer mystery of creation, and the limits to all human powers of understanding or controlling it.[17]

It is also true that all increase in our knowledge of natural law emphasizes the fact that mankind is the product not only of this earth but of the whole stellar universe, which is the setting, the cosmic order that has made possible the evolution of humanity on this particular planet. We are not to be stampeded by the *vastness* of creation into belittling ourselves; for quantity has nothing to do with quality, extension in space or time has nothing to do with significance or value. We do not know that we are the only beings in the universe capable of becoming children of God: but there would be nothing irrational in the supposition that we *are* the only such beings—unless it is irrational to suppose that a man is more "important" than a mountain. Nevertheless, these considerations do not justify us in affirming that the universe was made for man.

b. God, says the Creed, is the Maker of heaven and earth; and the Nicene Creed adds: "and of all things visible and invisible". "Heaven and earth" in the language of the creed-makers would naturally be taken to describe the material world known to us through our senses. The added clause makes it clear that the range of God's creation is not so limited: it widens out to embrace things beyond the reach of our powers of perception. For the creed-makers, the "things invisible" will certainly have included the "heavenly powers"—the angels who are God's "ministering spirits".[18] If there are angels, it would be gratuitous to suppose that their ministry is limited to us men. But whatever "powers" the universe contains— physical energies or spiritual agents unknown to us—all is of God.

We cannot then assume that even if the things that are "in subjection under our feet" extend far more widely than the author of Job supposed, it follows that God's universal purpose reaches no further than ourselves. The purpose of creation as a whole must be beyond our comprehension. But we can believe that God, in revealing himself to us in Christ, has therewith shown us his purpose *"for us men"*—what *man* is meant to be. And this should make it impossible for us to think that God has created all things with no other purpose than the satisfaction of men's natural desires and needs. We need not abandon the ancient insight, whereby the purpose of man's being, that in which he is to find his fulfilment, is embraced in the purpose of all creation—the *glory* of God. The glory of God in the Bible and Christian tradition has always been linked with the idea of light. The light of the sun enables those who have eyes to see the world lit up with splendour. God is glorified on earth when the eyes of men are enlightened, when they see his goodness in his works and come to worship him. But it would be presumptuous to imagine that the glory of God *depends* on the existence of the human eye.

REFERENCES

1. Ps. 103.19; cf. Amos 9.7; Isa. 19.25, etc.
2. Gen. 1.3.
3. Ps. 100.3.
4. Augustine, *Confessions*, XI.12ff.
5. F. R. Tennant, *Philosophical Theology*, II.184.
6. Ps. 95.4; Neh. 9.6; Ps. 33.6; 104.30.
7. John 1.3; Col. 1.17; Heb. 1.3.
8. John 5.17.
9. W. H. V. Reade, *The Christian Challenge to Philosophy*, p. 126.
10. Gen. 1.31.
11. 2 Cor. 4.18.
12. Augustine, *De Civitate Dei*, X.29.
13. Ps. 19.1.
14. Rom. 1.20.
15. John 1.1-3; Gen. 1.1-3.
16. C. H. Dodd, *The Fourth Gospel*, p. 277.
17. Ps. 8; Job 38-41.

CHAPTER 5

Man—as he should be

THE Creed, as we have said, sets forth our beliefs about the God in whom we believe. But our belief in God hangs upon an act of God performed "for us men and for our salvation". We must therefore have also certain beliefs about ourselves as the objects of the "salvation" which Christ wrought, and about the reasons why we stood in need of salvation. These beliefs are not stated in the Creed, but they are pre-supposed: we cannot properly understand the Creed without having its pre-suppositions in our minds.

That is our reason for interpolating at this point a consideration of what the Bible and Christian doctrine tell us about the nature of man. Man is part of God's creation, and the purpose of creation must therefore include the fulfilment of God's design in the making of man. We ask then: What is man meant to be? Is he what he is meant to be? If not, why not?

1. "Made in his image"

The creation story in Genesis ends with the making of man "in the image" of God, "after his likeness". Ancient commentators attempted to assign different meanings to the "image" and the "likeness"; but there is no ground for this in the text. In Gen. 5.3 the same phrase is used of Adam's begetting a son: the idea is the simple one of "like father, like son". The only indication in Gen. 1.26 of what is meant by the image and likeness of God is given by the conferring on man of *dominion* over the animals.

Direct references to the making of man in the image of God are not to be found in the Old Testament after Gen. 9.6, where it is ground for the ordinance that "whoso sheddeth man's blood, by man shall his blood be shed". The writer clearly does not suppose the "image" to have been lost by the Fall. Only in the Book of Wisdom do we find the image expressly interpreted as the gift of immortality[1]—an interpretation which shows the writer's affinity with Greek rather than with Hebrew thought.

In the New Testament the Genesis-text is recalled by St Paul in
1 Cor. 11.7, where curiously enough it is taken as ground for a
distinction between the sexes, and by the writer of the Epistle of
James (3.9) who appeals to it for his stringent warning against
misuse of the tongue. But in Col. 1.15 and Heb. 1.3 it is Christ
who is the image of God—no doubt in connection with the description in the Book of Wisdom of the divine Wisdom itself.[2] So St Paul
in 2 Cor. 4.4 speaks of the glory of Christ who is the image of God.
But a few verses earlier he has said that Christians by contemplating
the glory of God in Christ "as in a mirror" (cf. Wis. 7.26) are
"transformed into the same image". And this is no casual turn of
thought; for in Rom. 8.29 the elect are "fore-ordained to be conformed to the image of God's Son", and in Col. 3.9 the "new man",
whom Christians have "put on", is "renewed after the image of him
that created him". The new creation like the old is in the image of
God; but it is secure because it is "in" the New Man, the Second
Adam who is Christ.

Thus it appears that the image of God in the Bible is applicable
to three distinct things: (1) to man as originally created; (2) to
Christ the divine Wisdom as the revelation of God; (3) to the
destiny of man as redeemed or restored and re-created *in* Christ.

2. *Doctrinal interpretations*

This variation of meaning in Biblical texts has led to varying
doctrines of what is meant by the image of God in man.

a. The older tradition of the Church attached itself to the Genesis
story, in which there is a clearly-drawn contrast between man and
the animal creation. Greek thought found the main distinction
between man and beast in the rationality of man: man was defined
as a "reasoning animal"—a *logikon zoön*; and the image accordingly was generally held to consist in the gift of reason. This interpretation was easy to connect with the New Testament teaching
about the renewal of the image, by way of the *Logos*-doctrine
founded on the Prologue to St John's Gospel. The divine Word, the
Logos through whom man was created *logikos*, rational, is also the
instrument of his re-creation. But the Fathers of the Church did not
understand the *Logos* in this context in any narrowly intellectualist
sense: the gift of "reason" was held to include that of free will or
self-determination—which through the teaching of Origen became
an essential element in Greek Christian anthropology. St Augustine

distinguished a "lower" reason which guides us in our actions in temporal affairs from the "higher" reason which is made for the contemplation of God.[3] The gift of reason as the image of God remains in fallen man: its proper *use*, for the knowledge and service of God, is what sin destroys and what is restored in Christ.

b. St Thomas Aquinas, following St Augustine, placed the image of God in the human "mind" (*mens*); and he distinguished between the mind's natural aptitude or potentiality for knowing God, and its exercise of this aptitude—really though imperfectly in this life in the "state of grace", fully and perfectly in the life to come in the "state of glory".[4] But the Schoolmen also inherited from St Augustine the notion that Adam was created in a state of ideal perfection or "original righteousness"; and they asserted this to be a supernatural gift which was lost by the Fall, while the natural image of God, displayed in reason and conscience, remains in fallen men— albeit not unimpaired: fallen man is a being "injured even in his natural constitution".[5]

The Reformers simply identified the image of God with this "original righteousness", and declared that it was entirely destroyed by the Fall. But they had somehow to reconcile this with those texts of Scripture which speak of the image as existing in man as he is; and they could only do so by allowing that in reason and conscience there are "relics" of the lost image—which really comes to much the same thing as the doctrine of the Schoolmen.

c. Modern theologians of the Reformed Churches are usually unable to accept the picture of an original state of perfection as either historically probable or corresponding to the intention of the Eden story. Their tendency has been to say that the image of God is not to be found in any endowment of human nature regarded in itself, but consists simply in the fact that God has made man (in St Augustine's famous phrase) "for himself"—or more exactly "to be towards himself",[6] to be inescapably related to him; so that man can never shake off either his own need of God or God's claim upon him. It is claimed that mutual relationship is an essential element in personal being: we are persons inasmuch as we exist by and for one another. And if we take personality in this sense of "relatedness" as that which constitutes the image of God in man, it becomes possible for us to see both its connection with the doctrine of the Trinity (the Three divine Persons in mutual relationship), and also how it is that our own relationship to God is always bound up with our relationship to one another. God meets us in our meetings with our neighbour.

d. Yet we may still ask whether it is possible, if one thing A is "like" another thing B, that the likeness should consist in the relationship which A has to B. Likeness itself is of course a relationship between two things; but that relationship is constituted by the fact that A has certain characteristics which are also to be found in B. There is a relationship of likeness between a forget-me-not and the sunlit sky, because both in themselves are of a particular kind of blue. For one thing to be like another, there must be something in common between them which enables them to have the relationship of likeness—though this common factor may no doubt be itself a relation in which both stand to some third object: I may be like you in being fond of flowers.

Thus if man is in any respect like God, it must be possible to say more of the likeness than that it is a relationship—even a personal relationship. It is no doubt true that mutual relationships are necessary for the growth and functioning of personal life, and that mind and conscience could not exist without them. But the irreducible likeness between one human being and another does not consist in their being capable of personal relationships, but in the fact that they have the powers of thought, memory, feeling, and will, which give them that capacity.

We believe that man is so made that he may have communion with his Maker—that he may know as he is known. Upon what, then, in man's created nature, does the possibility of this communion rest?

3. The Image in the Creed

St Augustine, in common with the main tradition of Patristic teaching, believed that the image of God was to be seen in the spiritual part of man's nature, the human *mens*—not the thinking mind only, but the whole complex of self-conscious life. Now God is Trinity; and St Augustine was sure that the triune nature belongs to God as he is "in himself", and does not depend upon any external relation between God and the created world. He therefore looked for an image of the Trinity in the mind of man, not as that mind is related to other minds or to anything in the external world, but as it is "in itself", related to itself in its awareness of its own past and present and its self-direction towards the future—a triad of relationships which he called memory, understanding, and will.[7]

Thus the Augustinian theory of the image is at first sight directly opposed to the modern idea which identifies the image with relatedness to what is other than the self. Yet St Augustine insisted that the image of God is only realized, only achieves its fulfilment, when it does enter into a conscious relationship to the God whose image it is. Our self-centred and self-directed memory, understanding, and will must *become* re-centred and re-directed upon God—upon him whose image they represent.[8]

The Creed, once more, is a statement of Christian belief about God; and the Creed begins by applying to God the human notions of Fatherhood, of the Lordship or Mastery which is freedom, and of the Making which is the multiplication and preservation of good. This is plainly as much as to say that there *is* an image of God in man. But if these human characters are really the key to such knowledge of God as we need and as is given to us, then they must also point to that in ourselves which is like God, to the actual constituents of the image in which we have been made.

a. We may conveniently begin with the idea of *Mastery*; for it appears that for the writers of the Old Testament at any rate it is the dominion conferred upon man which is *par excellence* the point of likeness in God's image.[9] As God rules over all, so man rules over all that is below himself in the order of creation: he is God's viceroy. And this dominion belongs to man, not only because his intelligence, his power of forming and grouping general ideas, surpasses the capacities of the animal, but because he can use his intelligence for the furtherance of his purposes. Moreover, his purposes are not determined, imposed upon him. He can choose the purpose, the end which his intelligence is to serve. Man *can* be master, not only of sheep and oxen, but of himself and his actions: he can *decide* to do this or that.

So when we say that God is the Lord of history, it remains true that history is made by the decisions of men. Human freedom is the image of God's sovereignty. The difference between image and original lies just in the fact that man's power to do as he chooses is not determined, as the power of God is determined, by an unchangeable nature. Power in man, as in God, is ability to do as he wills. But man's will is not set, like God's, to what is good: it is directed to that which at the particular time or particular stage of his development *seems* to him good. And we can see that there had to be this difference, if God were to be Father as well as Sovereign. Children *made* to do their father's will—even if they were "conditioned" so as to imagine it to be their own—could not stand in a truly personal relationship to their father.

b. *Making.* God is goodness, and goodness can make nothing but what is good. The creative love of God is his constant will to bring what is good into being and to maintain it in being. But we cannot think of goodness without reference to someone for whom it is good—someone who can see that it is good and enjoy it. When God made heaven and earth, we are told that he saw that it was good: the Lord rejoiced in his works.[10] But when he made man, he made a creature who could see like himself that creation was good, and who could share in his rejoicing in it. God has given his own goodness to us in his creation, and given us eyes to see it, and a mind and heart to enjoy it.

And there is certainly in man a likeness of this creative love. Man *is* able to add to the goodness of creation, to bring new good into being and to preserve it when it is there. He can do this only by giving himself, by dedicating the power of vision that has been given to him to enable others to see. That is how artist, poet, and thinker do their work of creation. But the creative power in man is not confined to them. Whoever gives himself in love to his fellow-men is bringing new good into the world, and enabling others, to whom that good is given, to see that it is good and to rejoice in it.

c. *Fatherhood and Sonship.* We have already observed that in this first section of the Creed the terms "Almighty" and "Maker of heaven and earth" are not to be restricted to the First Person of the Trinity whom we call the Father, but are to be understood of the Godhead as such, and therefore of the whole Trinity in whom we believe. But Fatherhood in God belongs distinctively to him who is the Father of our Lord Jesus Christ. That means that in the eternal Godhead there is both Fatherhood and Sonship, mutually related to one another in an inseparable union. Christians become children of their Father in heaven by being "conformed", as St Paul says, "to the image of his Son":[11] we can only address God as "our Father" in Christ's name. But St Paul also prays to the Father who has given his name to every *patria*, every family or kin united by a common descent.[12] We must look then in our human nature, not for what may reflect the special character of either Fatherhood or Sonship in God separately considered, of either the First or the Second Person of the Trinity, but to that which makes us capable of the family relationship—that which is the secret of unity in any and every *patria*.

Parenthood as such does not distinguish men from the animals. Parental care and solicitude for the welfare of offspring is present in bird and beast, who will give their own lives to protect their young. The distinctively human element in the family relationship is most clearly pictured in the parable of the Prodigal Son. The relation between this father and his wilful son rises above anything traceable in the animal world, just because it is a *personal* relationship. Professor Farmer has suggested that the "heart and essence" of the personal world is found in the fact that "the persons are bound to one another by their common situation, yet free of one another, dependent on one another yet independent of one another".[13] The family, then, is the cradle of the world of persons; for in the family the life of mutual love and loyalty is incompatible with the will to dominate. To use Farmer's words, the "claim" of parent upon child must go with recognition of the child's "claim", not only to parental care, but also to freedom when he is ready for it. Conversely, the son who really loves his parents will not seek independence for its own sake. He will never cease to "honour and succour his father and mother",[14] or forget the debt of gratitude he owes them. It will be his aim to be a son of whom (in the common phrase) his parents can be proud.

The secret of the happy family is reciprocity—the will and the power to share a common life, to know the joys and the sufferings of others as one's own. And in this capacity for giving and receiving we may see the created likeness of that Love which is the eternal bond of Father and Son in the Godhead.

REFERENCES

1. Wis. 2.23.
2. Wis. 7.25ff.
3. Augustine, *De Trinitate*, XII. 21ff.
4. *Summa Theologica*, I, q.93, a.4, 6.
5. *Summa Theologica*, I, q.95; Ia IIae, q.85.
6. Augustine, *Confessions*, I. 1.
7. Augustine, *De Trinitate*, X. 17.
8. Augustine, *De Trinitate*, XIV. 15.

9. Gen. 1.28; Ps. 8.5f.; Ecclus. 17.3f.
10. Gen. 1.31; Ps. 104.31.
11. Rom. 8.29.
12. Eph. 3.15.
13. H. H. Farmer, *God and Men*, p. 48.
14. The Catechism in the Book of Common Prayer.

CHAPTER 6

Man—as he is

THE belief that man is made in the image of God is not inconsistent with acceptance of the evolutionary account of human origins. We may think of the "making" as a gradual process, leading in due course to the development of those powers in the human species which set man above the animals and give him the capacity for personal life in relation to his fellows and to God.

The present condition of mankind exhibits a perversion of this capacity, which has arisen through misuse of the powers upon which it rests. Intelligence and freedom have been used by men to dominate one another, so that the human family has become divided against itself. Man who was made to be a maker has become more destructive than any beast. The Bible teaches that this is the consequence of man's attempt to claim for himself an absolute mastery which he cannot have. Given dominion over the lower creation, he has refused to acknowledge the sovereignty of God. The Great Rebellion is the Fall: in St Augustine's words, "to be lifted up is already to be cast down".[1]

1. *Sin in the Old Testament*

a. This rebellion is pictured in a story set in immediate sequence to the story of Creation itself: there is no suggestion of a Golden Age. Apart from details, such as the nature of the forbidden fruit, which are left in an obscurity that tempts to the uncertainties of speculation, the purpose of the story is transparent and simple. It is the myth of lost happiness. The God whose sovereign will brought all things into being has also given *commands* to his creatures. The command is disobeyed, because its purpose is questioned and its sanction doubted. "Ye shall be as gods. . . . Ye shall not surely die." The moral is: God has the right to command because as Sovereign Goodness he can give no commands that are not for men's good. Doubt of God's goodness leads to disobedience, and disobedience to loss of true good.

b. The story of Adam and Eve is told for *Israel*. For Israel too has lost its Eden and learnt what it is to be a homeless exile. By the covenant with Abraham, confirmed and renewed at the Exodus and on Mount Sinai, Israel like Adam and Eve was set in a position of high privilege—in a relationship of mutual knowledge between God and the people whom he has chosen. "You only have I known of all the families of the earth."[2] But the privilege involved the acceptance of a Law in which God's will is made known and his sovereignty declared. "I am Jehovah, who brought thee out of the land of Egypt: thou shalt have none other gods beside me."[3]

Again as in Eden, unbelief, doubt of the power of God to enforce his commands or make good his promises, leads to the primal disobedience which is breach of the First Commandment in the Law —idolatry, the nature-worship of Canaan. Israel is mingled with the heathen and learns their works[4]—and so loses the knowledge of Jehovah. "The ox knoweth his owner, and the ass his master's crib: but Israel doth not know, my people doth not consider."[5] And when the knowledge of God is lost, all his commands are forgotten and disobeyed.[6] The ethical emphasis of the great prophets springs from their "knowledge" of the righteous God who loveth righteousness. Idolatry remains for them always the sin of sins: the corruption of religion is the cause of the corruption of morals. But both cause and effect are regarded by the prophet in terms of law and obedience. God's righteous commands have been disobeyed, and the disobedience is seen in particular actions which violate the Law and are called sins. As breach of law, every sin incurs guilt and brings upon itself punishment.

2. *Sin in the New Testament*

a. *The teaching of Jesus.* Jesus comes to fulfil the Law and the Prophets. His preaching of the Kingdom of God is Gospel, but it does not cancel the Law in which the kingdom of God and his righteousness are made known. It is the message of forgiveness, but demands repentance. Sin is still the act of transgression, and the word is nearly always used in the plural: "Thy sins are forgiven thee", "Her sins which are many are forgiven", "Forgive us our sins".[7]

But Jesus transforms the legal and prophetic conceptions of sin. He fixes attention upon the sinner rather than the sin, the person rather than the act. Only the good tree can produce good fruits:

the act expresses the man. He insists that outward obedience without love is hypocrisy, because it does not express the inward man, the real direction of the heart. He finds the worst of all sins where it is least suspected—in self-righteousness, and the contempt of the "open" sinner to which it leads; because God is like the father in the parable, and to be like God is to be merciful and forgiving. And the obedience which Jesus demands is an *entire* obedience—complete submission to the will of God. The Sermon on the Mount intensifies the Law's demand. The only actions that count in God's sight are those in which the real man and the whole man expresses himself.[8]

b. *St Paul and St John.* St Paul retains the conception of sin as disobedience or breach of law, together with the prophetic deduction of immorality from idolatry.[9] But he asks, *Why* are men sinful? —and answers by speaking of Sin in the singular as a spiritual power which has men in its grip: they are "slaves of sin", "sold under sin". This power has its hold on men through the "flesh"—which stands not for mere sensuality but for the whole life of man in its weakness and fragility apart from the Spirit of God.[10] Life "according to the flesh" is sin because it is the attempt to live without God in the world:[11] it is the opposite of faith, which is acceptance of the Gospel of forgiveness and the gift of the Spirit which is power to live by the Gospel. Faith "justifies" because instead of claiming God's verdict in its favour it throws itself on his mercy.[12]

The Gospel of St John develops St Paul's teaching of justification by faith into the simple equation of sin and unbelief. The Comforter who is to come will convict the world "of sin, because they believe not on me": "if ye believe not that I am he, ye shall die in your sins"; "he that believeth not is condemned already, because he hath not believed in the name of the only-begotten Son of God".[13] This unbelief is not mere incredulity, an attitude of mind: it is a perversity, both moral and intellectual, which takes effect in the rejection of God's revelation of his own goodness in Christ. For the "work of God", the service due to him, is simply to "believe on him whom he hath sent".[14]

3. *The Meaning of Sin*

Sin is defacement of the image of God, because it is wilful departure from God's purpose for man. God has given man life, to be lived *as* his gift: he has given it, that is to say, that man may accept it from his hands, "in quietness and confidence",[15] with grateful trust in the goodness of the Giver; and that man may live in the power of the love which has made him, as a brother among brothers, giving freely as he has freely received. In other words, life according to the purpose of God is the life of faith working through love. The man who will not accept the gift as it is given, and accept the Giver as his Father and his Lord, seeks to live "on his own", "from himself"—to be his own master and serve his own ends. It follows that instead of letting God's love rule in his dealings with his fellow-men, he seeks to dominate them, to compel them to serve himself. This is what the Bible calls "covetousness"—the craving for a larger share of the world's goods which can only be secured by power to command the services of others, the power of which the symbol in our modern world is money. And that is the rejection of the way of faith. "Because a man will not take the security he needs where God will give it to him, it follows that in the place where he should himself be a giver he will be nothing but a taker."[16] The natural egoism in which man is made impels him to seek his own welfare; but this natural egoism can only be saved from becoming self-worship by acceptance of the ultimate sovereignty of God.

4. *The Universality of Sin*

"All have sinned and come short of the glory of God." "If we say that we have no sin, we deceive ourselves."[17] We do not find such sayings in the Old Testament. In the Book of Job, Eliphaz can ask: "What is man, that he should be clean? and he which is born of a woman, that he should be righteous?"[18] Yet Job's comforters do not question the distinction between the "righteous" and the "wicked", which for so many of the Psalmists is as the difference between black and white.

But Christ says with terrible irony: "I came not to call the righteous, but sinners."[19] There are none who do not need to pray for forgiveness. What has made this difference?

The saying of St Paul just quoted is not a mere platitude to the effect that no man is morally perfect. That some men *are* morally better than others, that men can and do perform actions that in themselves are virtuous and noble, is not to be denied. Evil as we are, we do know, as Jesus says, how to give good gifts to our children.[20] Nor does universal sinfulness mean that everyone does some bad things sometimes as well as other good ones. It means rather that no man can claim that he is altogether pure in heart. Not only do we all have to contend with pride and selfishness in ourselves, but we know that even our best actions are never unmixed with self-assertion. We do not and cannot do all for the glory of God: we do not and cannot live altogether out of faith and love, trusting God and loving God with *all* our heart. And if we think we do, we "deceive ourselves". Indeed it is probable that the only men whose confession of sin is absolutely sincere are those whom we call the Saints.

Our wills are never wholly in the service of the will of God. Yet my will is my own will, and not something imposed upon me. When St Augustine honestly confronted the Manichean notion (with which he had soothed his own conscience) of an evil power not ourselves that works unrighteousness in us, he found himself obliged to confess that he alone was the agent of his misdeeds. *Totum ego eram*: "the whole of it was myself."[21]

5. Original Sin

The doctrine of original sin asserts not merely that men do in fact sin, but that they come into the world sinners—"by nature children of wrath".[22] The doctrine first appears not in the Old Testament but in late Judaism: it appears in our Apocrypha in the Second Book of Esdras, where we read of the "grain of evil seed" in Adam which has borne fruit in all his descendants.[23] In the Christian Church, the doctrine rested on two quite different foundations: the language of St Paul in the fifth chapter of the Epistle to the Romans, and the developing practice of infant baptism.

(1) St Paul's thought in Rom. 5 is obscured by the presence of two separate ideas: that death is the inevitable consequence of sin, and that sin is always transgression of a revealed law of God. But he begins by saying clearly enough that death, which entered the world with Adam's transgression, has passed to all men "inasmuch as all sinned". He is asserting the *universality* both of sin and of death, and drawing his parallel and contrast between the sin and death to which mankind is subject "in Adam", and the righteousness and life which are given to the redeemed "in Christ". His thought moves in terms not so much of physical heredity as of

corporate identity—the inclusion of mankind in the person of Adam, and the inclusion of believers in Christ.

(2) The Church's baptism was from the first "for the remission of sins".[24] If baptism was to be administered to infants, the sacrament could not change its significance: there was but "one baptism".[25] It was difficult to avoid the conclusion that the infant recipient of baptism, though he has transgressed no law, is nevertheless a "sinner"; and it seemed to follow that he must in some sense have inherited the universal sinfulness of mankind.

a. The Pelagians boldly denied the existence of any such inherited sinfulness. Their view of sin was individualistic and legalistic: a sin (they held) is a responsible action contrary to the known law of God; therefore an infant cannot be a sinner. The denial evoked the particular formulation of the doctrine of original sin which we associate with St Augustine. It runs as follows. The sin of Adam was pride, refusal to be subject to God; and this revolt against the eternal order was punished by *dis*order in the rebel—the subjection of man's spirit to that which is below it in that order, namely, the flesh. This enslavement appears in the form of "concupiscence"— the "lust of the flesh" in all its manifestations, i.e. not sensual desire in itself, but the "inordinate", uncontrollable desire which vainly seeks satisfaction in things which cannot satisfy. St Augustine saw this inordinate desire most plainly exemplified in the sexual craving which had once enslaved himself; and he concluded that the way in which original sin is propagated is just this particular activity of concupiscence—the desire "out of which and in which we are born".[26]

b. This plausible but most disastrous theory was never accepted by the Church, though unfortunately the reputation of St Augustine was too great for it to be pronounced a heresy. Roman Catholic teaching as represented by St Thomas defines original sin in negative terms as the loss of "original righteousness" and sanctifying grace through Adam's fall—its "form" is a deprivation rather than a depravation—but retains the idea of concupiscence as the "material" or positive element, which results from loss of the power given by grace to control the lower nature.[27] On the other hand, St Thomas substitutes for the Augustinian theory of transmission *via* physical generation the idea of an organic or mystical unity of mankind in Adam. We are all members of the body of which Adam is head, and as such we share in his responsibility for the sin which he committed by the act of his own will.[28] And here St Thomas is probably nearer to the real thought of St Paul in Rom. 5 (as we have suggested) than either St Augustine or Pelagius.

c. The sciences of biology and psychology have drawn the links which bind us to our ancestors closer than St Thomas could have imagined—though he would have welcomed the evidence they bring. We know now that there is no such thing as the isolated individual which Pelagius believed every man to be. We are in great part what our descent has made us; and most of the rest is what our environment is making us. We come of a line of sinful beings, men in whom faith and love have always been at odds with self-assertion. We are "born in sin"—not because the natural process of generation has anything sinful in it, but because (as Job said) the clean cannot come out of the unclean.[29] The fearful reality of human godlessness is nowhere so glaringly evident as in nationalism, where the naked worship of the collective Ego becomes the supreme virtue. Yet none of us can separate what he is "in himself" from what he has inherited or received from others. We cannot throw back our own sinfulness upon our inheritance or our environment, and so disclaim our own responsibility. For whatever be the factors that have contributed to the making of me, the result is "I".

6. The Fall

a. It can hardly be denied that the sin of mankind has a history. Schleiermacher said that "sin is in everyone the work of all and in all the work of everyone". The social interdependence of mankind means that no one's sin can be without its effect upon others. Thus there has arisen what Ritschl (following Schleiermacher) called the "kingdom of sin", extending itself through evil example, evil habit, and evil institutions—the guilt of which cannot rest upon any particular individual in isolation. But this, though it is certainly true, cannot serve as a substitute for the doctrine of original sin; for it gives an account of sin's propagation, but says nothing of sin's origin.

b. For sin to be propagated it must first exist. Christian doctrine can dispense with any theory of sin's propagation: it needs nothing more than the observable fact of sin's terrible fecundity—its power of propagating itself. But Christian doctrine must affirm, and affirm clearly, what it believes to be sin's origin. And upon that there can be no compromise. God is not the author of sin, and there is no rival god of evil from whom it can come: the story of Genesis contains

C

no hint that the serpent is more than one of the "beasts of the field" —for all his "subtlety". The one and only origin of sin is the perverted will of the created human being; and since there can be no sinful act until the will is perverted, we cannot escape belief in the Fall of Man. We may, if we like, invent (as Origen did in the third century) a pre-mundane world of created spirits whose fall preceded and occasioned their descent into bodily existence. But such an invention is entirely without ground in the teaching of the Bible. If the Fall belongs to this world, it must in some sense belong to history; but it need not be regarded as a single event of past and very ancient history. The embryo in the womb appears to reflect in the stages of its growth the history of the species. In the development of humanity there must have come a moment when man became able to choose, plan, and act as a person—and therefore to sin. So there is a moment in the spiritual growth of every child when he becomes able consciously to resent his inability to have everything his own way—and therefore able to take his little self for his god. And there is no grown man who has not yielded to that temptation, as Adam did in the story.

REFERENCES

1. Augustine, *De Civitate Dei*, XIV. 13.
2. Amos 3.2.
3. Ex. 20.2f.
4. Ps. 106.35.
5. Isa. 1.3.
6. Cf. Hos. 4.1,2.
7. Luke 5.20; 7.47; 11.4.
8. Matt. 7.17ff.; 23.23; Luke 18.9ff.; 6.35f.; Matt. 6.1–24.
9. Rom. 1.23ff.
10. See especially Rom. 7 and 8.
11. Eph. 2.12.
12. Rom. 10.1–10.
13. John 16.9; 8.24; 3.18.
14. John 6.29.
15. Isa. 30.15.
16. R. Seeberg, quoted by P. Althaus, *Die Christliche Wahrheit*, p. 356.
17. Rom. 3.23; 1 John 1.8.
18. Job 15.14.
19. Mark 2.17.
20. Matt. 7.11.
21. Augustine, *Confessions*, V. 10.
22. Eph. 2.3.

23. 2 Esdras 3.21; 4.30; 7.48.
24. Acts 2.38.
25. Eph. 4.5.
26. Augustine, *Contra Julianum*, VI. 55.
27. *Summa Theologica*, Ia IIae, q.82, a.3.
28. Ibid., q.81, a.1.
29. Job 14.4.

CHAPTER 7

And in one Lord Jesus Christ, the only-begotten Son of God

THE Second Article of the Nicene Creed begins, like the First, with words taken from St Paul. "We know", he writes to the Corinthians, ". . . that there is none other God but one. For though there be that are called gods, whether in heaven or in earth (as there be gods many, and lords many), yet to us there is but one God, the Father, of whom are all things, and we in him; and one Lord Jesus Christ, by whom are all things, and we by him."[1] Plainly, neither for St Paul nor the Creed is the Lordship ascribed to Jesus any infringement of the unity of God. We shall presently consider what is meant by giving to Jesus the title of "Lord". For the moment, the important point to observe is that the Christian faith in the one God, which the Creed is concerned to express, *can* only be expressed adequately by making certain statements about a person and events belonging to *history*.

In the Creed, as generally in St Paul, "Jesus Christ" forms a proper name. At first, "Christ" was the title claimed for Jesus of Nazareth: what the Apostles told their Jewish compatriots was that this man *is* the predestined and expected Messiah. For Gentile converts, the functional significance of the title tended to disappear: for Tacitus and Pliny, "Christ" is simply the executed Jew who gave his name to his followers. But to set the person in his historical context, we need both names. The Jesus of whom we speak is a certain Nazarene who was called the Christ and on that account was put to death under Pontius Pilate. That there actually was such a person is not a matter of belief but of historical knowledge, whereas the Creed as a whole is concerned not with what we may reasonably claim to know but with what we believe. The Gospels which give us our knowledge of Jesus were all written that we might believe that Jesus is the Christ, the Son of God:[2] they supply the ground for the Church's beliefs about Jesus of Nazareth. But what, in fact, do they enable us to know about him? Is the ground for these beliefs sufficient?

A. THE JESUS OF HISTORY

The Gospels give us "doctrine", but they give the doctrine's ground in what is not doctrine but historical fact. St Luke's preface puts it exactly. The Gospel "narrative" (A.V. "declaration") is designed to give the believer a "secure foundation" (A.V. "certainty") for the teaching he has received.[3] The teaching rests firmly, he means, upon the testimony of eye-witnesses to that which they have seen and heard. And this testimony must be subject like any other historical evidence to the examination of the historian: he wants to know how far it is a reliable record of facts, and for that purpose he must analyse and "criticize" the record itself, i.e. he must submit it to questioning.

1. *Criteria of historicity*

Contemporary records of events are hardly ever disinterested or unprejudiced; and they are the less so, the greater the importance attached to the events by those who record them. The tradition of the Church which lies behind and in the Gospels is certainly not unprejudiced, impartial; and the historian who studies the record may share the prejudices of the writers—or he may not. If he does not, he can hardly avoid being prejudiced *against* the interpretation which they have put upon the story they relate; and that prejudice will dispose him to detect them as adapting or even inventing features in the story in order to support their interpretation.

In all historical investigation there are certain criteria or tests by which the reliability of an account is estimated. The estimate will be affected (1) by the date and place of origin of the document, the closeness or remoteness of the writer to the events related, and (2) by the degree of internal consistency in the account itself: whether it contains contradictions or incompatibilities. But it will be affected also (3) by the historian's personal and *a priori* judgements of what is probable, i.e. what conforms to our general experience of the way men behave and things happen, what can be paralleled in our knowledge of other times and places. A story is held to be improbable if it goes against the measure of uniformity generally observable in history—a uniformity notoriously less than the "uniformity of nature".

2. The Gospel History

What then is the result of the application of these criteria to the study of the Gospels?

(1) The study of the Gospels as historical documents has concentrated upon the attempt to reconstruct the process by which they came into being. This attempt has been directed in two ways: first, the "source-criticism" which traces the priority or dependence of the various documents in relation to one another, and later the "form-criticism" which tries to go behind the written documents to the formation of the oral tradition which (it is reasonably supposed) must have preceded them, and the manner in which that tradition became crystallized. The object in all this is to arrive at the evidence for what happened in its earliest form. It is generally assumed that what is later in date is less reliable than what is earlier, even if there is no inconsistency. Yet this is by no means self-evident. Later accounts are not always less accurate than earlier; for they may be based on equally good authority, and the first form in which a story circulates may need correction by more careful inquiry.

(2) The criterion of consistency is not always an objective one. It can be applied with confidence only in cases of directly contradictory statements of fact, place, or time. But often it will depend on a judgement upon what is compatible with consistency of character in word or behaviour: the critic asks himself, Is this "like" Jesus? *Would* he have said or done this? And in such cases the answers will be subjectively affected in varying degrees.

(3) In all *a priori* judgements on the Gospel history, the effect of prejudice is not to be escaped. If the critic is an unbeliever, he will regard all elements in the story as suspect which attribute supernatural power to Jesus. If he believes in the uniqueness of the person of Jesus, he is much more likely to accept as probable the presence of the unique in his story. But the critic may also be a believer who shares some of the prejudices of the unbeliever. Whereas the faith of the first readers was no doubt aided or confirmed by what was marvellous in the story, his faith may rather be offended by it: he may *want* to find nothing that could separate the humanity of Jesus from the humanity of every man. He will then be prejudiced in favour of any argument tending to show that the real humanity of the man of Nazareth has been here and there obscured by legend.

Thus none of the criteria generally applicable to historical evidence can give complete security. But their application to the study of the Gospels has led in recent times to one fairly generally agreed conclusion. It seems overwhelmingly probable that *before* the Gospels reached the form in which we have them there was a period during which the common tradition about Jesus was already being used for the instruction of converts and the edification of the Church. And there is reason to think that this use will have led to modifications in the tradition itself: e.g. that the parables in many cases were twisted from their original purpose in the preaching of Jesus to "them that were without",[4] so as to give guidance for situations in the common life of the Christian community. It becomes increasingly difficult and hazardous to disentangle what Jesus may actually have said from what the development of the Church's tradition may have made him say, and not less difficult to distinguish what he actually did from what the Church had come to think of him as doing. So we find a devoutly Christian scholar like the late Professor R. H. Lightfoot concluding that "the form of the earthly no less than of the heavenly Christ is for the most part hidden from us";[5] and Rudolf Bultmann confessing that in his opinion "we can now know almost nothing concerning the life and personality of Jesus".[6] And both Lightfoot and Bultmann make it clear that they see in this nothing that should discourage the faith of the Christian.

3. *History and the Faith*

Are we then to infer that the whole business of New Testament criticism is irrelevant to Christian faith and life? Would it make no difference to what we believe and teach, to Creed and doctrine, if the historical study of the Gospels should lead in the future to results ever more and more negative? Is faith in Christ compatible with almost complete agnosticism about Jesus?

a. The first thing to be said here is that a Christianity which had cut itself loose altogether from its moorings in history would certainly be something quite different from what it has been from its beginning. For it could no longer say that God has visited and redeemed his people: it could not even say that the story of Jesus gives us a true picture of what God is "like". For the Gospel picture is actually a picture of God coming to seek and to save the lost—not of a God who must be sought and found with such aid as pictures may give. However, even the fairly extreme agnosticism of such a scholar as Bultmann does not go so far as to dispense with history. He does believe that Christian faith hangs upon the act of God in Christ, for us men and for our salvation, which took place under Pontius Pilate. But he does not believe that God was in Christ because the human "personality" of Jesus—the Jesus of the Gospels —displayed the likeness of God: he believes it because the death of Jesus has opened to men the way of escape from their past selves which is the forgiveness of sins. So Kierkegaard said that if the Apostolic witness had been no more than that "in such and such a year God appeared among us in the humble figure of a servant, that he lived and taught in our community and finally died".[1] it would be more than enough.

b. Enough—but for what? Christianity is more than trust in a forgiving God: it is life in Christ. A Christianity which admitted that the Christ of faith is not the Jesus of history would have virtually deprived the Resurrection of the meaning it had for the Church from the first. For according to the New Testament it was the "Jesus of history", the man who was crucified, who rose from the dead and is with us always. But we come to know this Jesus only through the Gospel story. Unless that story, taken as a whole, makes him known to us as he was on earth, it is not making him known to us as risen and alive for evermore. The life of Christian devotion is not "Jesus-worship"; but it is the knowledge of God *in Christ*, and it cannot be maintained on a fiction. We cannot follow as our Lord one whose person is to us no more than an X.

c. It follows that Christian doctrine cannot be indifferent to historical research. Christian theology must always be confronted by the questions posed to it by particular conclusions of contemporary New Testament study; and it can never be sufficient reason for accepting or rejecting any of these conclusions that one or the other will support or conflict with a traditional form of doctrine. If our faith is grounded—as the Creed implies—on particular events of history, we cannot screen off the events from the historian's scrutiny. That does not mean that we must be dupes of the prejudices of any historian. Historical certainty is beyond our reach, for all history rests upon an assessment of probabilities. But Christian faith can never be grounded on a set of historical improbabilities.

B. THE TITLES OF JESUS

The three titles—Christ, Son of God, and Lord—express the significance which Jesus bore for the Church of the New Testament.

No doubt, it was the Resurrection that made it possible for the Apostles to justify these titles. But it was the Jesus of history for whom the titles were claimed; and their significance cannot be for us any more than it was for them independent of what can be known about this same Jesus.

1. *Christ*

The first of the titles by which the followers of Jesus expressed their belief about him was that of "the" Christ—the Anointed One of Jewish expectation.

a. The ceremony of anointing was the setting apart and empowering of a chosen individual for a sacred office, especially the office of priest or king. But both priest and king were representatives of the nation. Israel believed itself to be God's chosen people—his "anointed ones",[8] the elect community in which the rule of God was to be effectively displayed, the place where his kingdom should come on earth as it is in heaven. The prophets looked forward to the coming of a prince in David's line who would rule in righteousness, in the name of God, and by the power of God's Spirit.[9] The hope implied the establishment of the nation in political freedom and independence; and it was easily enlarged into a grandiose anticipation of Israel's dominance over other nations—whereby the universal sovereignty of Israel's God would be manifested.[10] This hope was certainly alive in the time of Jesus: a classical expression of it is found in the *Psalms of Solomon* which date from the middle of the first century B.C.[11] Jesus was undoubtedly put to death as a pretended Messiah in this sense. Yet there was nothing in his activity or teaching which suggested claims to the throne: his followers insisted that even the Roman governor who condemned him did not take the charge of treason very seriously; and we know that he actually challenged the teaching of the "scribes" that the Messiah would be a son of David—though the prophets might well seem to be on the side of the scribes.[12]

b. In the literature of Apocalypse, in which the prophetic hope was clouded by a despair of secular history, the functions of the prophetic Messiah were transferred to a supernatural being whose appearance is linked with a catastrophic end of the whole present order of things. Or, if such a generalization be disputed, this was at least a prominent form of apocalyptic prediction.[13] In Jesus' preaching of the kingdom of God, there is no mistaking the note of crisis and urgency, even of impending catastrophe.[14] He calls men to *decide* before it is too late—to repent, for the kingdom is *at hand*. What remains uncertain and as keenly debated as ever is the meaning of his application to himself of the term "Son of Man". The Gospels clearly represent him as in some sense identifying himself with the figure of apocalyptic whose "coming" is still future.[15] The "Son of Man" in the Book of Daniel stands for the "people of the saints"; and the "Servant of the Lord" in the Second Isaiah is not easy to take as a purely individual figure.[16] It is probable enough that Jesus found a representative character in both. But it seems to have been by a combination of these two that he foretold that before the Son of Man will "appear" he must die at the hands of his own people.[17] Only prejudice can raise a doubt that Jesus himself made that startling correction of Messianic hope. Certainly it was as the Messiah of apocalyptic rather than of prophecy that he was proclaimed after his death.

2. Son of God

Nowadays "Christ" is for most people hardly more than a kind of surname of Jesus, with no implications of faith or allegiance. We need to remind ourselves that when we call Jesus "Christ" we mean "the Christ": we are committing ourselves, as St Peter did at Caesarea Philippi, to a tremendous claim on his behalf. What is involved in the title is the relation of Jesus himself to the Kingdom of God whose coming he proclaimed; and that is more clearly seen in another of the Creed's titles—"the only-begotten Son of God".

In the Gospels this title appears as a synonym for "Christ".[18] There is not much evidence from Jewish sources that "Son of God" was a common title of the Messiah. But in the Old Testament sonship to God is the privilege of Israel; and that sonship is as it were concentrated in the person of Israel's king:[19] the ideal king of Israel must incorporate the character of the ideal Israel—which is to know God as Father and obey him as King of kings.

We recall here what was said earlier about the meaning of sonship for Jesus himself and his "knowledge" of the Father.[20] The temptation story, whether told by Jesus to his disciples or a product of their later understanding of him, marks the difference between a Messiah whose kingdom should be of this world, and the Son who comes to do his Father's will. That will is indeed the rule of righteousness, but it can only be set up on earth by the changing of men's hearts, and their reconciliation to God through repentance and forgiveness.

The word "only-begotten" in the Fourth Gospel and in the Creed has nearly the same meaning as the word "beloved" in the Voice from heaven that designates Jesus as God's Son at Baptism and Transfiguration. It marks the difference that separates Jesus as the Christ from all Christians, but points at the same time to the gift of "adoption" that is offered to men "in Christ". As the Son of God, Jesus is fulfilment, not so much of the Jewish Messianic hope in any of its forms, as of the destiny of Israel as a people. The Bible compels us to think of God's purpose in history as working itself out "according to election".[21] God chooses a people to know him, as the means of making himself known to all nations. He chooses his prophets from within the chosen people to recall them from their wanderings. He chooses the son of Mary in whom the whole purpose shall be brought to fulfilment, and he is named Jesus ("Jehovah is salvation") because he will save his people from their sins.[22]

3. Lord

In the Gentile world of the Near East in the first century there were (as St Paul says) "lords many", worshipped in the various mystery-cults of saviour-gods. In that context, "lord" signified the relationship of the god to his worshippers: they *belong* to him as slaves to a master, and so look to him for protection. It was easy to suggest that this was how the title came to be applied to Jesus in Gentile Churches: this so-called Christ was another, and perhaps a more powerful, dying and rising god. But there is good reason to think that the title did not in fact originate in Greek-speaking Churches, but in Palestine itself; for it appears in the Aramaic prayer *Marana-tha* ("Our Lord, come!") which St Paul quotes in writing to the Corinthians.[23] Moreover, Jesus had cited the 110th Psalm ("The Lord said unto my Lord") as Messianic prophecy, and that text must have been used early and constantly in Christian preaching, for it recurs all through the New Testament: it is the Jesus who is ascended and sitting at God's right hand who is "Lord".[24]

At the end of St Matthew's Gospel, the risen Christ says: "All authority is given to me in heaven and on earth." And in John 17 Jesus prays to his Father: "Glorify thy Son, that thy Son also may glorify thee: as thou hast given him authority over all flesh, that he should give eternal life to as many as thou hast given him."[25] That authority is what the New Testament ascribes to Jesus when it calls him "Lord". In Jesus, the Jesus who was obedient to death, Christians recognize the plenipotentiary of God, who can speak to men the divine word of forgiveness. He has the right to be called Master, because he is the *good* Master, to whom they can entrust themselves with a confidence that is absolute, because he is clothed with the Lordship, the absolute sovereignty, of God. So, already in the New Testament, the prayers of Christians are being addressed to the Lord Jesus; and Gentiles are neither the first nor the only Christians to "call upon the name of the Lord" who is Jesus Christ.[26] Because God has given to his Servant the name which is above every name, the name of "Lord", St Paul can find the glory of God the Father manifested in the bowing of every knee before the name of *Jesus.*[27]

REFERENCES

1. 1 Cor. 8.4ff.
2. John 20.31; cf. Mark. 1.1.
3. Luke 1.1,4.
4. Mark 4.11.
5. R. H. Lightfoot, *History and Interpretation in the Gospels,* p. 225.
6. R. Bultmann, *Jesus and the Word*, p. 8.
7. Quoted by D. M. Baillie, *God was in Christ*, p. 49.
8. Ps. 105.15 (R.V.).
9. E.g. Isa. 11.1ff.; Jer. 23.5f.; Ezek. 34.22f.
10. E.g. Isa. 60.
11. Psalms of Solomon, xvii (ed. Ryle and James).
12. Mark 12.35ff.
13. Enoch 37–70 (ed. Charles); cf. 2 Esdras 13.
14. E.g. Matt. 24.37ff.; Luke 17.20ff.
15. Mark 8.38; 14.62.
16. Isa. 44.1; 49.3.
17. Mark 9.12; 10.44f.
18. E.g. Matt. 16.16.
19. Ex. 4.22; 2 Sam. 7.14.
20. See p. 24.
21. Rom. 9.11.
22. Matt. 1.21.

23. 1 Cor. 16.22.
24. Mark 12.36; cf. Acts 2.34; Rom. 8.34; Eph. 1.20; Col. 3.1; Heb. 1.13, etc.
25. Matt. 28.18; John 17.1f.
26. Acts 7.59; 22.16; 1 Cor. 1.2.
27. Phil. 2.10f.; cf. Isa. 45.23ff.

CHAPTER 8

Begotten of his Father before all worlds, God of God, Light of Light, Very God of very God, Begotten, not made, Being of one substance with the Father, By (Through) whom all things were made

IN the Nicene Creed and the Apostles' Creed alike, the Second Article begins, as we have seen, with the ascription to Jesus of three titles, all of which are primitive, drawn from the earliest confession of the Church as we find it in the New Testament. But at this point the Nicene Creed inserts seven phrases, which set forth not what the primitive Church believed about the "Jesus of history", the man who lived and died and rose again, but what was later declared to be implied, by these beliefs about Jesus, in regard to the eternal being of God. Only the last of these seven phrases—"through whom all things were made"—has clear authority in the New Testament.

1. Nicaea and Constantinople

Three of the seven phrases—"Very God of very God, Begotten not made, Being of one substance with the Father"—were introduced for the first time into the Church's statement of belief by the Council of Nicaea in the year 325, with a specific purpose: viz. to exclude the Arian doctrine that Christ, as the *Logos* (Word) of the Father, was not co-eternal with the Father but created by him and therefore inferior in being.

The Creed which we call "Nicene" was not the formula adopted by the Council of Nicaea. We know that our Creed's Catholic authority was recognized at the Council of Chalcedon in 451, but its previous history is obscure. It had probably been in some way accepted by the Council of Constantinople in 381, when the original "faith of Nicaea" was found to need supplementation in order to assert the Catholic doctrine of the Holy Spirit. It may have existed as a local Creed before that date. In any case, it included the three anti-Arian phrases of Nicaea; though it left out a fourth—"that is, from the substance of the Father"—which had been inserted at Nicaea in order to make it clear that to speak of the Son as "begotten of the Father" implies a process "within" the being of God, not an act of external creation.

2. Pre-Nicene elements

For the moment we disregard the particular anti-Arian phrases of Nicaea, and consider the other four; "Begotten of his Father before all worlds, God of God, Light of Light, Through whom all things were made." These were all part of the baptismal Creed of Caesarea, to which Eusebius its Bishop appealed in defence of his own orthodoxy at Nicaea; and the first and last of them (at least) seem to have had a place in nearly every Eastern Creed by the beginning of the fourth century. What the last phrase asserts is the teaching of the New Testament, common to St Paul and St John, that Christ who is the Wisdom or Word of God is therefore God's instrument in the creation of the world. The first phrase asserts in accordance with this that the divine Sonship of Christ cannot be "dated" from the birth from the Virgin, but must "precede" the very beginning of the created world.

a. The early Church declared that Jesus is Christ, Son of God, and Lord of men. We cannot say when or how it came to affirm what we call the "pre-existence" of him who was so entitled—that in some sense he "came down from heaven" to be born and live on earth. St Paul seems to take it for granted; for he uses it more than once as ground for exhortation to Christian conduct. Christians ought to give generously, for they know the generosity of him who, *though he was rich*, for their sakes became poor.[1] Christians should be unselfish, for their pattern is one who was "in the form of God", but took upon himself the "form of a servant".[2] If, as many think, that great passage in the Epistle to the Philippians is not St Paul's own composition, but a Christian hymn already familiar when he wrote the Epistle, the belief that Christ's existence did not begin with his human birth must have arisen very early indeed.

The Rabbis taught that the Torah, the Law given through Moses, was created by God before the world; and apocalyptic writers could speak of the Messiah as existent in heaven before his appearance on earth.[3] But such "pre-existence" does not necessarily carry with it the idea of a cosmic Christ, the agent of God in creation; and this is what is asserted by St Paul, St John, and the author of the Epistle to the Hebrews.[4]

b. "The Jews", says St Paul, "require a sign", a miraculous demonstration of God's saving power. "The Greeks seek after wisdom": they look for knowledge to bring them salvation. "Christ crucified" is "unto the Jews a stumbling-block, and unto the Greeks foolishness" . . . but "unto them which are called, both Jews and Greeks, Christ the power of God, and the wisdom of God."[5] "Power" and "Wisdom" here are not abstract qualities or attributes. The Hebrew thinker does not deal in abstractions; and when the writers of the early chapters of Proverbs and of the Book of Wisdom spoke of the divine wisdom by which the world was made, it came naturally to them to use the language of personification: "Wisdom" speaks and acts.[6]

This conception of God's Wisdom, his purposing and designing Mind, as the agent or instrument of his creation, is evidently anthropomorphic, derived from our human experience of the use of tools in construction and manufacture. In Philo the Platonizing Jew, who was St Paul's contemporary, the *Logos*, which is the equivalent of the divine Wisdom, is the instrumental medium, the link between the transcendent and eternal God and the world of things that come into being and pass away—like the eternal "Forms" or thoughts of God in later Platonism. But the *Logos* of St John's Prologue is both the Word of command, the Word of the almighty will whose speaking brought all created things into being, and also the Light by which God reveals his purposes to men—his self-utterance. And here the metaphor of instrument, though it still moulds the language, really breaks down. The tool is no longer separable from its user. "The Word was God."

c. This creative self-utterance of God himself, this divine and eternal Wisdom, has been "made flesh"—visible, audible, tangible in a man like ourselves. How was it that the writers of the New Testament were drawn to make so tremendous a claim on behalf of the Jesus of Nazareth whose human figure still lived in the memories of men?

Jesus became Lord for the early Church because it was *through* him that God's kingdom was being established: *through* his word God had spoken, *through* his victory over sin and death God's own salvation was being wrought, *through* identification with him men were reconciled to God. "No man cometh unto the Father, but *through* me."[7] J. M. Creed in his Hulsean Lectures suggested that there was an "inner logic" in the early faith of Christians which issued in this doctrine of the "cosmic" Christ, and that we can see the movement taking place in the last verses of Rom. 8. "When St Paul has proclaimed his persuasion that the love of God which is in Christ Jesus is the sovereign power to which all things created must give place, the way has been opened for the belief that through Christ all things created came to be."[8]

Yet the love of God which comes to us through Christ is not at first sight the *same* as the love by which the Creator was moved in the beginning. The way indeed was opened, and the idea of an instrument in creation lay ready to hand. But even so a leap in thought was necessary. If we look for some connection in New Testament teaching between the Christ through whom we are redeemed and the Christ through whom we were made, we may perhaps find it in St Paul's saying that life in Christ is a "new creation".[9] The "newness" of the being into which we enter in Christ is nothing less than a coming to be of that which was not— a creation "out of nothing". And he who is God's instrument in the new creation cannot be other than God's instrument in all creation.

3. *"Very God of very God, Begotten not made, being of one substance with the Father"*

The belief that Christ is to God as the instrument or agent through whom both creation in the beginning and re-creation in these latter days are performed, thus became an expression of the Church's faith. Yet it was just this *form* in which Christian faith had been led to express itself that occasioned the crisis of Arianism in the fourth century.

The Arians thought they were contending for the pure and absolute monotheism which had been affirmed in Hebrew Scripture and confirmed in Greek philosophy. They took the Gospel story at its word, as telling of a Christ who was in truth subject, obedient in all things to the Father, and not the Father himself in human disguise; and they argued that if Christ was God's obedient tool in the work of creation as in that of redemption, he could not be God himself in either function. Again, the term "Son" (they said) is

meaningless if it does not connote the priority of him who is called
Father as well as the subordination of him who is called Son.

But if Christ is neither co-equal nor co-eval with the Father, he
must belong to the sphere of things which God has made—though
no doubt St Paul was right in calling him the "first-born of all
creation".[10] When we speak of God, the Arians maintained, there
is no real difference between the act we call "begetting" and that
which we call "creating". Both are free actions of the divine Will:
there was no more necessity in one than in the other: God was not
compelled by his nature either to create or to beget. "By his will
the Father begat the Son": so (they said) it must be, if God is
personal being and not mindless nature-process. The Arians did not
reject the phrases of the older Creeds—"God from God", "Light
from Light"—the purpose of which had been to clarify the sense in
which the language of fatherhood and sonship is to be taken, by
affirming both likeness and distinction. The metaphor of light and
ray was traditional and based on Scripture;[11] and even the word
"God" could still be used in the speech of Greek Christians as a
general term to denote a *kind* of being which is superhuman and
immortal—like the stars. There could be inferior divine beings, but
only one supreme and absolute God. Did not Christ himself
sanction such usage when he quoted the Psalmist's "I have said,
Ye are gods"?[12]

So the defenders of orthodoxy could call the Arians "pagans",
because they made Christ a demi-god, and "Jews" because they
denied his true divinity. In fact they were insisting that *if* our
salvation comes "through" Christ, *if* Christ is really an instrument,
he can in the proper sense be neither Creator nor Redeemer. Christ
is the means, but no more than the means, by which the one God
both creates and redeems—the one and only true God in the knowledge of whom is eternal life.

4. *The rejection of Arianism*

Arianism was rejected by the Church for two reasons.

(1) It is by union with Christ that Christians are given a share in
the eternal life which is the life of God "who only hath immortality".[13] All things created are transient, perishable. If Christ were
a creature, he could not have "life in himself",[14] and therefore could
not impart life to the Church which is his Body. This was the

central argument of Athanasius. To be united to a creature cannot give union with God.

(2) To admit that Christ is less than God would be to falsify the Christian religion which is expressed in prayer and worship. The Church refused to deny that which had been the mainstay of its devotional life. Arius, said Athanasius, has no right to worship a creature; but the Church cannot exist without the worship of Christ.

The formulae of Nicaea were the best that could be found at the time to protect the Church from the possibility of Arian teaching; and the possibility was serious, because there were Bishops who sympathized with Arius. Looking back, we may feel that "Very God of very God" would have been enough. "Begotten not made" simply insisted that the human language of fatherhood and sonship, taken from the world of creation, must not be understood of God in the creaturely sense in which it is used of men. The much-disputed term *Homo-ousios* ("of one substance") really adds nothing: the word itself was ambiguous—even Athanasius could apply it to the relation between human fathers and sons[15]—and it was objected to because of its vagueness as well as because it was "philosophic" and not Scriptural. Its orthodox defenders had to hedge it with negations: it did *not* mean that there is nothing to distinguish Father and Son, or that the Godhead was a composite substance like all the material objects of our experience—as though Father and Son were "parts" of God like the members of a body. But what it *did* mean was never and never could be stated more clearly than in the simple "Very God of very God". We repeat "of one substance" in the Creed today, though few of us are much less vague about its meaning than were most of the Bishops at Nicaea, because we must needs stand by the Nicene decisions.

5. The indispensability of Nicaea

Why is that decision so vital for the Christian faith?

a. Arianism, though it has had its revivals, is not in its original form a live option for anyone today. No one is likely to defend the notion of a superhuman being, brought into existence to be the instrument of the world's creation, and in the fullness of time appearing on earth to be the instrument of man's redemption.

b. Nevertheless, the fact remains that the offence of Christianity in the modern world is still the dogma of the divinity of Christ. Is it not possible, we are asked, to believe in God, to believe that the power which sustains the universe is good—a power not ourselves making for righteousness—without putting on our minds the intolerable burden of declaring that God was in Christ in any different sense from that in which he is present and active in all good men and all good things? Can we not believe that Christ by his life and death has taught us how to think of God, taught us to think of divine goodness as the power of self-giving love—without demanding acceptance of a theological inference about the person of the teacher which is really gratuitous, and pretends to knowledge of what we cannot know?

The answer must be that Christianity is not a "teaching", not a "doctrine", but a *Gospel*. It does not ask us to put our faith in the goodness of God despite the obvious evils of the world. It tells us why such a faith is possible for us. God is not the sort of being who might or would give his only Son to save the world. He has actually done it: God so loved that he gave—once upon a time and once for all.

c. Still, there remains the question, What is meant in this context by speaking of "Father" and "Son"? If the Son here simply meant a human being devoted to the love and service of the common Father of mankind, then Jesus Christ would be no more than a typical figure—one of the many "sons of God" whose self-devotion may inspire others to follow their example. God would have "given" this son, as he gives all good men to the world, as the good Creator is the Maker and Giver of all good. But in such "giving" there would be no uniqueness and nothing decisive or final.

To acknowledge with the Creed that our Lord is of one substance with the Father, is to acknowledge that what God gave in the giving of his Son was *himself*—and that nothing less than God's giving of himself could bring into this world of change, sin, and death the power of his own endless life.

REFERENCES

1. 2 Cor. 8.9.
2. Phil. 2.4ff.
3. E.g. 2 Esdras 13.26 and Enoch 48.6.
4. Col. 1.16f.; John 1.2; Heb. 1.2.
5. 1 Cor. 1.22ff.
6. See especially Prov. 8.22ff., and cf. Ps. 104.24; 136.5
7. John 14.6.

8. J. M. Creed, *The Divinity of Christ*, p. 140.
9. Gal. 6.15; 2 Cor. 5.17.
10. Col. 1.15.
11. Heb. 1.3; cf. Wis. 7.26.
12. John 10.34.
13. 1 Tim. 6.16.
14. John 5.26.
15. Athanasius, *De Synodis*, 51.

CHAPTER 9

Who for us men and for our salvation came down from heaven, And was incarnate by the Holy Ghost of the Virgin Mary, And was made man

THE clauses which we have just considered constitute the most important of the differences between the Nicene Creed and the Apostles' Creed. The Apostles' Creed says nothing about the Godhead of Christ: at least, it makes no attempt to define the nature of the divinity which is to be ascribed to the Jesus who is Christ, only Son of God the Father, and our Lord. Instead, it proceeds at once to state that the manner of his coming into the world was miraculous: "conceived of the Holy Ghost, born of the Virgin Mary".

1. *Who for us men . . . came down from heaven*

a. The grammatical structure of this part of the Nicene Creed is remarkable. For the relative pronoun "who" links all that precedes, including the theological phrases of the anti-Arian insertion, with what is now to be stated about the life and death of a man. In fact, the whole Article from beginning to end is *about* the Jesus who performed the work of the Christ and is to be confessed as Lord. It is "this same Jesus" whom we believe to be the eternal Son of God, of one substance with the Father.

Does that mean that the man Jesus of Nazareth existed from all eternity in the personal relationship of divine Son to divine Father, so that his earthly life was no more than a temporal episode in his existence? The framers of the Creed certainly did not so intend it. The suggestion that the humanity of Christ came down from heaven was actually made in some quarters towards the end of the fourth century; but it had only to be made to be rejected, although there was a text that might be taken to support it: "No man hath ascended up to heaven but he that came down from heaven, even the Son of Man which is in heaven."[1] The text had to be otherwise interpreted. The Church took it for granted that the manhood of Christ—all that he has in common with ourselves—came into being by way of conception and birth in the days of Herod the king. It was only Resurrection and Ascension that exalted this manhood into a continuing heavenly existence "at the right hand of God". But the structure of the Creed, by keeping Jesus Christ as the grammatical subject of the whole Article, did serve to rule out in advance any separation or division between the eternal Son of God and the man of Nazareth. It speaks throughout of one subject, one agent or actor, one person. And this unity of the divine-human person of Christ was underlined at the Council of Chalcedon in its famous Definition by the emphatic repetition of the word "the same": "We confess one and the self-same Son our Lord Jesus Christ . . . the self-same complete in Godhead, the self-same complete in manhood, truly God and truly man, the self-same of a reasonable soul and body, of one substance with the Father as to the Godhead, the self-same of one substance with us as to the manhood . . . before the ages begotten of the Father as to the Godhead, and the self-same in the last days born of the Virgin Mary as to the manhood; one and the self-same Christ, Son, Lord, Only-begotten."[2]

b. The Creed can say "came down from heaven", *because* he who was born of Mary is "the same" as he who was begotten of the Father before all worlds. In so saying, it uses language which for us, if not for those who framed it, is unquestionably symbolic: it speaks of a non-spatial event in spatial terms as a "descent", in order to convey its assertion that what Jesus Christ did for us men and for our salvation was an act of God in the course of history. The Eternal submitted himself to the measures of time, the Infinite consented to become finite; and that (to us) inconceivable act of "self-emptying" or "self-humiliation" was the way God chose to save mankind. We may believe that it was indeed the only way in which our salvation could be accomplished: as St Augustine loved to put it, the only remedy for the pride of man was the humility of God.[3]

There is here no doctrine of Atonement: we are not told *how* the "coming down" was "for our salvation"; and we shall postpone our consideration of that question till we reach the end of this Second Article of the Creed. But we must observe that the words "came down" exclude any form of Atonement-doctrine which might concentrate or isolate the saving efficacy of Christ's work in what he did or was "as man". If we acknowledge the Godhead of Christ because we know him as our Saviour, he is able to save us only because he is God. It was *God* and not man who reconciled the world to himself. But on the other hand the reconciliation was "in Christ"—the "man Christ Jesus" who is the mediator between God and men.⁴ There was no other way.

2. *Was incarnate . . . And was made man*

Neither of the two Greek verbs here used (*sarkousthai* and *enanthropein*) occurs in the New Testament. The first is an adaptation of the text of St John's Prologue "was made flesh" (*sarx egeneto*). But the Greek verb *sarkousthai* in secular usage meant literally to "put on flesh" or "grow fleshy"; and it was felt that some further definition was required of the sense in which St John's text is to be understood. The "flesh" which the Word "became" means humanity as we know it—not merely its outward appearance, the visible bodily structure, but the complete human being—body and soul with the human soul's powers of thought and will. So the creed-makers coined the verb *enanthropein* by compounding the preposition "in" and the substantive "man", to give the sense of "enter" or "assume" manhood. The English "was incarnate . . . and was made man" derives from the Latin form of the Creed; and the retention of "incarnate" serves to remind us that in the text of St John the word "flesh" carried the Biblical implications of weakness and fragility which always characterized "flesh" in contrast to "spirit". The human nature into which the Son of God entered was no less subject than our own to "the thousand natural shocks that flesh is heir to".

Arianism compelled the Church to realize to the full what it must mean to speak of Christ as God. But that realization made it all the more difficult to understand how the same Christ could be man as we are; and the Christological controversies which began with the final rejection of Arianism turned upon the meaning of the words "was made man". How was it possible for Godhead and manhood to be united, without either one or the other being deprived of the fullness and reality of its essential nature? What made an answer to that question so important was the Christian conviction that we men *are* united to God through Christ: which could not be, unless Christ and God are truly one. And what makes the story of these ancient controversies of living interest for us still is the fact that modern attempts to answer the same question are apt (as we shall see) to follow one or other of the roads which were found long ago to lead belief astray.

a. There was, first, the answer given by Apollinarius, which took the incarnate Christ to be a "miraculous mixture" of the divine and the human. The living body (it was supposed) was that of a man; but the "mind", the reasoning and active subject by which its workings were controlled, was nothing but the Word of God, the divine *Logos*—which, as we remember, could be understood as the divine Reason. This was in effect to deny that Christ was wholly and completely man; for our minds are the distinctively human element in our nature. Apollinarius believed that only a divine "mind" could be entirely free from sin; but he could not meet the objection that if the *Logos* was to redeem our human nature by entering into it, he must have entered into it at the very point where sin begins—and that is in our "mind", our rational will. Yet it is probable that many simple believers are Apollinarian today, and imagine the "mind" of Christ as though it were the mind of God *and not* the mind of a man at all: that is to say, imagine him as conscious *only* of a divinity exempt by its nature from all human frailty, and therefore incapable of serving as an example for frail men to follow.

b. On the opposite side stood a group of theologians whose teaching got its name from Nestorius, the Bishop of Constantinople. The great merit of their theology, which has made Nestorianism congenial to the "modern Churchman", was its insistence that the picture of Christ which the Gospels paint for us must be accepted as it stands and not explained away. That picture shows a real man, tempted to false choices, touched by doubts and uncertainties, suffering in body and mind—and not only suffering but *praying*. Jesus of Nazareth was most certainly a man; and the Nestorians could see no way of representing the union between God Almighty, changeless and impassible, and a man who "learnt obedience by the things which he suffered", except as a union of *togetherness*, "conjunction": the invisible God was present *with* the visible man—the Son joined to the heavenly Father in the moral unity of love and obedience. The reason why this Nestorian answer was found unsatisfactory was that it could hardly be stated without appearing to *divide* the one Christ into two really independent centres of personal life and activity; while the mode of union seemed to leave no difference but one of degree between Jesus and the prophets and saints, in whom also the Spirit of God could be said to dwell as in his temples.

c. The Church's final decision was taken at the Council of Chalcedon in the year 451. It was maintained that Christ *is* "one altogether", that he who lived and died and rose again is personally identical—"the same"—with the eternal Son of God; but that both Godhead and manhood in him are "perfect", i.e. complete.[5] We can see that this was not to offer any solution of the Christological problem, but simply to uphold what appeared to be endangered by either of the solutions offered. The formula of Chalcedon—"Two Natures, One Person"—no longer conveys to us the meaning which it had for those who thought in the manner of the fifth century: neither "nature" nor "person" carries in our modern speech the sense in which Chalcedon used the word. But the effect of the decision was to rule out *any* theory of the Incarnation which fails to preserve the two poles of Christian faith: that our Saviour is God, and that he saves by entering without reserve into the conditions of our human existence. Nothing less can justify Christian worship while accepting the account of Jesus which the Gospels give. For he to whom we pray lived himself by the power of prayer.

In principle, then, Chalcedon warns us against *all* theories of Incarnation. For theories must aim at making an idea or an event intelligible; and they can only do that by bringing their subject into line with the rest of our experience. But the event of the Incarnation is strictly unique, and therefore can have no parallel: we can never *understand* how God could become man. If a miracle is an event which can never be accounted for as the product of ascertained laws or regularities of the natural world, the Incarnation is in this sense the miracle *par excellence*.

d. Nevertheless, the warning of Chalcedon has not deterred modern theology since the Reformation from attempts to devise more satisfactory theories.

(1) Some have begun, where the Nestorians began, with the assured fact of the real manhood of Jesus. This manhood, it is said, was perfect, i.e. not merely complete in the sense of Chalcedon but fulfilling the ideal of manhood, realizing in man the image of God. So God is revealed in Christ in the only way in which he could be revealed to men, namely, in human terms: for us men, Christ is the "adequate symbol" of Godhead.

Now the moral perfection of Jesus is not a fact demonstrable from the Gospel history[6]: if we believe it, our belief is not grounded upon assured knowledge, but upon an act of faith which is not separable from our belief in the uniqueness of Christ's person. But the real weakness of a theory which reduces the divinity of Christ to a perfect humanity is that it abandons the old conviction that only God himself, and no man however good, can be our Saviour. We cannot be redeemed by being shown in a perfect man what God is "like".

(2) Others have begun, like Apollinarius, with the Church's assertion that Christ is Very God, and then asked what it must have meant to God to become man. An answer is sought in the various forms of Kenotic theory, so called because their Scriptural ground is the great Christological passage in the Epistle to the Philippians, where it is said that Christ who was in the form of God "emptied himself" (*ekenosen heauton*) by taking the form of a servant.[7] Here the *difference* between God and man, between Creator and creature, is taken as axiomatic. If God really became man, if God was really in Christ, his infinite Being must have accepted limitations; and in fact the Jesus of the Gospels is plainly limited by the nature of his humanity. The Son of God must then have limited himself—in the phrase of a fifth-century Apollinarian, "allowed the measures of humanity to prevail over him"[8]—accepted the conditions of finite existence under which all men have to live. Living, acting, thinking, and praying *as* man, he may have known himself only as a creature: we remember that for Biblical thought there is no contradiction between "son of God" and "son of man".[9]

There is force in this argument for all who accept its premises. If there is to be a theory at all, a Kenotic theory is open to the fewest objections. It makes no pretence of showing *how* God could limit himself or be unaware of his own Godhead. It does not violate the *mysterium Christi*.

e. We may, however, refuse to theorize, yet still seek some light upon the mystery by looking for analogies in our Christian experience; and such analogies may be found in what we are led to believe: (1) about the working of divine Grace; or (2) about the relation between the outward and visible and the inward and spiritual in the Sacraments.

(1) The saint, the "man in Christ", knows that it is by the grace of God that he is what he is. It is not that his own strength is supplemented or reinforced by a divine power. His good works are not partly but wholly his own, and yet he knows them to be wholly

the work of God's grace. So St Paul can say: "I live, yet not I but Christ in me."[10] Grace does not supplant or extinguish freedom, but brings the free human personality to its fulfilment in the service of God. Thus we can know something of how it is possible for one and the same activity to be both human and divine.[11]

(2) Again, we may take the analogy of the Sacraments, in which the outward sign is both expression and instrument of the gift of God. So we may regard the "flesh", the human life of Christ, as the effectual sign, the expression and the instrument of God's saving act. God was in Christ, we may think, after the manner in which we find Christ really present and active in and through the outward sign of Holy Communion. The Sacrament has sometimes been called an "extension" of the Incarnation; but it is better that we should regard it rather as an image or analogy of the unique and unrepeatable act of God's becoming man.

3. "By the Holy Ghost of the Virgin Mary"

The miracle of the Incarnation, God becoming man, is an event altogether inaccessible to human observation. No one saw or could see it happen, no one can describe or explain how it was possible. There can be no history of the Incarnation itself. But the Creed records an event which does fall within the range of things observable and describable, and records it as the outward and visible sign of the Word being made flesh. The birth of Jesus from a virgin, if it is a fact, is a fact of human history as much as any other. There was at least one person who could have been called as a witness to its actual occurrence.

It is probable that an increasing number of Christians in these days are finding it difficult to profess belief in the Virgin Birth as a fact of history; and we will consider the reasons for this in some detail, before we try to say what is signified by these words in the Creed, whether they are understood as history or as symbol.

a. We must recognize that the difficulties do not arise simply from a sceptical attitude to the miraculous in general: they are peculiar to this miracle, and they are twofold, concerned both with the evidence for the event and with the doctrines based upon it.

(1) The evidence for the event comes from the early tradition of the Church. But in the New Testament this tradition is strikingly confined to the Birth narratives in St Matthew and St Luke, which in other respects present features of a much more legendary charac-

ter than most of the Gospel story. There is no reference to the Virgin Birth in the earliest Gospel, in any of the Epistles, or in St John. It is very difficult to avoid the conclusion that it formed no part either of the Church's first missionary preaching (which may be understandable), or of the teaching given to converts by St Paul, the author of the Epistle to the Hebrews, or St John. We can only account for this by supposing that it was not known to the Apostles themselves at first, but only disclosed by the mother of Jesus at a later date. Even then, the silence of the Fourth Gospel is remarkable. Whereas the fact of the Resurrection, as an event no less miraculous to which the Apostles bore witness, is central both to preaching and teaching in the primitive Church, the Virgin Birth must be admitted to have had no place in the faith of the first Christians. Can it then be an essential part of the Church's faith? As an attestable fact of history, its case is plainly different from legitimate developments in doctrine.

(2) In the first chapter of St Luke's Gospel, what the miraculous conception signifies, its Christological bearing, is that Mary's child is the Son of God.[12] St Luke's Gentile readers would be familiar with the widespread tales of heroes and holy men born of a human mother and a divine father. And there is no stress on the uniqueness of the miracle: the conception of the Baptist is only one degree less marvellous.

But in the doctrinal treatment of the Virgin Birth, the point is the *absence* (in contrast with all pagan parallels) of any male factor in the conception. Ancient ideas of human generation supposed that the male was the only active element: the female was believed to be purely passive and receptive—which we know is not the case. Thus ancient and mistaken physiological ideas were adapted, as the real facts are not, to convey the notion that the sole agent in the conception of Jesus was the divine Spirit: the flesh of Mary was no more than the receptacle for the miraculously created Seed.

Later came the growing tendency to regard all sexual intercourse as impure. Reverence for the Virgin Mother of God contributed to the exaltation of virginity and the depreciation of marriage as an inferior state, which can only be sanctified inasmuch as it makes a good "use" of what is in itself (as St Augustine was accustomed to say) a "bad thing". With this vilification of sexual desire was linked the Augustinian theory of original sin as a corruption of human nature transmitted from parents to children by the process of generation; and the Virgin Birth was represented as the necessary condition for the exemption of the Saviour from this hereditary taint.

Nowadays, even a convinced and ardent believer in the Virgin Birth like Karl Barth can actually reject the doctrine that Christ's human nature was exempt by virtue of the manner of his birth from anything to which our own is subject: it was the "fallen" nature which belongs to us all. "There must be no weakening or obscuring", he writes, "of the saving truth that the nature which God assumed in Christ is identical with our nature as we see it in the light of the Fall."[13] Moreover, Barth thinks it impossible for us to say "that the reality of the Incarnation had by absolute necessity to take the form of this miracle. The true Godhead and the true humanity of Jesus Christ in their unity do not depend on the fact that Christ was conceived by the Holy Spirit and born of the Virgin Mary."[14]

This is not far from an admission that the acceptance of these words of the Creed as a statement of historical fact is not inseparably bound up with acceptance of the Christian faith—even if birth from a virgin were the most "fitting" manner in which the Incarnation could take place. Some, however, would go further, and say that a natural birth of human parents is *more* fitting, more in keeping with the real marvel of the Incarnation than a Virgin Birth. The divine condescension—what St Augustine called the "humility of God"—is displayed in his entering the *common* life of men and making it holy through and through. If anything in the outward conditions of his human existence was different from those of our own, Christ is by so much less our brother man.

b. No doubt others will feel that none of these difficulties are insuperable. It may be urged that if God chose to give that sign which would speak most clearly to those who first received it, we should accept it even if it speaks less clearly to us. Those who doubt whether such a sign was ever given must be content to treat this statement of the Creed as symbolic rather than historical; and they may appeal to the more evident necessity for a symbolic treatment of the later statement: "He ascended into heaven."

But if it is symbolic, the truth symbolized must be the same truth which would be conveyed by the historical fact. What then is that truth? That Christ was born of a virgin is a negative statement: it means that he was *not* brought into the world by a human act as all other men are brought into it. The statement, whether it be understood as history or as symbol, excludes any understanding of the Incarnation as the natural product of man's seeking after God, as outcome of a process of human ascent towards the divine. We may think (as Barth does) that such a misunderstanding would not necessarily follow if Christ had had a human father. But if there is at the least a symbolic truth in the Virgin Birth, we *cannot* so mistake the meaning of God's becoming man. "Conceived by the Holy Ghost" means that the Incarnation was a totally *new* beginning in the world's story, in which the initiative lay solely with God. He came down from heaven; and that divine descent was into the weakness and fragility of human nature, not its strength. All that humanity, in Mary's person, could do was to accept the miracle of grace. "Behold the handmaid of the Lord: be it unto me according to thy word."

REFERENCES

1. John 3.13.
2. For the full text of the Definition, see T. H. Bindley, *Ecumenical Documents of the Faith*, 4th (revised) edition, p. 234.
3. E.g., *De Catechizandis Rudibus*, 8.
4. 1 Tim. 2.5.
5. See reference on p. 79 above.
6. The Gospels are not concerned with a "pattern man", but with the Saviour of mankind.
7. Phil. 2.7.
8. Cyril of Alexandria, *Quod unus sit Christus*, 760. (Migne, *Patrologia Graeco-Latina*, LXXV.)
9. See p. 66.
10. Gal. 2.20.
11. See D. M. Baillie, *God was in Christ*, c. 5.
12. Luke 1.35.
13. K. Barth, *Church Dogmatics*, I, 2 (English translation), p. 153.
14. K. Barth, *Dogmatics in Outline*, p. 100.

CHAPTER 10

And was crucified also for us under Pontius Pilate. He suffered and was buried

THE Creed passes straight from Christ's coming into the world to his leaving it. Nothing is said about his ministry in Galilee or Judaea, his teaching, or his miracles—though these things had their place in the earliest Apostolic preaching, if we may judge from the little sermon of St Peter in the house of Cornelius.[1] It is only by way of exception that we find an early creed inserting such a phrase as "lived as a man among men".[2] In general the absence of any reference of the kind is characteristic. It means that the things concerning Christ on which the faith rests are the four "moments" of Birth, Death, Resurrection, and Ascension; and of these the second and the second only is a matter not of faith but of knowledge. The Apostles' Creed simply states the bare facts: "suffered under Pontius Pilate, was crucified, dead, and buried". That is no more than what the Roman historian Tacitus was able to say: he explains the odd name of the sectaries who were made to suffer for the burning of Rome as derived from "Christ, who suffered capital punishment in the reign of Tiberius under Pontius Pilate the procurator".[3]

The Nicene Creed, which has inserted "for us men and for our salvation" into its statement of the Incarnation, here also inserts "for us". But we must observe that the preposition translated "for" in both cases changes in the second clause from the Greek *dia* and Latin *propter* to *huper* and *pro*. This is not accidental. It was for the sake of us men or on our account, in order to achieve our salvation, that the Son of God came down from heaven: his crucifixion and death was more specifically "on our behalf". *Huper* is the preposition constantly used by St Paul and St John of Christ's dying "for us". Thus the Creed keeps the redemptive significance of Christ's person and work in view throughout. It implies a doctrine of Atonement as well as Incarnation.

1. *"Crucified under Pontius Pilate"*

That Christ was crucified is not a doctrine but a crude fact admitted by unbelievers. For the believer, the fact of the crucifixion may be evocative of awe, penitence, adoration—*because* he believes that the Crucified was God. But our theology of the Cross must not omit to take account of the crude fact; we ought to reflect upon the historian's question, Why did this happen? And it is possible to answer this question without doctrinal presuppositions.

a. The death of Jesus, considered by the historian as a fact of history, is an instance—and by no means the only instance—of a particularly ugly human phenomenon, judicial murder. Jesus was put to death as a malefactor, under the forms of law. The purpose of all law is justice: law exists to secure that right shall not be at the mercy of might. In the ancient world, and in Israel as elsewhere, justice depended more than it does now upon the judge: it was largely for him to decide what was "right". The prophets saw in current perversion of justice a sin which more than most sins must provoke the indignation of the God who is Judge of all the earth, the God whose inviolable holiness is nothing else but his transcendent righteousness.[4] The Jewish law in our Lord's time was held to be the direct expression of the righteous will of God: the supreme court of justice in Jerusalem was therefore concerned to maintain a right which was not human but divine. Theft and adultery, blasphemy and Sabbath-breaking, were alike and equally violations of the Law *of God*. To fail in the infliction of due punishment for any of these offences was to do what the righteous God will never do—to "justify the wicked", to treat him as righteous.[5]

"We have a law, and by our law he ought to die, because he made himself the Son of God." What decided the fate of Jesus was the verdict of the Sanhedrin: "guilty of blasphemy".[6] Was it, like the sentence of Pilate, a dishonest verdict? or an honest one, like that of the Inquisitor in Shaw's *Saint Joan*? We should not be over-hasty in answering that question. Worldly prudence may have moved the Sadducees, resentment against the prisoner's disregard of their authority may have moved the Pharisees. Jesus had in fact claimed for himself an authority above the Law of Moses as well as above the traditions of the elders. But there is no sufficient reason to doubt that all his Jewish judges were convinced that this man was a blasphemer, a despiser of things sacred, a rebel against God's holy Law.

D

If we ask how it was possible for them to be so mistaken, we must answer that nothing can so effectively deaden the moral sense and darken the light of reason as *religion*. There is no disputing the justice of the Roman poet's indignant reproach: "So great a tale of evils has issued from religion's promptings"[7]—and not only from the promptings of a religion which is primitive superstition divorced from morality. The Pharisees had turned the Law into an idol; and like all idolaters they must constitute themselves as guardians and protectors of their idol, since the idol is powerless to look after itself. And the history of the Christian Church is a warning that such idolatry is an ever-present danger. Christians have given their worship to Bible, Creed, or Sacrament, making their religion and its institutions an ark to be defended instead of a faith to be preached and lived in the love and service of the living God.

b. Jesus died—of so much there can be no question—*because* of the sins of men, sins of which Christians are no more innocent than Jews. He had to die, because the religious leaders of his own people saw him as a menace, not only to properly constituted authority, but to the sanctity and the survival of the religion in which they believed.

But for the manner of his execution there was a different reason. He was crucified as a potential, if not an actual, leader of revolt against the imperial government of Rome; and that was an offence of which neither the Jews who denounced him nor the Roman governor who sentenced him really thought he was guilty. Neither Jewish nor Roman law made crucifixion the penalty for blasphemous or insane pretensions. For a pretended king of the Jews, the cross was quite in order; and no one who read Pilate's malicious placard would question the appropriateness of the sentence, whether it was a just sentence or not.

And Jesus himself did not, could not deny that he was the Christ, whose mission was indeed the deliverance of his people. In St Mark's account of the trials, the high priest's question is, "Art thou the Christ?", and he answers, "I am." That, for Caiaphas, was not treason but blasphemy. Pilate's question is, "Art thou the king of the Jews?"—which implies that the charge against Jesus has been brought to him in some such form. Jesus answers, "Thou sayest"— and will say no more. He makes no attempt to rebut the charge in the sense in which he must have known it would be taken—"so that the governor marvelled greatly".[8] There would have been nothing for us to wonder at if Pilate had taken the answer as a plea of guilty and pronounced sentence without more ado. The historian may suspect that Christian tradition has attributed to the Roman governor a greater reluctance to find his prisoner guilty than he is likely to have shown, if we may judge from what we otherwise know of this particular governor. But however that may be, the fact remains that Jesus was crucified *because* he would not disown his calling to be a Saviour. In that sense, at least, he was crucified "for us".[9]

2. *"For us"*

But of course the Creed's "for us" means more than that the sins of men and his own faithfulness to his divine calling brought Jesus to the Cross. The Gospel as St Paul learnt it was that Christ died "for our sins".[10] The writers of the New Testament commonly say that he died "for us", but the meaning is the same: he died "for us sinners". The Greek preposition is regularly *huper*, which means "on behalf of", and not "instead of" or "in place of" for which the Greek is *anti*. It is not everyone (St Paul says) who is ready to die "for" another, even if the other be a good man: Christ died for us "while we were yet sinners".[11] The Good Shepherd gives his life "for" the sheep, and Christ's giving his life "for" us is reason why we should give our own lives "for" the brethren.[12] In such connections there is no suggestion of one dying instead of another, but only of death in the service of others: the other may or may not be saved himself from death by the action of his friend.

In the First Epistle of St Peter, the sufferings of Christ "for us" are expounded in terms of the Suffering Servant prophecy in Isa. 53.[13] We can hardly be mistaken in associating all such phrases in the New Testament with a reference to that prophecy. In its Greek version, the Servant was wounded "because of our sins": he was "brought to death by the iniquities of my people": he "bore the sins of many".[14] It is worth noting that the word here translated "bore" is most frequently used in the sense of "carry up" to the altar, "offer" in sacrifice; and in the First Epistle of St Peter and the Epistle to the Hebrews, both of which have it in quotations from Isa. 53, it is also used with its commoner meaning: "offer up spiritual sacrifices", "offered up himself".[15] The "carrying" or "bearing" of sin in Isa. 53 recalls the ritual of the Scapegoat upon whose head the transgressions of Israel are laid on the Day of Atonement, and who "bears" them all into the wilderness.[16] But the Scapegoat is *not* sacrificed: his bearing away of the people's sins represents simply their removal, their putting out of sight.

On the other hand, what is said of the Suffering Servant does seem to convey the idea of vicarious *punishment*. Yet in the New Testament here is no single text in which Christ is clearly presented as bearing in his death the punishment of our sins. In one passage St Paul compares the "curse" which lies upon the transgressor of the Law, the curse from which Christ has redeemed us, with the curse pronounced upon the dead body of the executed malefactor according to the Deuteronomic law.[17] But St Paul can hardly have conceived God's curse as resting upon the innocent victim of legal injustice. He is using here (as elsewhere in the Epistle to the Galatians) the methods of Rabbinic argument. And when he writes of the deliverance "provided in Christ Jesus, whom God put forward as the means of propitiation by his blood . . . to demonstrate the righteousness of God",[18] when he says that God "hath made him to be sin for us, who knew no sin",[19] he is speaking in terms not of transgression and punishment, but of the Levitical conceptions of sin and atonement, the priestly religion of Israel. In that context, God's provision for dealing with sin is not punishment but sacrifice; and the death of the sacrificial victim is *not* penal. Christ has converted the unholy death of a malefactor into a truly atoning sacrifice to God "for us". Of this there will be more to say later.

3. *"He suffered and was buried"*

The Apostles' Creed says "dead and buried". "Suffered" in both Creeds means "endured the extreme penalty of the law". The word does not stress either physical or mental suffering—"the pains that he endured". The clause states simply: (a) that Jesus was sentenced as a criminal to capital punishment; and (b) that the sentence was carried out. The death and burial are affirmed in order to make it clear that the resurrection from the dead was not survival but a real bringing back to life after a death no less real. The burial, we remember, had its place in the Gospel which St Paul "received".[20] But the fact that Christ died, apart from the manner of his death, is also the seal upon the full reality of his being made man; for death is the common lot of men. The Son of God shared our humanity in its ultimate weakness and transience. "All flesh is grass . . . the grass withereth."[21]

(1) In the Old Testament, "death" means simply the physical dissolution which is the end of life—the earthly life which is the sum of all good for man. Mortality is just the sad condition of human existence, to be accepted uncomplainingly when it comes in due time, in ripe old age. Premature death is all the more felt to be a calamity, because after death there is no more life worth living. Thus a violent death may be a punishment for sin, but mortality as such is not. It is fairly generally agreed that no such idea is present in the Genesis story of the Fall: it was lest he should *become* immortal that Adam was driven out of Eden.[22]

On the other hand, "life" in the Old Testament is much more than bare physical existence. True life, life as God gives it, is life with God, the life of faith and obedience.[23] So the "sting" of death is separation from God: the dead cannot praise him.[24] And since it is sin that breaks the union between man and God,[25] the way is open for an understanding of death in a deeper sense than the merely physical. There is a death which is purely penal—the death of the malefactor; and "the soul that sinneth, it shall die".[26] But Balaam prays that he may die the death of the righteous, and the Psalmist knows that in the sight of the Lord the death of his saints is precious.[27] Finally, the death of the sacrificial victim is a *holy* death, because it represents the surrender of life as the dutiful return to God of his own gift.

(2) Between the Old Testament and the New, the belief in a resurrection in the "Last Day" and a life to come became established in Judaism. This belief is quite different from the Greek and dualistic conception of an immortal soul which is unaffected by the death of the body. In the New Testament as in the Old, life belongs to the whole man and not to a part of him. In the New Testament, this belief in a resurrection has transformed the meaning of "life", and we find that the word *zoé* is nearly always used in the sense of the "true" life, over which death can have no power. In St John this true life is the life eternal which begins here and now for the believer in Christ.[28] In St Paul, only the life "in Christ" is life indeed, both here and hereafter. Correspondingly, the word "death" has three distinguishable references in St Paul's use of it. It can mean the end of our natural life on earth, and it can mean the spiritual death which is the "mind of the flesh", the attempt to live without God;[29] but it can also and often refer to the death of Christ which as a "death unto sin" must be shared by Christians, but which is nothing less than an entry into the true life.

There is indeed one passage in which St Paul does represent death as the consequence of sin—the sin which "came into the world" through Adam's disobedience.[30] St Paul speaks here of the death which "reigned" from Adam to Moses in the absence of any law to be transgressed, and of death as having "reigned" by the transgression of one man. It is implied that mortality itself is God's judgement upon sin, which was "in the world" even before the giving of the Mosaic Law. Here St Paul is following the beliefs in which he had been brought up—those of the later Judaism which appear (for example) in the Second Book of Esdras in our Apocrypha.[31] So in the fifteenth chapter of the First Epistle to the Corinthians, which is concerned throughout with the resurrection of the body, the death which "came by man" and is "the last enemy" must be or at least include physical death.[32]

Nevertheless, the real significance of death for St Paul is a spiritual fact. Were it not for sin, the death of the body would have no sting. The "body of death", from which the slave of sin cries for deliverance, is not mere mortality.[33] And since we must all stand before Christ's judgement-seat,[34] the moment of bodily death cannot be the real judgement for any man: it is no more than a passing, a transition from one state to another.

(3) We can no longer think of natural death as a punishment, and we need not do so. Death belongs to the finite nature of man as God created him, and the knowledge that we must die is the emphatic and salutary reminder of our human finitude. By death, the generations make way for one another: resentment of death is self-worship, its acceptance "for others" is the supreme test of self-giving love. All holy death is a sacrifice in which God is well pleased.

Yet if Jesus had died a natural death, we cannot imagine that in such a death we should have found atoning power, reconciliation to God. Not the death of Christ, but his death *on the Cross* is our salvation. For the central fact about the Cross is that it was sin-inflicted. It does not need Christian faith to see that. What Christian faith sees in the Cross is God giving himself to sinners to do with him as they would.

4. *"Descended into hell"*

Although this clause of the Apostles' Creed is absent from the Nicene, a word may here be added about it. It first appears in

Creeds of the fourth century, where the word for "hell" means the "nether regions"—not the place of punishment, but, like Hades in Greek or Sheol in Hebrew, the abode of the dead. Originally the clause may have meant no more than that Christ "went" at death where we must all "go". There are New Testament texts that might suggest this, as in the saying that as Jonah was three days and three nights in the whale's belly, so shall the Son of man be three days and three nights in the heart of the earth.[35]

But there are two places in the First Epistle of St Peter where it is said that Christ preached to the spirits in prison, or the dead;[36] and Cyril of Jerusalem in the fourth century already interprets the clause in the Creed as meaning that Christ descended into Hades to deliver the saints of the Old Testament from Satan's fetters. Later this idea was extended to suggest that the salvation wrought by Christ has availed for men before as well as after his coming, without restriction—which indeed we should find it hard *not* to believe.

A different interpretation arose, however, when the Latin word *inferna* was understood to mean Hell in the sense not of a place of detention but of a place of punishment. In medieval art, the Harrowing of Hell represents the accomplishment of Christ's victory over the devil and the death which is eternal. Luther, connecting the clause with the fourth word from the Cross, went further still. Christ, he said, not only descended into Hell but endured its pains in their extremity which is God-forsakenness. Karl Barth, in effect, is ready to follow Luther.[37] But it must certainly be admitted that this is to read into the Creed something which it was not meant to affirm.

REFERENCES

1. Acts 10.38.
2. The Creed of Caesarea recited at the Council of Nicaea by Eusebius: literally, "lived as a member of human society".
3. Tacitus, *Annales*, XV. 44.
4. Isa. 5.16.
5. Ex. 23.7; Pro. 17.15; Deut. 25.1.
6. John 19.7; Mark 14.64.
7. Lucretius, *De Rerum Natura*, I. 101.
8. Mark 15.2–5.
9. Parts of this section are taken (by permission) from a sermon published in *Good Friday at St Margaret's* (ed. C. H. Smyth).
10. 1 Cor. 15.3.

11. Rom. 5.7f.
12. John 10.11; 1 John 3.16.
13. 1 Pet. 2.21ff.
14. Isa. 53.5,8,12.
15. 1 Pet. 2.5,24; Heb. 7.27; 9.28.
16. Lev. 16.21f.
17. Deut. 21.23; Gal. 3.13.
18. Rom. 3.24f.
19. 2 Cor. 5.21.
20. 1 Cor. 15.4.
21. Isa. 40.6ff.
22. Gen. 3.19,22.
23. E.g. Deut. 30.15ff.; Amos 5.4ff.; Hab. 2.4.
24. Isa. 38.18; Ps. 88.10f.
25. Isa. 59.2.
26. Ezek. 18.20.
27. Num. 23.10; Ps. 116.15.
28. John 5.24; cf. 1 John 3.14.
29. Rom. 7.9ff.; 8.6.
30. Rom. 5.12ff.
31. 2 Esdras 3.7.
32. 1 Cor. 15.21,26.
33. Rom. 7.24.
34. 2 Cor. 5.10.
35. Matt. 12.39f.; cf. Acts 2.27ff.; Rom. 10.7.
36. 1 Pet. 3.19; 4.6.
37. So in *Dogmatics in Outline*, p. 118f.

CHAPTER 11

And the third day he rose again according to the Scriptures

THE words are those of St Paul in his recitation of the Gospel which he had "received".[1] They state a fact which, if it is a fact of history, is datable and dated. But it is not, like the Crucifixion, a "public" fact, about which there is no room for reasonable doubt. For it is only inferred from certain other happenings—visions which the disciples claimed to have seen, and the alleged disappearance of a dead body—both of which could be accounted for otherwise. The fact of the Resurrection is not one which could have been attested by any impartial observer. Nevertheless, as a historical fact, it rests upon attestation like any other. The Christian Church arose on the basis of the Apostolic witness to it. The Apostles were confident that Jesus had appeared to them alive after his death and burial.

We cannot *know* that Christ rose from the dead, as we know that he was crucified. But if we believe that he rose again, we must be ready to face a historical investigation of the origin of our belief.

1. *The Background of Belief*

We know that in the time of our Lord there were Jews who believed, as well as other Jews who did not believe, in a resurrection of the dead as a preliminary to the Judgement of God in the Last Day. The belief hardly appears at all in the Old Testament, and then only in its latest parts.[2] It probably arose in consequence of reflection on the destiny of the individual and his relation to God. So long as the main concern of religion was with the corporate life of the community, the religious hope of Israel need look for no more than a national restoration. But after men like Jeremiah had shown the way to a personal relationship between the soul and God, it came to be felt that the righteousness of God must provide not only a new life for a repentant people but a share in it for all who had served him faithfully yet not received the promises.

So, when the hope of the Messianic kingdom moved from this world to another, and its realization was looked for in the ending of this present world-age, the resurrection of the dead became associated with the End—the End which would also be a new beginning. But since the Kingdom of the Age to come demanded a new heaven and a new earth, the dead would be raised not to a life like the present but to a life transformed, glorified, and unending. This appears in Christ's answer to the Sadducean sceptics. "The children of this world marry, and are given in marriage; but they which shall be accounted worthy to obtain that world, and the resurrection from the dead, neither marry, nor are given in marriage; neither can they die any more."[3] Thus the resurrection "in the last day" would be a different thing from the return of the dead to the life which death had cut short. There was nothing incredible for the Jew in the raising of the dead to life by a "mighty work"—a miracle such as both Testaments record; but that was not *the* Resurrection, which would be final and lasting in its effect. The raising of Lazarus was not his "rising again at the last day"—of which Martha had no doubt.[4]

Wherever the Hebrew conception of man's nature was dominant, resurrection could not mean the return to life and activity of a disembodied soul. The few relevant texts of the Old Testament plainly imply the restoration of life to bodies buried in the earth.[5] For man in Hebrew thought is not an immortal soul imprisoned in a corruptible body of flesh: he is an organic unity of personal life, in which soul and body are correlative. "The Hebrew idea of the personality is an animated body and not an incarnated soul."[6] Only where later Judaism was influenced by Greek thought was there a tendency to substitute the notion of a purely "spiritual" immortality of the soul for that of resurrection. When we read in the Book of Wisdom that "the corruptible body presseth down the soul",[7] we know that we are in the atmosphere of Hellenism. The idea of rising from the dead was Hebraic—whatever it may have owed to Persian antecedents—and it was an absurdity to the Greeks.

But for the Palestinian Jew of the first century who followed the teaching of the Pharisees, the resurrection of the body to a new and glorious life was an inseparable element in his hope of the *End*— the coming of the Kingdom of God; and that is the most important point in the background of belief upon which we must regard the faith of the Apostles.

2. *"According to the Scriptures"*

We know little of how this belief in a general resurrection in the
Last Day was related to Jewish hopes of a Messiah, a Deliverer who
should come. But if it was not easy to find in Scripture predictions
of the Messiah's suffering and death, it was harder still to discover
prophecies of his rising from the dead. In St Peter's sermon on the
Day of Pentecost, the resurrection of Jesus is presented as the fulfilment of the words of the Psalm: "Thou wilt not leave my soul in
hell, neither wilt thou suffer thy holy one to see corruption"—
treated as a prophecy which is clearly inapplicable to the Psalmist
himself.[8] No other Scripture is quoted by any New Testament
writer in this connection; but it has usually been supposed that when
St Paul says that Christ "rose again the third day according to the
Scriptures", he can only be referring to the text of Hosea: "after
two days he will revive us: in the third day he will raise us up, and
we shall live in his sight".[9] The passage in Hosea describes a hope
of Israel for restoration on repentance; and the context hardly suggests that either the hope or the repentance are genuine.

It is possible, however, that the tradition of the Church spoke of
the resurrection "on the third day" simply because that was when
the first appearance to St Peter actually took place, and that it
was the fact and not the date of the resurrection for which appeal
was made to prophecy. Had the body of Jesus remained more than
three days in the tomb, it would according to the belief of the time
have "seen corruption".[10] If we must look elsewhere than to the
Psalm which St Peter quoted, the likeliest place seems to be the same
chapter of Isaiah which was held to have foretold Christ's suffering
and death. For the last verses of that chapter (in spite of textual
and exegetical difficulties) are naturally taken as affirming that the
Servant will be restored and vindicated *after* having been "cut off
out of the land of the living".[11]

3. *The Fact*

a. *The Appearances.* St Paul's account of the Church's tradition
was written down twenty years or so after the Crucifixion, and he
must have "received" this tradition several years earlier. What he
says is evidence, which no historian will be disposed to reject, that
a number of persons did believe themselves to have seen the crucified Jesus alive. That there *were* such visions may be called a public

fact, sufficiently attested. The only question is, How should this fact be interpreted? What, if anything, does it prove?

(1) There can be no reasonable doubt of the Apostles' belief in the reality of the Resurrection, or of the extraordinary strength with which the belief was held. A belief which gave such power to those who held it, which changed the men of whom we read in the Gospels to the men we know from the Acts, must have been not only sincere but intense. The fact of the appearances gives an explanation of the intensity of the belief which is otherwise lacking.

(2) But what caused the appearances themselves? We know that there are such things as visions which are hallucinatory, i.e. which are produced by the psycho-physical condition of the person who sees them, and not by anything outside him. Now there is no indication that the disciples were expecting their Master to rise from the dead: as it stands, the tradition implies the contrary, and suggests that the predictions of his own resurrection which the Gospels attribute to Jesus were not made as directly and unambiguously as they are recorded.[12] We cannot then say that the appearances were produced by a belief that Jesus *must* have conquered death, for we have no reason to assume any such belief. The Cross cannot (to say the least) have strengthened the disciples' faith in their Master. They must have been overwhelmed by what had happened, and no doubt psychologically unstrung. Was such a condition likely in itself to give rise to hallucinations?

(3) The New Testament writers obviously take it for granted that the Apostles came to believe that the Lord was risen again *because* he had shown himself to them alive, and not because his body had disappeared from the tomb. The appearances caused the belief and not *vice versa*. If anyone refuses to accept this account of the matter, it can only be on the ground of a presupposition that such visions can *never* have any basis in a reality that is objective, external to the minds of those who see them. Of course, if the visions *were* subjectively caused, it would not follow that the faith of the disciples was a delusion. It could still be believed that Christ passed through death to become the life of his Church, and that the resurrection appearances made it possible for the Apostles to be assured that this was so. We ought not to use the argument that the foundation of Christianity upon a "mistake" is incredible. What the appearances led the Apostles to believe could be true, however the appearances themselves might have been caused.

(4) When we turn from St Paul's statement of the Church's

tradition to the accounts in the Gospels of what happened after the Crucifixion, we find that no consistent or consecutive narrative can be constructed out of them. They do not conform to the exact order of St Paul's tradition, and they contradict one another at many points. The earliest account in Mark is extremely reticent, and a case can be made out for the opinion that the Evangelist intended it to end where his authentic text does end—with the words "they said nothing to any man, for they were afraid"[13]—without recording any appearance at all of the risen Christ. Matthew seems to describe the tremendous event itself, with the earthquake and the descent of the angel; and he adds the apologetically motivated story of the guards, and the Jewish "common report" that the disciples had removed the body. Luke alone relates the beautiful (and probably very early) story of the two disciples at Emmaus; and he alone alludes to the appearance to St Peter, though without describing it.[14] His account, on the face of it, excludes the appearances in Galilee to which Mark points, and which Matthew makes the only appearances to the disciples.[15]

We get the impression that the visions were variously described in the tradition which St Paul summarizes, and that the Gospels show the effect of this variety. In this, however, there is nothing at all surprising, and nothing to cast doubt on the actuality of the appearances themselves. But it does make it unsafe to argue from details in the conflicting accounts: though it is worth noting that in Luke there is a recurring theme of the risen Lord's presence at a common meal, which suggests a connection of the Resurrection appearances with the primitive Eucharist.[16]

b. *The Empty Tomb.* In Luke and John the fact that the tomb was found empty is stressed not as in itself a conclusive proof of the Resurrection but as an invitation to faith.[17] In Mark and Matthew, the women are told by the "young man" or the angels that "he is not here, he is risen", and are only invited to "see the place where the Lord lay".[18] Neither in Acts nor in the tradition given by St Paul is there any mention of the Empty Tomb.

What has already been said about the background of Jewish belief leaves no room for doubt that for the Apostles the raising of Jesus from the dead must have implied the restoration of his body to life; and it is difficult, if we accept the story of the Burial, to suppose that it would have not occurred to them to see whether Jesus was not still lying where he had been laid. But the Empty Tomb has often been used by Christian apologists as an irresistible proof of the historical fact of Christ's resurrection. It is urged that if it had been possible for the Jewish authorities to "produce the body" in order to refute the Apostles' story, they must have done so. The argument seems strong, but it is quite ineffective; for the sceptic will answer that the burial story itself is a legend, that the body of Jesus is most likely to have been thrown into a common criminals' grave and soon become unidentifiable, and that the disciples who "forsook him and fled" in Gethsemane were probably scattered to their Galilean homes within the next two days. In any case, was it beyond the Sanhedrin to produce *a* body which they could assert to be that of Jesus? In fact, the only trace of any attempt to cast doubt on the Resurrection story in the early days of the Church is the tale "commonly reported" among the Jews (according to Matthew) that the Apostles had removed the body—a tale which is altogether incredible.

According to the New Testament, no proof of the Resurrection was offered to unbelief. The faith of the Apostles did not rest upon any public fact, but upon the appearances of the risen Christ. The only unbeliever to whom Christ showed himself alive after his Passion was Saul the Pharisee. It is with the Empty Tomb as with the Virgin Birth: if we believe it, we believe it because we believe that the Son of God who came down from heaven to be born as a man has overcome death in the manhood which he made his own.

4. *The Faith*

The historical evidence is enough to assure us that something happened which was a sign to the Apostles that God had raised their Master from the dead, and that he was living, not as he was before but in a changed or sublimated form of existence, for which the only conception at hand was that of the risen life of faithful Israel in the Last Day.

(1) *Resurrection and the New Age.* It is clear from Acts that what the resurrection of Jesus first meant to the Apostles was the removal of the "stumbling-block" of the Cross. "God hath made this same Jesus whom ye crucified", they tell the people of Jerusalem, "both Lord and Christ."[19] The resurrection in the Last Day, which was the hope of contemporary Judaism, was to be the vindication—in St Paul's word the justification—of the faithful people of God. It was fitting, then, that the Messiah himself should be the "first-born from the dead", the "first-fruits of them that sleep".[20] The resurrec-

tion of the Messiah was the confirmation of the hope of Israel, and
the unmistakable sign that the time was fulfilled and the Kingdom
of Heaven at hand. The New Age had begun, and the New Creation,
the new heaven and earth, had received the divine word of command
which should bring them into being. The Resurrection was the firm
ground for that confidence with which the early Church looked
forward to the final "restitution of all things" as a consummation
that could not be long delayed.[21]

(2) *Resurrection and the Church.* In the opening verses of the
Epistle to the Romans, St Paul seems to be reproducing this primitive Messianic Christology. He speaks of Christ as "designated" or
"invested" Son of God with power, from the resurrection. But in
nearly every other reference in his Epistles to the resurrection, he
speaks of it not as an event confined to the person of the Messiah,
but as having immediate application to Christians as members of
the Messiah's people—or (as he puts it) members of Christ. It is in
the first place the pledge and promise of something to come in the
future—the general resurrection, when "we shall not all sleep, but
we shall all be changed".[22] But since the Last Day will be no more
than the final and public manifestation of the New Age which has
already begun with Christ's rising from the dead, the resurrection
of Christians can be spoken of in the past tense as well as in the
future.[23] What makes it possible for St Paul to think of this "resurrection" as an accomplished fact is the doctrine which was the centre
of his understanding of the Gospel—the doctrine of the unity between Christ and his Church. In the Epistle to the Romans baptism
means union with Christ in his death and resurrection; and the
union can be expressed in the figure of marriage: Christians who
have become "dead to the Law through the body of Christ" (i.e. the
body that was crucified) are wedded to him who has been raised
from the dead, in order that they may bear fruit unto God. They
have become one flesh with him.[24] The Church *is* the Body of
Christ which has passed through death to resurrection.

(3) *Resurrection and the Cross.* In the early chapters of Acts, the
death of Christ at the hands of wicked men is accounted for simply
as having been foretold in Scripture. It happened "by the deter-
minate counsel and fore-knowledge of God". The saying in the
Gospels that the Son of Man must suffer, and the teaching of the
risen Christ in Luke's last chapter, preserve this early appeal to a
divine "must"—which means simply the unchangeable will of God
declared in the Scriptures.[25]

But it was impossible not to ask *why* such necessity should be; and (as we have already seen) the answer was soon found. The Gospel which St Paul received was that Christ died *for our sins* according to the Scriptures. The Cross was now seen to be the pre-destined means of the Messianic redemption. But a further step in thought was needed to bring Cross and Resurrection so closely together that they could be viewed as obverse and reverse of a single divine action. In the "Christ-hymn" of the Epistle to the Philippians, the voluntary self-humiliation and obedience of Christ, even unto the death of the Cross, is the *reason* why God has exalted him.[26] No mention is made here of the purpose of his death: the point of the hymn is that it was the humility of Christ that won for him the name above every name—the name of "Lord". "He that humbleth himself shall be exalted." Man fell by Adam's pride: he is raised again by Christ's humility. Submission and exaltation are related as act and consequence.

It is only in St John's Gospel that the word here used by St Paul with clear reference to Resurrection and Ascension (*hupsoun*) is applied deliberately to the "lifting up" of the Son of Man upon the Cross, so as to convey the profound implication that the suffering of Christ is itself the manifestation of his true glory. Cross and Resurrection, therefore, form an inseparable unity. The Resurrection is simply the divine comment on the Cross; and that is why the risen Christ bears the marks of his crucifixion—his "glorious scars".[27]

But this Johannine interpretation is firmly based upon one of the most indubitably authentic sayings of Jesus, which appears in every strain of the Gospel tradition. Luke has it twice; once as he found it in Mark, and again in a different and peculiarly significant form—"Whosoever seeketh to gain his soul for himself shall lose it, and whosoever shall lose it shall bring it to life."[28] The resurrection is the conclusive manifestation of the Gospel: it means that the one true and abiding life is the life that is *given* to the uttermost—surrendered whole and entire to God.

It is this that takes the sting from death. The death of Christ was no tragic end to a beautiful life. It was the accomplishment, the fulfilment (in Greek the *telos*) of all that he had set himself to do.[29] The *Via Crucis* did not begin with the last journey to Jerusalem. And so Christians bear the sign of the Cross from their birthday in the Church. We are not to think of dying with Christ simply as a metaphor. It is true of course that the Christian is called in a meta-phorical sense to die daily: St Paul will exhort those who are risen

with Christ to be continually putting to death their corrupt affections, the covetousness which is idolatry, the lust for possession and
superiority.[30] But they will be enabled to do this because they look
upon their life on earth no longer as a possession to be clung to
and enlarged to the uttermost, but as a gift of God to be given back
to him who gave it. And the fulfilment, the *telos* of this lifelong
giving back, is the moment of actual death. The pains of death and
its approach may be great or small: we cannot help fearing them,
if not for ourselves, at least for those with whom our own lives are
bound up. But to live with Christ is to know not only that death
cannot separate us from his love, but that in death we shall be
nearer to him than ever.

REFERENCES

1. I Cor. 15.4.
2. Isa. 26.19; Dan. 12.2; cf. 2 Esdras 7.32.
3. Luke 20.34f.
4. 2 Kings 4; Luke 7.11ff.; John 11.24.
5. See references in note 2 above.
6. H. Wheeler Robinson, *The People and the Book*, p. 362.
7. Wis. 9.15.
8. Acts 2.24ff.
9. Hos. 6.2.
10. Cf. John 11.39.
11. Isa. 53.10ff.
12. Mark 16.11ff.; Matt. 28.17; Luke 24.11,25,37,41.
13. Mark 16.8.
14. Luke 24.34.
15. Mark 14.28; 16.7; Matt. 28.7,10,16; cf. Luke 24.13,33,36,50f.
16. Luke 24.30,43; Acts 10.41.
17. Luke 24.3ff.,12,23f.; John 20.1-9.
18. Mark 16.5f.; Matt. 28.5f.
19. Acts 2.36.
20. Col. 1.18; I Cor. 15.20.
21. Acts 3.21.
22. I Cor. 15.51.
23. Col. 2.12; 3.1ff.
24. Rom. 6.3f.; 7.4; Eph. 5.31f.
25. Mark 9.12, etc.; Luke 24.26.
26. Phil. 2.5ff.
27. John 3.14; 8.28; 12.32ff.; 20.20,25ff.
28. Luke 17.33.
29. John 19.30 (*Tetelestai*).
30. Col. 3.5.

CHAPTER 12

And ascended into heaven, And sitteth on the right hand of the Father

A. THE ASCENSION

WHEN Bishop John Pearson wrote his *Exposition of the Creed* in the seventeenth century, he was still able to be "fully persuaded that the only-begotten and eternal Son of God, after he rose from the dead, did with the same soul and body with which he rose by a true and local translation convey himself from the earth on which he lived, through all the celestial orbs, until he came into the heaven of heavens, the most glorious presence of the majesty of God". And he insisted that "the ascent of Christ into heaven was not metaphorical or figurative, as if there were no more to be understood by it but only that he obtained a more heavenly and glorious state or condition after the resurrection".[1]

In the nineteenth century, Bishop Westcott would tell us "not to think of the Ascension of Christ as of a change of position, of a going immeasurably far from us. It is rather a change of the mode of existence, a passing to God, of whom we cannot say that he is 'there' rather than 'here', of whom we all can say 'God is with me', and if God then Christ who has ascended to the right hand of God."[2]

And at the present day a distinguished Protestant theologian will say frankly that the story told in the first chapter of Acts is a legend, for which the motive is simply the fact that the appearances of the risen Jesus came to an end. The story "expresses, in the language of ancient fancies of men rapt away from earth to heaven, the certainty of the faith that Jesus by his resurrection has been exalted into God's presence".[3]

1. History or legend?

The historicity of the Ascension story in Acts is not of course bound up with an understanding of it as naive and literal as Pearson's. It could have been a vision, no less actually experienced than the Resurrection appearances, adapted to the minds of the disciples, and serving for a sign to them that their risen Master was now and for ever with God. The only reason for regarding it as a legend of later origin is that in other parts of the New Testament there seems to be no clear distinction between Resurrection and Ascension. The speeches of St Peter in Acts do not separate the two events, and St Paul's account of the Resurrection appearances says nothing of the Ascension as bringing them to an end: the last appearance is that to St Paul himself, long after the Ascension of which Acts tells —which indeed makes it difficult to suppose that the story was known to him. Again, both in the "Christ-hymn" of the Epistle to the Philippians and in the other primitive hymn preserved in the First Epistle to Timothy, Resurrection and Ascension seem to coalesce.[4]

On the other hand, in the Fourth Gospel one at least of several references to the Ascension does expressly separate it from the Resurrection. The risen Christ says to Mary Magdalene: "I am not yet ascended to my Father"; though the message she is to bring to the disciples ("I ascend" in the present tense) does not suggest an interval of forty days during which the appearances would continue.[5] It does imply that some at least of the Resurrection appearances were not appearances of the ascended Lord. It would probably be a mistake, however, to suppose that the Evangelist thinks of the Ascension itself as happening *between* the appearance to Mary Magdalene and that to the disciples: so that while Mary might not touch him (*for* he was not yet ascended), Thomas could be invited to do so. The mysterious "Touch me not" is best interpreted as it was by Westcott (following St Augustine): "Christ says, 'Do not cling to me, as if in that which falls under the senses you can know me as I am; for there is yet something beyond the outward restoration to earth which must be realized, before that fellowship towards which you reach can be established as abiding. I am not yet ascended to the Father. When that last triumph is accomplished, then you will be able to enjoy the communion which is as yet impossible.' . . . The spiritual temper of Mary will be seen to be the exact opposite of that of St Thomas. She is satisfied with the earthly form which she recognizes. Thomas, having thought that the restoration of the earthly life was impossible, rises from the recognition of the earthly form to the fullest acknowledgement of the divine."[6]

2. *The Meaning of the Ascension*

Whether the vision itself be fact or legend, few nowadays will doubt that it is to be understood symbolically rather than literally. We may or may not be inclined to see the value of the story of the Virgin Birth rather in what it signifies than in the actuality of its occurrence. But we shall probably feel that this is the case at any rate with the story of the Ascension. What then is its symbolical meaning?

a. In the Creed, the words "ascended into heaven" are counterpart to the *descendit de caelo* which introduced the statement of the Incarnation. The Son of God who "came down" to save the world has "returned" to the heaven whence he came, when his work was done. This is the characteristic language of the Fourth Gospel. "What and if ye shall see the Son of Man ascending where he was before?" "I came forth from the Father and am come into the world: again I leave the world and go to the Father.'" Similarly for St Paul, he who was in the form of God but forwent his divine prerogative to suffer and die has been exalted to a glory no less—perhaps greater?—than was his before.[8] St Paul like St John teaches that he who ascended is one who first descended.

b. But this interpretation is not hinted at in the Ascension story in Acts. For the Apostles on Mount Olivet, who beheld him taken up and a cloud receiving him out of their sight, it was "this same Jesus", the man approved of God among them by miracles and wonders and signs, whom God has raised up and who was now exalted.[9] In the terms of later doctrine, it was the humanity of Christ and not his Godhead that was translated from earth to heaven—as Bishop Pearson said, with the same soul and body with which he was raised from the dead. Resurrection and Ascension alike are events concerning Jesus of Nazareth. And this means that the human life of the Incarnate Lord was not an episode, a temporary and transient form assumed by the eternal Word of God as the necessary means of revelation and redemption, and discarded when it had served its purpose. In the words of the ancient prayer: "For love of our fallen race the Son of God did most wonderfully and humbly choose to be made man, as never to be unmade more, and to take our nature, as never more to lay it off."

c. This has always been the Christian faith. But the Greek Fathers of the ancient Church had their own way of applying it to their doctrine of salvation. They were nearly all Platonist in their way of thinking. Man, the form or essence of Humanity, was more real because more enduring than individual human beings. Human nature itself, as it exists in the mind of God, is the concrete and abiding reality in which individual men are somehow included, and from which they derive such imperfect being as belongs to them. It was this essential Humanity—Man, not a man—that was united to God in the Virgin's womb, offered as a sacrifice on the Cross, restored to fullness of life in the Resurrection, and exalted to God's right hand in the Ascension. Henceforth, Man is one with God; and by sharing in the humanity of Christ we become at the same time "partakers in the divine nature".[10] For, as Athanasius put it, Christ was made man in order that we might be made divine.[11] And this Platonist conception lay behind the doctrine that the humanity of Christ was "impersonal"—in the sense that the centre or subject of his personal life was *not* "a man" but God. For if God had united to himself nothing more than *a* man, a single individual, then mankind would not have been redeemed.

d. We can see that the Fathers might claim descent for such a doctrine from St Paul as well as from Plato. In fact they were taking St Paul's teaching of the Body of Christ of which all Christians are members, the "new man" whom Christians must "put on", in whom they have their life and are indeed a new creation, and re-stating it in terms of their own Platonist philosophy so as to commend it to thinking men of their time. But not many of us today are Platonists in this matter—or at any rate as unqualified in our Platonism as the Fathers were. We do not attribute to the idea of Man an importance or reality greater than that of the individual human being. Humanity is an abstraction, men are real; for the touch-stone of reality is the living, thinking, acting, and loving individual—the *person*. Indeed we are on our guard against the exaltation of the collective—race, class, society—at the expense of the individual human being. Moreover, we have found it impossible not to see in the Jesus of the Gospels *a* man in the fullest sense of the word. A manhood from which individuality has been deducted is not for us manhood. If in Christ manhood has been taken into God, it is the manhood of Jesus—a manhood perfect because whole, entire, lacking nothing that makes manhood what we know it to be.

e. The orthodoxy of Chalcedon did assert that Christ was perfect man as well as perfect God in this sense of completeness, in order to exclude the Apollinarian theory that he was a compound of divine "mind" with human soul and body. But Chalcedon retained the doctrine which Cyril of Alexandria had maintained against Nestorius, viz. that the "person" of Christ—the *hypostasis* or determining ground of his being, the centre of its unity—was not human but divine. Nestorius had in fact stood for just that conviction that Jesus was *a* man, which seems to us so imperatively demanded by the Gospel picture. Where he had failed was in showing how to avoid the implication that in Christ God and man were present (as it were) side by side—two *hypostases* and not one—and so to do justice to the real union of divine and human in the Incarnation. But it is possible to go much of the way with Nestorius, and still believe that God and man are one Christ.

f. If the Incarnation means that the Son of God took upon himself the life of *a* man, we shall naturally believe that he who has ascended into heaven is this same Jesus whom the Apostles knew, and whom not having seen we love. It is one made like unto his brethren in all things through whom we have our access to the Father. For all Christians, the misery of this world's condition is separation from God—that separation which is brought about by sin and which alone gives its sting to death. According to the ancient way of thinking, this separation could be ended only by a change in human nature. In Christ, human nature has been transformed into the likeness of God. The Christian is as it were grafted into this transformed humanity; and the Ascension stands for this very lifting up or exaltation of humanity into the divine sphere of being. But the original message of the Gospel spoke of a movement not from man to God but from God to man. The gulf was bridged by God's stepping across it to our side, when he came down from heaven to share our life. The grace of God is Emmanuel—God with us, not we with God. Then the Ascension into heaven of the man in whom God has reconciled the world to himself will signify for us rather the once-for-allness of the Incarnation itself. God's gracious entry into human life was not for a time but for ever. The fact that Jesus is now in heaven does not mean that human nature has been deified. Men we are, and men we remain. But in the man Jesus, the same yesterday, today, and for ever, God is with us. In Luther's words, we have a Brother in heaven.

B. THE HEAVENLY SESSION

1. *The King*

The words of Acts—"a cloud received him out of their sight"—
recall the prediction in the Gospels of the coming of the Son of Man
"in the clouds". The angels in Acts say that he will come "in like
manner as ye have seen him go". In the seventh chapter of Daniel,
"one like a son of man" comes with the clouds of heaven and is
brought near before the Ancient of Days. The picture, in Daniel, is
not of a descent to earth, but of an exaltation to heaven. In the
Gospel sayings as we have them, the direction of the movement
seems to be reversed: they imply rather a descent, a coming down.
But the Ascension narrative in Acts is clearly modelled upon the
original sense of the Daniel vision. The Son of Man is taken up
with the clouds of heaven, and there is given unto him "dominion
and glory and a kingdom, that all people, nations, and languages
should serve him". Christ comes (in the words of the dying thief)
"into his kingdom".[12]

Now the words of the 110th Psalm—"The Lord said unto my
Lord, Sit thou on my right hand . . ."—had been quoted by Jesus
as an acknowledged Messianic text; and that text is combined with
the one from Daniel in the answer to the high priest's question at
the trial: "Ye shall see the Son of man sitting on the right hand of
power, and coming in the clouds of heaven."[13] St Peter's sermon to
the Pentecost crowd in Acts ends with the appeal to the same text.
He has claimed Ps. 16 ("Thou wilt not leave my soul in Hell") as a
prophecy of resurrection not for David but for the Messiah; and
Ps. 110 furnishes the prophecy of the exaltation. "For David is not
ascended into the heavens: but he saith himself, The Lord said
unto my Lord, Sit thou on my right hand, until I make thy foes
thy footstool. *Therefore* let all the house of Israel know assuredly,
that God hath made that same Jesus, whom ye have crucified, both
Lord and Christ."[14] The same "testimony" or proof-text, in quotation or allusion, appears frequently all through the New Testament.
It recurs twice in Acts, three times in St Paul, once in the First
Epistle of St Peter,[15] and it is central to the argument of the Epistle
to the Hebrews. Dodd has no hesitation in numbering it among
the fundamental texts of the primitive Apostolic preaching.[16]

Its primary meaning there, as in Acts 2, was that "God hath

made this same Jesus . . . Lord": that, in the words of the risen
Christ in Matthew's Gospel, all authority was given to him in
heaven and on earth.[17] The "enemies put under his feet" are the
"principalities and powers" whom he overcame on the Cross, the
"rulers of this world" who stand for all that is in opposition to the
Kingdom of God.[18] In other words, the ascended Jesus is clothed
with the sovereignty of God himself. And conversely, it is implied
that the power of God, by which he rules the course of history,
despite all that the powers of evil can do to mar it, is none other
than the power which was manifested in the Incarnate Lord. The
world is subject to the victory of the Cross, which is the victory of
God's love.

2. *The Priest*

In the Epistle to the Hebrews the same proof-text from Ps. 110
is cited or alluded to at least five times.[19] But the theme of the
Epistle is not the the *royal* power of the ascended Christ. The author
takes up another verse of the same Psalm—"Thou art a priest for
ever after the order of Melchizedek"—and represents the entrance
of Christ into heaven in terms of *priesthood*. The theme is stated
at the outset: the Son of God who is the brightness of the Father's
glory and the express image of his being, when he had by himself
purged our sins, sat down on the right hand of the majesty on
high.[20] In fact, the priestly attitude is not sitting but standing; but
later passages make it clear that the writer does not envisage the
priestly work of Christ as preceding the Ascension and Heavenly
Session or coming to an end with them.[21] The priest is ordained
to represent his fellow men to God, to approach God on their
behalf, to offer sacrifice for sin and so to open the way for sinners
to come into God's holy presence.[22] And this is the thought that
governs the Collect for Ascension Day: "so we may also in heart
and mind thither ascend and with him continually dwell"; and
also the Proper Preface in the Liturgy: "that where he is, thither
we might also ascend". Thus the significance of Christ's ascension
into heaven is intimated by the figure of the Jewish high priest's
entrance into the Holy of Holies on the Day of Atonement; and
the appropriateness of Melchizedek as type lies in the Psalm-text's
assertion of an unceasing priesthood, i.e. one that is not ended by
death—"a priest for ever".[23] But it is the true and complete *humanity*
of Jesus that qualifies him for the priestly office: "it behoved him

in all things to be made like his brethren".[24] Nestorius found in this Epistle the strongest Scriptural support for his Christology.

The author of Hebrews has succeeded, by comparison and contrast with the provisions of the Old Testament for dealing with sin, in presenting a view of the work of Christ which links the Cross to the Resurrection and Ascension in a comprehensive doctrine of Atonement. The death of Christ is the sacrament of our reconciliation to God. It happened in this world of time and space, but its significance and effectiveness are enduring. The author does not say in so many words that Christ in heaven still offers or pleads the sacrifice of himself: he insists that the sacrifice was completed on earth[25]—just as the old atonement sacrifice was complete before the high priest entered the sanctuary. But it is as being in himself the complete and perfect sacrifice for sin that "he is able to save to the uttermost (absolutely) them that come to God by him, seeing that he ever liveth to make intercession for them".[26]

So St Paul had spoken of "Christ Jesus who died, nay rather who is risen from the dead, who is on the right hand of God, who also maketh intercession for us";[27] and this is our assurance that we who have God's justifying decision for us need fear no condemnation. The word translated "intercede" which both writers use (*entunchanein*) is not a synonym for "prays for us": it means rather "stands before God on our behalf", so that *our* prayers "in his name" may be heard. The royal Judge is himself our advocate.

Yet it is "from thence"—from his place of perpetual advocacy—that the Apostles' Creed goes on to say that "he will come to judge the quick and the dead". That final "coming" belongs to the Last Day, and it will be best to speak of it when at the end of the Creed we pass beyond history to the Last Things and the affirmations of Christian eschatology. But we may add a note here on the words *Whose kingdom shall have no end*. The words are taken from the Annunciation of Gabriel to the Virgin Mary in Luke.[28] They owe their place in the Nicene Creed to an episode of the Arian controversy. The anti-Arian Marcellus of Ancyra had troubled his own side by elaborating a doctrine according to which the "dispensations" of the Son and the Spirit were temporary and would pass away. His Scriptural authority was the text in which St Paul says that in the end Christ will deliver up the kingdom to the Father, that "God may be all in all".[29] St Paul of course is as far as possible from the Sabellian or unitarian theology with which Marcellus was charged by his opponents; but he does not hesitate to speak of the

subordination of Christ as Son to his Father.[30] The verse from Luke
provided the required refutation of Marcellus; but its effect is not
to deny the eternal sovereignty of the Father, but rather to assert
that there can be no question for Christian faith of an absorption
of the being of Christ the Lord into the being of the Father. "The
kingdom of this world is become the kingdom of our Lord and of
his Christ: and he shall reign for ever and ever."[31]

REFERENCES

1. Pearson, *On the Creed* (ed. Burton 1847) Vol. I, pp. 317, 323.
2. Westcott, *The Historic Faith*, p. 80.
3. P. Althaus, *Die Christliche Wahrheit*, pp. 489f.
4. See Acts 2.32f.; 1 Cor. 15.3ff.; Phil. 2.9; 1 Tim. 3.16.
5. John 20.17.
6. Westcott, *The Gospel According to St John*, Vol. II, p. 345.
7. John 6.62; 16.28.
8. Phil. 2.9ff.
9. Acts 1.9,11; 2.22,32f.
10. 2 Pet. 1.4: a text unique in the New Testament.
11. Athanasius, *De Incarnatione*, 54.
12. Cf. Dan. 7.13f. with Acts 1.9ff. and Mark 13.26; 14.62 and parallels.
13. Mark 14.62.
14. Acts 2.34ff.
15. Acts 5.31; 7.55f.; Rom. 8.34; Eph. 1.20; Col. 3.1; 1 Pet. 3.22.
16. See C. H. Dodd, *According to the Scriptures*, pp. 34f.
17. Matt. 28.18.
18. Col. 2.15; Eph. 1.20ff.; 1 Cor. 2.8.
19. Heb. 1.3,13; 8.1; 10.12f.; 12.2.
20. Heb. 1.3.
21. See Heb. 8.1ff.
22. Heb. 5.1; 9.24; 10.19ff.
23. Heb. 7.23f.
24. Heb. 4.15–5.10; 2.17f.
25. This is implied by the repeated "once for all", 7.27; 9.12; 10.10.
26. Heb. 7.25.
27. Rom. 8.34.
28. Luke 1.33.
29. 1 Cor. 15.28.
30. 1 Cor. 3.23; 11.3.
31. Rev. 11.15.

CHAPTER 13

For our salvation

THE salvation of mankind is the reconciliation of sinful men to God—the Atonement wrought by Jesus Christ. There have been many theories of the meaning and method of this Atonement, but none of them has been found so defective or so misleading as to evoke from the Church a formal statement of "orthodox" doctrine. It was characteristic of the Greek tradition in the ancient Church to see the focal point of God's reconciliation of the world of men to himself in the act of Incarnation whereby man and God were made one. The Latin tradition, on the other hand, has fixed rather upon the Cross as the place of Atonement. But Birth, Death, Resurrection, and Ascension of our Lord were *all* "for our salvation", and our understanding of that salvation must be inadequate unless we take account in it of the whole story of Jesus Christ. An exposition of the meaning of the Atonement in terms either of the Cross or of the Incarnation alone is sure to be imperfect.

1. *The word and the idea*

The English word "save" suggests immediate reference rather to the danger or evil *from* which deliverance is brought than to the condition of safety or "salvation" which results from the deliverance. In the Bible, salvation means health, wholeness, and implies the removal of whatever impairs or hampers the fullness and vigour of life. "Thy faith hath saved thee" translates the same Greek word as "Thy faith hath made thee whole." To be saved is not merely to escape, but to *live*. "God save the king!" is the same prayer as "Let the king live for ever!" and the versicle "O Lord, save thy people" has the same sense as its response "And bless thine inheritance." But since men can have no fullness or wholeness of life apart from God, salvation can also stand for an act which breaks down any obstacle to such life; and the ultimate obstacle to life in union with God is sin.

Thus salvation in Christian doctrine has a double aspect, backward and forward-looking. Over-emphasis on either gives a one-sided form of doctrine. So we find concentration on the retrospective element leading to "satisfaction"-theories of Atonement, concerned more with the removal of sin's consequences than with its cure. Sin *must* be punished by death; therefore Christ must have borne sin's punishment instead of us: we are saved by the Cross. Or on the other hand, concentration on the prospective element leads to the theory, common to the Greek Fathers, of divine life (immortality) imparted to men by God's becoming man and overcoming death in man. We are saved by the Incarnation and its corollary in the Resurrection.

In the New Testament as a whole the balance is preserved. The work of Christ has both removed the obstacle to life and enabled men to live. St Paul sees the Cross as giving the backward aspect, and the Resurrection and gift of the Spirit as pointing forward; but he will never separate the one from the other.

2. *The Language of the New Testament*

The New Testament writers naturally saw the salvation brought by the Gospel in the light of Israel's faith. In the Old Testament the people of Jehovah are bound to him both by the Law which rules their common life, and by the cult, the sacrificial worship of Tabernacle and Temple, in which God dwells with men. So in the New Testament we find the doctrine of salvation expressed (a) in legal and (b) in sacrificial terms. In both cases the ancient usage of the terms breaks down: they can do no more than point towards the truth which it is attempted to express by means of them. But the fact that we are thus given as it were two compass-bearings taken from different angles should make it easier for us to avoid mistaking our objective.

A. JUSTIFICATION

(1) St Paul's word "justify" (*dikaioun*) is the verbal form in active or transitive sense of the adjective "righteous" and the noun "righteousness" (*dikaiosunē*). Justification is God's righteousness in action: it is an act of "righting". But St Paul takes the word with its Old Testament contexts, which belong to the law-court where "justice" is done. There it means neither to make a person righteous or just, nor to treat as righteous or just someone who is not in fact either. It means to pronounce sentence in favour of one of the parties

to a legal dispute.[1] The procedure is like that of the causes which we call civil. In Hebrew justice there was no distinction between civil and criminal procedure: unless some private person made a complaint against another, there was no trial. A just judge, then, will always justify, "right" the person who deserves to be righted; for he must act like the Judge of all the earth who will never "justify the wicked".[2] But the judge's action is more than a mere declaration, more than a verdict. It is *effective*: it puts the justified party "on top" of his adversary. And since the chief purpose of law is to maintain right against might, to prevent oppression, justification carries with it the idea of *delivering* the weak and oppressed. Thus St Paul's "justification" means not simply "accounting as righteous", but conferring upon the justified person the status and the security that follows from the decision in his favour. He leaves the court free and fearless: he is "saved".

(2) We best understand what St Paul means by "justification" if we come to the Epistle to the Romans from a reading of the Second Isaiah. That great evangelist of the Old Testament sees in the deliverance of Israel from Babylonian captivity an act of God which is at once "righteousness" and "salvation". "I bring near my righteousness: it shall not be far off, and my salvation shall not tarry."[3] The "just God" is the "saviour": "in the Lord shall all the seed of Israel be justified, and shall glory".[4] God has righted, delivered, those who were indeed sinners but have already suffered punishment for their sins.[5] St Paul goes further than that, and almost turns his legal categories upside down. God in Christ has done what no human judge ought to do: he has *"justified the ungodly"*, even in the midst of their sin.[6] Incredible, but true! for it was what had actually happened to Saul the Pharisee. Neither prophet nor Apostle thinks that God is justifying his people in the sense of declaring them to be righteous, in the right. But the Apostle has left further behind him than the prophet the guiding principle of legal justice, which is that none may be justified unless he deserves it. The best and simplest illustration of the Pauline doctrine is Christ's parable of the Pharisee and the Publican. The Pharisee's thanksgiving assumes that he is entitled by his good works to the divine recognition and reward. The publican who can do nothing but confess his sins, his lack of all claim, is justified rather than the other.[7] He is not declared to be more righteous, a better man, than the Pharisee; but God will do for him in his humility what he cannot do for the Pharisee in his pride.

Archbishop Cranmer, in the Homily to which the Anglican Article XI refers, identified Justification with "the remission, pardon, and forgiveness of sins". Forgiveness is certainly a nearer equivalent of the Pauline word than any other, but it is hardly a complete equivalent. St Paul seems deliberately to avoid the ordinary words for forgiveness, as though he felt them to lack the forward-looking implication which he needed to convey; and "justification" does look forward rather than back, to what is to be made of the sinner rather than to what he was. For similar reasons the translation "acquittal" is unsatisfactory. It suggests to us the wrong kind of legal procedure, criminal instead of civil; a decision given in favour of the defendant is not an acquittal. But as we have already seen, the language of the law-court was bound to break down when it was applied to God's dealings with sinners in Christ. St Paul was led to use it by the need to settle his account with the Judaism of those who "seek to establish their own righteousness"[8] —to stand on their "rights", to claim God's recognition of their meritorious service.

We can only be justified "out of faith"—by trusting acceptance of a decision in our favour which we cannot claim but which is given *gratis*, unearned, undeserved. But this justification is a real deliverance, not a formal declaration. And if we ask St Paul, Who then is the adversary, the oppressor from whom God's justifying act has delivered us? he will answer "Sin". For he thinks of Sin as a spiritual power which hales us before the divine judgement-seat, but instead of securing our condemnation is itself "condemned" by the act of God in Christ.[9] Justified, we are free from the chain in which Sin held us, set free to realize in actual righteousness the status to which we have been restored.

(3) In the hands of Luther the doctrine of Justification became the palladium of Protestantism, because Luther saw in the teaching and practice of unreformed Catholicism a relapse into the works-righteousness of Judaism. We are "accounted righteous" by the free act of God which is to be accepted *sola fide*, by faith alone: nothing that we *do* has any part in it. But this "being accounted righteous" is not, for Luther, confined to the beginning of the Christian life of faith. It is much more than a preliminary. God's justification has to be received in penitence and humility day by day, in order that the transforming work of grace may have effect in us. The Christian all along the way is *simul iustus, simul peccator* —which of course does not mean that he is righteous and sinful

at the same time, but that he is always in the position of having to pray the Publican's prayer and receive the divine mercy.

The Catholic theologians of Trent strongly asserted that the Church does *not* teach justification by works. The grace of God, they said, must always be given first; but the gift of grace must be freely accepted, so that men by faith and penitence dispose themselves under the influence of grace for their justification. But the Tridentine theologians at the same time stuck to St Augustine's mistaken understanding of St Paul's "justification" as meaning "being made righteous"; and so they had to assert that justification in its proper sense is *not* merely remission of sins, but "a sanctification and renovation of the inner man", a spiritual renewal which enables us "both to be called and to be righteous".[10] Between what they believed and what Luther believed about essential Christian experience there was less difference than might appear; but on the question of the meaning of words the Catholic reply to Luther had a certain ground in the fact which we have been emphasizing, that justification for St Paul did mean more than either "accounting righteous" or "remission of sins": it included a real deliverance from sin's power.

There was a corresponding difference between the Catholic and the Protestant use of the word "faith". Cranmer in his Homily on Faith called it "a sure trust and confidence in the mercy of God through our Lord Jesus Christ". For the Catholic theologian, faith in the strict sense of the word meant simply belief—the mind's assent to a proposition.[11] To say that we are justified by faith alone, if you are using the word in its proper sense, is to say that nothing more is needed than an act of mental assent. If what you mean by faith is a "sure trust and confidence", you are saying that nothing is needed but a particular kind of feeling: we are justified because we feel sure of it![12] For St Paul, faith is not a feeling: it is not to be identified with the confidence which it gives, but still less is it the mere act of mental assent, the belief which St James sardonically ascribes to devils.[13] It is the act of trusting self-commitment to the mercy of God held out to us in Jesus Christ.

B. SACRIFICE

Justification by Faith was very far from being the whole of St Paul's doctrine of salvation. The faith which is not so much the "ground" or preliminary condition of God's justifying act as the

only possible response to it is not simply reliance on God's mercy:
it is belief in and acceptance of that which *Christ* has done for us.
We are justified "through the redemption (the deliverance) that is
in Christ Jesus";[14] and we cannot avoid asking, How has this deliverance been achieved? How has Christ removed the barrier to
our reconciliation with God which our sins have set up, and made
it possible for us to accept the free forgiveness offered to us?

To this question St Paul gives an answer which is in no way
peculiar to himself but common to all the writings of the New
Testament—and therefore presumably part of the earliest teaching
of the Church. We ought then to hesitate before we dismiss it as
one of a number of possible analogies for the work of Christ, and
one which is too much involved in obsolete religious ideas to have
retained particular value for us. We have deliverance in Christ Jesus
(says St Paul), because God has given him to be the "means of
atonement", of sin's expiation, *by his blood*. We are "justified by
his blood"—not *sola fide*.[15] In this belief, that we are reconciled to
God by the blood of Christ, the entire New Testament is at one.[16]
We may safely assume that the early Church did not invent for
itself so startling an understanding of Christ's death. It can hardly
have rested upon anything but the unforgotten and unforgettable
words of Christ himself at the Last Supper: "This is my blood
which is shed for many." What did those words mean?

(1) Israel like other ancient peoples believed that there was a
means by which the chain of sin could be broken and fellowship
with God restored; and this means was the solemn rite of sacrifice.
The blood of the consecrated victim is constantly said in the Old
Testament to "cover", "put away", "make expiation for", sin. The
Hebrew verb is generally rendered "make atonement for" in our
versions; but the Septuagint used the word *exilaskesthai*, which in
classical Greek means to "propitiate". The Hebrew original, however, never has this meaning: its object is not God but sins. It is
most unfortunate, therefore, that two cognates of *exilaskesthai* which
occur in three New Testament texts have been translated "propitiation"[17]—a word which inevitably suggests the appeasement of an
angry God rather than the "covering" or expiation of sin.

No doubt, the belief that the blood of sacrifice is "given upon
the altar to make an atonement for your souls"[18] has its roots in the
primitive notion of the blood as the mysterious vehicle of life: contact with the blood of the sacred victim was believed to renew the
fading or weakened life of the worshipper. But in the Israel of

historic times sacrifice was always understood primarily as a gift to God, a rendering to him of what was due. Sin is the neglect or refusal to offer to God the service of the life received from him. God accepts from sinful men their offerings from the flocks and herds which he has given them for the sustenance of their natural life, as a pledge or token of the debt they owe him; and so their sins are "covered", deprived of lasting power to separate from God.

Such a form of worship was only too easily degraded in practice to a commercial transaction, a payment for services rendered or expected; and it was just this degradation, by which the meaning and intention of sacrifice was destroyed, which was attacked so ruthlessly by the great prophets. God could not and would not accept any gift that did not truly represent the devotion of the giver's own life. But so long as sacrifice remains a token, a symbolic action, there can be no security that the reality will correspond to the action that symbolizes it.

(2) The words of Jesus at the Last Supper meant that he went to the Cross as a sacrifice to God. The Paschal sacrifice, by which Israel was delivered from the death which fell upon the first-born of Egypt and at the same time from Egyptian slavery, must certainly have been in his mind; but if he spoke also of a new covenant in his blood, he must also have thought of the covenant sacrifice on Mount Sinai which made the background of Jeremiah's prophecy of the New Covenant.[19]

If Christ's death was a sacrifice, a flood of light was thrown both upon the true meaning of sacrifice, and upon the reason why the blood of bulls and goats could never take away sin. For the death of Jesus was not a symbolic substitute; it was the final seal upon a life completely devoted to the service of God. His sacrifice was (in the words of the Liturgy) a perfect sacrifice, because in it offerer, priest, and victim were all one. What is not so clear is how it can be a "sufficient" sacrifice for the sins of the whole world. If it were a substitute for the offering which sinful men are incapable of making themselves, it could be no more effective than the ancient sacrifices, in which the life of the victim was offered *instead* of the life of the offerer. It must be possible for the sacrifice of Christ to be in some more real sense the sacrifice *of* those "for" whom it is offered.

(3) The answer which the New Testament suggests to this question begins with the idea that the Messiah acts in all things as the representative of his people. But "representative" here is not what

E

the word means in modern usage, in which a representative is hardly more than a delegate for some particular purpose. The identification of the Messiah with those whom he represents is much closer. Just as the righteous remnant of Israel in prophetic thought *is* the true Israel, so Jesus, the purpose of whose ministry was to gather that remnant round himself, to "build his church",[20] finally goes to his death personifying in his isolation the remnant which in the persons of his chosen disciples has failed him at the last. Jesus in himself *is* the fulfilment of Israel's destiny: he is its "inclusive representative".

And this is the ground of St Paul's most characteristic phrase "*in* Christ", and of his teaching that the Church is the "body" of the Messiah. The Church is the Body of Christ, because the Christ who gave his life *for* the Church upon the Cross is risen from the dead and now gives his life *to* the Church through the Spirit. For St Paul, the pattern of justification by faith is Abraham, whose trust in God's promise that he should have a son in his old age was belief in a God "who quickeneth the dead and calleth those things which be not as though they were". So Christian faith is faith in him "who raised up Jesus our Lord from the dead, who was delivered for our offences and was raised again for our justification".[21] The justification of believers by the sacrifice of Christ rests not upon the Cross alone but upon the Resurrection of the Crucified. For it is by the Resurrection that God has justified, vindicated the righteousness of his Suffering Servant. In Isaiah's prophecy, the Servant who will be exalted after suffering, who will "divide the spoil with the strong because he hath poured out his soul unto death", stands for Israel as the inclusive representative of his people.[22] So St Paul argues that the Christian belief that "one died for all" *means* that "all have died"—and *therefore*, because they have shared in Christ's sacrificial death, must of necessity live a sacrificial life: not "to themselves, but to him who died for them and rose again". But what "constrains" us, compels us to accept this identification of ourselves with Christ, is simply the love of Christ manifested in his dying for us.[23] St Paul is applying to all Christians what he had to confess of himself: "I am crucified with Christ, and my life now is not my own, but Christ's . . . who loved me and gave himself for me."[24]

We may call this, if we like, St Paul's "Christ-mysticism". But it is not something quite out of touch with the experience of ordinary men. We know that what we *are*—the kind of person we have become or are becoming—is not a private creation of our own.

It is, to a degree which we cannot measure, the product of influences which from our birth have been continually at work upon us in the persons of those among whom we have grown up. And much the most powerful of those influences comes from those who love us and whom we love. St Augustine said that we cannot help becoming like that which we love. We can scarcely put a limit to the extent to which our own lives are shaped by the very existence of men and women better than ourselves, of whose fellowship and affection we are impelled to make ourselves more worthy. We *owe* the best of ourselves to them. And we know that the love between man and man or man and woman has the power of breaking down the barriers between person and person, and enabling them to share in one another's life.

The knowledge that Christ loved us and gave himself for us, the knowledge of that love as a living and present reality, binds us to him in death and life. And those who are so bound together with Christ in at-one-ment with God are at the same time at-oned with one another. The sin which separates man from God is also the cause of all estrangements and enmities between man and man. In the last resort, what prevents the ending of these estrangements is our human pride. To be made one with Christ in his sacrifice is the death of pride, and the receiving not only of forgiveness but of power to forgive as we have been forgiven—to love as we have been loved.

REFERENCES

1. See e.g. Deut. 25.1.
2. Ex. 23.7.
3. Isa. 46.13; cf. 45.8; 51.5ff.
4. Isa. 45.21ff.
5. Isa. 40.2.
6. Rom. 4.5.
7. Luke 18.9ff.
8. Rom. 10.3.
9. Rom. 8.3.
10. See c. 7 of the Decree of the Council of Trent *De Justificatione*.
11. Cf. p. 12.
12. See H. A. Hodges, *The Pattern of Atonement*, p. 86.
13. Jas. 2.19.
14. Rom. 3.24.
15. Rom. 3.25; 5.9.

16. Cf. e.g. Acts 20.28; Eph. 1.7; Heb. *passim*; 1 Pet. 1.19; 1 John 1.7; Rev. 1.5.
17. Rom. 3.25; 1 John 2.2; 4.10.
18. Lev. 17.11.
19. Jer. 31.31f.
20. Matt. 16.18.
21. Rom. 4.17ff.
22. Isa. 53.12.
23. 2 Cor. 5.14ff
24. Gal. 2.20.

CHAPTER 14

I believe in the Holy Ghost

1. *The Spirit in the Old Testament*

THE epithet "holy" is attached to "Spirit" in only two passages of the Old Testament: (1) Isa. 63.10,11, where the rebellion of Israel is said to have "vexed" God's "holy Spirit", by the power of which Moses had brought them out of Egypt; and (2) Ps. 51.11: "Cast me not away from thy presence, and take not thy holy Spirit from me." In both these passages, which probably date from after the Exile, "holy Spirit" signifies the presence and power of Jehovah, which as "holy" must be in reaction again sin. We must therefore consider separately the Old Testament ideas of "holiness" and "Spirit".

a. *Holiness.* The most general meaning of this word is that of *appropriation* to Jehovah. Places, persons, and actions are holy as being set apart, reserved out of the common life of the people as the special sphere or point of contact between Jehovah and Israel. Holiness is not, at first, a term of ethical character: it has the primitive connotation of "aweful", "mysterious", "unapproachable", "numinous"; and what is "reserved" to Jehovah is holy because this character of the "aweful" belongs to Jehovah himself.

Yet we read in the nineteenth chapter of Leviticus: "Speak unto *all the congregation* of the children of Israel, and say unto them, Ye shall be holy, for I the Lord your God am holy." The nation as a whole is set apart, appropriated to Jehovah. And the rest of the chapter expounds the requirements of this holiness, which the entire community and not only a special part or parts of it must exhibit, in an apparently indiscriminate mixture of ethical and ritual precepts, in which the ethical in fact predominates—culminating in the "great commandment": "Thou shalt love thy neighbour as thyself." The chapter belongs to what is known as the "Holiness Code" of Leviticus, which is generally assigned to the beginning of the Exile. It shows affinities with the book of Ezekiel; and we see in it how the content of the idea of the Holy has been transformed by the work of the great prophets of the eighth and seventh centuries B.C. The prophets did not invent the belief that Jehovah is a God of righteousness: he was that already when he established his covenant with Israel; for the covenant rests upon faithfulness, upon love and loyalty. But whereas holiness in itself had been a non-ethical conception, the prophets come near to *identifying* the holiness of Jehovah with his righteousness. That does not mean that the moral is substituted for the "numinous": it is just the white heat of Jehovah's righteousness that is both aweful and unapproachable.

In the post-exilic period, the holiness which Jehovah requires of his people takes on once more the special character of separation, apartness. In the priestly legislation the emphasis naturally falls upon ritual holiness; but this was in part at least an expression of the deeply felt need to maintain the purity of Israel's religion by a pure worship. It was because Israel in Canaan had been "mingled with the heathen and learned their works"[1] that the knowledge of Jehovah as the God of righteousness had been lost. The eventual product of this struggle of Israel after the return from Babylon to "keep itself to itself" as a holy people was Pharisaism—with its high achievements as well as its tragic failures.

b. *Spirit*. (1) The Hebrew word (*Ruach*) means "wind" or "breath". Since the wind though invisible is mighty, works powerfully and irresistibly, Spirit stands for the *power* of God as recognizably displayed in its effects—for the supernatural experienced as an invasion of the natural, especially as the source of extraordinary powers in men. Joseph the dream-interpreter, Samson the mighty man, Bezaleel the skilled craftsman of the Tabernacle—all are raised above themselves, above the normal capacities of human nature, because the Spirit is in them.[2] Thus from the first "Spirit" denotes what we may call the immanence of the transcendent. It does not belong to man's natural constitution, it enters into him from without, but it works in and through the men whom it thus possesses. Especially it marks the beginnings of *prophecy*: its presence is shown in the wild infectious ecstasy of the bands of prophets of whom we read in the First Book of Samuel.[3] These early prophets (*Nebiim*) are plainly patriots, who inspire the resistance of God's people to their enemies and oppressors. And it is the Spirit again which rests upon Elijah and Elisha as the champions of Jehovah-worship against the infiltration of the foreigner in religion.[4]

(2) But what is most noticeable in the great writing prophets

down to the Exile is that they very rarely attribute their inspiration to the Spirit.[5] They are strongly conscious of a difference between themselves and the ecstatic *Nebiim*. To the captains of Israel, the "young man the prophet" who brought Elisha's message to Jehu was a "mad fellow"; to Hosea, "the prophet is a fool, the man with the spirit is mad"; and the exiles in Babylon complained that Jeremiah was still at large in Jerusalem, instead of being imprisoned and put in the stocks—the proper treatment for "every man that is mad, and maketh himself a prophet".[6] In fact, when Isaiah, Micah, or Jeremiah use the word "prophet" it is more often than not in a bad sense. A prophet is generally one of the "false prophets"— sanguine nationalists like the four hundred in whom God put a "lying spirit" to persuade Ahab to go up and fall at Ramoth-Gilead, just as Hananiah the son of Azur, Jeremiah's rival, "made the people to trust in a lie".[7] For the method of true prophetic inspiration, the experience of Elijah on Mount Horeb is classical. There, "the Lord was not in the wind" (*Ruach*), but in the "still small voice".[8] So for all the pre-exilic prophets it is not the spirit but the *word* of the Lord which is given to them and enables them to speak, not like "mad fellows", but with intelligence and reason.

(3) With the Exile comes a change, plain to see in the Book of Ezekiel. Not only is Ezekiel himself subject repeatedly to the supernatural impulsion and control of the Spirit,[9] but he foretells the renewal and reformation of the people as a whole through God's putting his Spirit within them: the Spirit will *cause* them to walk in God's statutes and do them.[10] Spirit, like holiness, now involves and includes the righteousness which comes from the knowledge of God. It is the "Spirit of wisdom and understanding" which will rest in fullest measure upon the promised "shoot out of the stock of Jesse", the girdle of whose loins will be righteousness.[11] Finally, Joel prophesies an outpouring of the Spirit in the "last days" upon "all flesh" (which can only mean all the people of God—"your sons and your daughters", etc), accompanied by wonders in heaven and earth, "blood and fire and pillars of smoke".[12] Here the decay of prophetic hope is made good by the daring imaginations of Apocalyptic. The Spirit has been projected into the Age to come.

(4) Yet at the same time we find in the Psalms and the Wisdom writers a remarkable extension of the sphere of the Spirit's working to creation as a whole. The creative word is equated with the breath or spirit of God, by which the "face of the earth" is "renewed",

and from whose reach there is no escaping.[13] In the Book of Wisdom, the Holy Spirit is indistinguishable from the wisdom of God. "The Spirit of the Lord filleth the world": his "incorruptible Spirit is in all things"; and so Wisdom "reaches from one end to another mightily, and sweetly ordereth all things": she is the "breath of the power of God", a "spirit quick of understanding, holy", and penetrates "all spirits that are quick of understanding" like herself —"in all ages entering into holy souls and making them friends of God and prophets".[14] In this book, in short, we see already the Judaism of the Dispersion coming to terms with Greek thought of the cosmic or universal reason or *Logos*, immanent in the world and in the rational power of the human mind.

2. *The Spirit in the New Testament*

a. *Synoptic Gospels.* For the Rabbis, the Spirit was less a hope for the future than a thing of the past, the Spirit which "spake by the prophets". What appears in John the Baptist is a sudden revival of this prophetic spirit.[15] But the descent of the Spirit on Jesus at his baptism is described, not as prophetic inspiration, but as the anointing of the Lord's Servant, who is also the Son-Messiah.[16] Yet after the Baptism and Temptation, and the first sermon at Nazareth with its text from Isa. 61, there are scarcely more than two references to the Spirit in the sayings of Jesus recorded in the Synoptic Gospels. One comes in the dispute about the casting out of devils (the "blasphemy against the Holy Spirit"), and the other in the promise to the disciples that the Holy Spirit will speak for them when they are called to witness for their faith.[17] This "Synoptic silence" is all the more remarkable when we recall the ubiquity of the Spirit in Acts and Epistles. If Jesus had really spoken more frequently of the Spirit, it was not likely to have been forgotten in the tradition of his teaching formed in the Pentecostal Church. How should this reticence be accounted for?

(1) It is clear that the miracles of Jesus, and especially the mastery over "evil spirits", were for him signs of the present working of the power of God.[18] He could not have believed himself called to the destiny of God's Messiah, without believing that the promised gift of the Spirit was his.

(2) But we know that he would not publicly claim the title of Messiah, because of the difference between the popular conceptions of Messiahship and his own. It may be that he was silent about the

Spirit for the same reason. When the Baptist sends to ask, "Art thou he that should come?" Jesus points in answer to the fulfilment of Isaiah's prophecy—to the healing of the blind, the lame, the deaf, and the preaching of the Gospel to the poor. But he adds: "Blessed is he who is not offended in me."[19] The signs would not tell the whole story to those who were looking for the wrong kind of Messiah. And so he tells the Sons of Thunder who would call down fire, like Elijah, on the inhospitable Samaritans: "Ye know not to what kind of Spirit ye belong."[20]

(3) The key to the problem may well be found in the saying of the Fourth Gospel: "There was not yet Spirit, because Jesus was not yet glorified."[21] The general outpouring of the Spirit is reserved to the Last Days; but before those days could come, the Son of Man must suffer. The Spirit is indeed the power of God, but God's kingdom will come "with power" only when the true meaning of divine power has been displayed in the death and the resurrection of the Messiah.[22] The Spirit is the bequest of the glorified Jesus to those who have believed on him.

b. *Acts and Epistles.* (1) At Pentecost the prophecy of Joel and the promise of Christ are fulfilled. The Spirit replaces the visible presence of Jesus, and becomes the centre and support of the life of the new-made people of God. The Church *is* the Spirit-possessed community, and the gift of the Spirit is available to all who will enter that community by the acceptance of baptism. Evidence of the reality of the gift is seen in the manifestly supernatural powers displayed by the baptized—especially the "speaking with tongues", which the references of St Paul in 1 Cor. 14 show to have been a form of ecstatic utterance, distinguished from prophecy by its unintelligibility.[23] We are reminded of the manifestations of the Spirit in the *Nebiim* of the Old Testament. But the writer of Acts interprets the strange phenomenon (which it is difficult to suppose that he can have witnessed) as the Spirit's testimony to Christ—the Spirit-given power to make known to all men the mighty works of God.[24] And this is by no means for him the only proof of the Spirit's presence; it is to be seen also in the unity of the infant Church which makes it "of one heart and one soul", and in the consequent impulse to the sharing of goods, to having all things "in common".[25] Again, Stephen and Barnabas are "full of the Spirit", not merely because they perform miracles, but because of their convincing witness to Christ, their Christian eloquence and Christian character.[26] Finally, the Spirit is the guide of the Church, both in its critical decisions and in the day-to-day movements of its missionaries.[27] It is still the Spirit of "wisdom and counsel", as well as of "ghostly strength".

(2) We cannot then sharply distinguish St Paul's teaching about the Spirit from that of the writer of Acts, or contrast the one as "ethical" with the other as "sensational". St Paul too recognizes abnormal phenomena as gifts of the Spirit. "Powers", miracles were wrought among the Galatians when they "received the Spirit".[28] St Paul does not substitute an exalted human morality for supernatural manifestations—any more than the great prophets of Israel substituted righteousness for holiness. We can compare his noble words on the "fruits of the Spirit" in Gal. 5 with the account of the Spirit in Isa. 11, 42, and 61. But his guiding principle is fully in line with what we have noted in the writer of Acts. It is that the Spirit's supreme gift is *koinonia*—communion, sharing—the *koinonia* of the Spirit which is linked with the grace of our Lord Jesus Christ and the love of God in the familiar benediction.[29] The Spirit gives nothing to the individual that is not to be used for the service of the one Body. The "unity of the Spirit" requires the transformation of character by the *Agapé*, the charity which is the ethic of Christ; and the love of God—the love which comes from God and returns to him—is "poured out in our hearts by the Holy Spirit which was given to us".[30]

(3) Yet, just as for the eighth-century prophets the righteousness of Jehovah was virtually identical with his transcendent holiness, the Christian "life in the Spirit" loses nothing for St Paul of its supernatural character, as a manifestation of the New Age. It is only by virtue of the Spirit's presence that Christian faith is possible—that we can say "Jesus is Lord", and approach God with his "Abba, Father" on our lips.[31] And as the Spirit of promise, the Spirit which brings freedom from the domination of all hostile powers, it is an "earnest" or pledge of the Christian "inheritance"—a first-fruit or advance instalment of that perfect liberty of the sons of God for which we still must wait.[32] For life in the Spirit is the same thing as life in Christ; and Christ and his kingdom are future as well as present—present in his Body the Church, but to come in the End in final glory.

St Paul speaks most commonly of "the Spirit" simply, often of "the Spirit of God", only occasionally of "the Spirit of Christ". But we cannot read the eighth chapter of the Epistle to the Romans without observing how nearly the terms "Christ" and "the Spirit"

are interchangeable in his use of them. The whole tenor of that
chapter makes it impossible to describe the Spirit in St Paul as an
impersonal influence. The Spirit is the mode of Christ's presence in
the Church—"Christ in you, the hope of glory".[33] We may probably
understand that when St Paul speaks of "Christ after the flesh" as
one whom now we "know no more", he is thinking of the limitations within which every human individual, even the Lord himself
in his earthly life, must be confined.[34] It is the Spirit's dwelling in
each and every individual believer which makes it possible to say
that as the many members are one body, *so also is Christ*.[35] Christ
"after the Spirit" is super-individual Person.

c. *St John*. This same conception of the Holy Spirit as the *alter
ego* of Christ is what we find in the Last Discourses of the Fourth
Gospel. These discourses in the Upper Room replace in the structure of the Gospel the discourse upon the Signs of the End in Mark
and the Synoptics. There, we remember, Christ had promised his
disciples that the Holy Spirit would give them their answer or testimony when they should be brought before rulers and kings to
witness for him. So in the Upper Room Jesus promises that the
Father will send "another Paraclete", the Spirit of truth, who will
"bear witness" of him with them and in them.[36] Neither "Comforter" nor "Advocate" is a wholly satisfactory translation of the
word "Paraclete". In St John's Epistle, the word is used of Christ
himself in connection with his atoning work which speaks for us
to God; and here "Comforter" is of course impossible.[37] In the
Gospel there is no reference to the Holy Spirit as our "advocate
with the Father", though Christ makes himself our advocate in the
great intercession of chapter 17. It is best on the whole to take
"Paraclete" in the general sense of "Helper"—remembering that
the help is given by *speaking*, to, in, and for those who need it.

In any case the word "another" in John 14.16 emphasizes the
identity of the "help" which the Spirit will bring with that which
the Christ on earth has given to his disciples. In the promised
coming of the Spirit, Jesus himself will come again to them. There
is the same relation of dependence and self-effacement between the
Spirit and Christ as that which holds between Christ and the Father.
The Spirit will not speak of himself, but will take of what is
Christ's and declare it to the disciples.[38] The chief function of the
Spirit is the same as Christ's in the Gospel—to *reveal*. He will
teach, guide into all truth, both by recalling the words of Jesus and
by revealing truth for which the disciples are not yet ready.[39] No

doubt, the writer of the Gospel regards his own work as part of this promised inspiration. Through him, the Spirit is taking what is Christ's and declaring it to the Church of his day.[40]

REFERENCES

1. Ps. 106.35.
2. Gen. 41.38; Judges 14.6,19; Ex. 35.31.
3. 1 Sam. 10.5ff.; 19.20ff.
4. 2 Kings 2.9,15f.
5. Mic. 3.8 is a notable exception.
6. 2 Kings 9.11; Hos. 9.7; Jer. 29.26.
7. 1 Kings 22.23; Jer. 28.15.
8. 1 Kings 19.11f.
9. Ezek. 2.2; 3.14; 8.3, etc.
10. Ezek. 36.26f.
11. Isa. 11.1ff.
12. Joel 2.28ff.
13. Ps. 33.6; 104.30; 139.7.
14. Wis. 1.7; 12.1; 8.1; 7.25,22f.,27.
15. Luke 1.15,17; 7.26ff.
16. Mark 1.10f.; cf. Isa. 42.1; Ps. 2.7.
17. Mark 3.29; 13.11, and parallels.
18. Luke 11.20.
19. Luke 7.19ff.
20. Luke 9.55.
21. John 7.39.
22. Mark 9.1; Acts 1.8.
23. See 1 Cor. 14.2f.
24. Acts 2.11.
25. Acts 4.31ff.; 5.3,9.
26. Acts 6.5; 7.55; 11.24.
27. Acts 13.2; 15.28; 16.6f.
28. 1 Cor. 12.9f.; Gal. 3.5.
29. 2 Cor. 13.14.
30. Eph. 4.2f.; Col. 3.14; Phil. 2.1–5; Rom. 5.5.
31. 1 Cor. 12.3; Gal. 4.6.
32. See Rom. 8.16ff. and Eph. 1.13f.
33. Col. 1.27.
34. 2 Cor. 5.14ff.
35. 1 Cor. 12.12.
36. John 14.16; 15.26f.
37. 1 John 2.1.
38. Cf. John 16.13 with 5.19.
39. John 14.26; 16.12f.
40. For much in this chapter I am indebted to J. E. Fison's *The Blessing of the Holy Spirit*.

CHAPTER 15

The Lord and giver of life, Who proceedeth from the Father and the Son, Who with the Father and the Son together is worshipped and glorified, Who spake by the Prophets

1. *The Biblical Doctrine*

BEFORE considering the Creed's statements about the Holy Spirit, we must try to sum up the conclusions to which the study of the Biblical evidence may lead us.

(1) The Holy Spirit is known as the presence and power of God within the world he has made, and especially (though not exclusively) in the activity of men.

(2) But just as God, though the whole world is in his hands, has chosen a particular people to be his "peculiar treasure", and the history of this particular people to be the place where he will reveal himself, so the Spirit is observably and conspicuously present in certain chosen members of that people.

(3) In this manifestation of the Spirit's presence there is no uniformity; for the Spirit does not suppress or replace the individuality of the man in whom his presence is shown. His power is active in the measure in which the chosen individual responds to his promptings.

(4) Only in *the* Elect One who appears in the fullness of time, only in Jesus, is the Spirit present "without measure"[1], because the response is full and absolute. In this one Man, God and man through the Spirit are completely one.

(5) The at-one-ment of men with God, which is the work of Christ, takes effect through the creation of a *community* that shall be representative and instrumental of the Spirit's power to overcome the divisive and disruptive power of sin.

Accordingly, this conception of a *unifying power* may give us the direction for all Christian doctrine of the Spirit's place in the

Godhead as well as in the work of creation, redemption, and sanctification.

2. The Godhead of the Spirit

All Creeds mark the intimacy of connection between the Spirit and the Church which is to be his instrument in the world. The further statements introduced into our Nicene Creed were intended not so much to define the work of the Spirit as to assert his Godhead in relation to the Church's faith in Father and Son. For the application to the Spirit of the Son's title of "Lord" there was indeed little Scriptural authority. But St Paul had been led, through a somewhat tangled process of Old Testament exegesis, to say that "the Lord is the Spirit"—thereby identifying the "Lord" who is revealed to us in Christ with the Spirit which confers liberty.[2] Inverting this Pauline text, the Creed claims that the same Lordship which belongs to Father and Son is shared by the Spirit, who alone can give us the freedom of the sons of God. The Spirit, that is to say, is greater than a "minister" or "angel".[3] And the clauses which say that the Spirit proceeds from the Father and the Son, and that he is worshipped and glorified together with them, have the same purpose of asserting his divinity.

a. Down to the fourth century, Creeds both Eastern and Western generally had the simple phrase "I believe in the Holy Spirit", without any addition or elaboration. This reflects a general vagueness of teaching about the Spirit in the early Church. Tertullian indeed, that erratic genius of the African Church who was seldom vague in the expression of what he believed at any one time, had as early as the beginning of the third century clearly formulated a Trinitarian theology of Three Persons and One Substance, in which the Spirit equally with the Father and the Son is called "God and Lord".[4] But Origen of Alexandria a little later could still speculate, without (as he believed) transgressing the Church's "rule of faith", on the implications of the text of St John's prologue: "All things were made through him." Are we to infer that the Spirit is one of the things made through the *Logos*—and therefore a creature?—Origen is not sure of the answer.[5] But the Arian denial of the Godhead of the Son carried with it the corollary of a creaturely nature in the Spirit, inferior to the Son as the Son to the Father. Even when Arianism had been rejected, there was reluctance among some of the Eastern Bishops to call the Spirit God; and Athanasius, followed by the Cappadocian Fathers Basil and the two Gregories, had to urge in respect of the Spirit the same arguments which had been used to prove the Godhead of the Son. What our Christian experience assures us that the Holy Spirit *does*, in the work of our salvation and sanctification, is what can be ascribed to nothing less than Deity.

The Arian controversy had turned on the application of the word *Homo-ousios*—of one substance—to define the relation between the Son and the Father. The Council of Constantinople in 381 is said to have pronounced that the same word is applicable to the Spirit, that he is "of one substance" with both Father and Son. But if our Creed was approved at the same time, it is remarkable that the Nicene test-word was not introduced into the developed statement of the Creed's Third Article. The Council may have been anxious not to give avoidable offence to conservative Bishops—a motive which certainly influenced St Basil of Caesarea, when about this time he wrote his great treatise *On the Holy Spirit*. For in this work Basil not only avoids the word *Homo-ousios*, but never actually calls the Spirit God. His friend Gregory of Nazianzus had no such hesitations: in his celebrated *Theological Orations*, the question "Is the Spirit God?" is put and answered with an emphatic affirmative; and that is said to compel us to answer the question "Is he then *Homo-ousios*?" no less affirmatively.[6] But Basil had already shown that both the language of Scripture and the faith of the Church require us to give the same honour to the Spirit which we render to Father and Son. The Church's traditional doxology, in all its varying forms, implies that the Spirit is worshipped and glorified together with the Father and the Son. The phrase of the Creed exactly represents the teaching of St Basil's treatise.

b. The words "proceedeth from the Father" are taken from John 15.26. The phrase corresponds to what is said in the Second Article of the Son: "begotten of the Father". There the words "not made" were added to define the sense of "begotten"; and although these words are not repeated here, the same difference from things created is implied. What "proceeds" from God belongs to his divine being, whereas all created things are called into being by his command; and their being cannot have the eternity which is his.

How then does the "procession" of the Spirit differ from the "generation" of the Son? The Greek theologians of the ancient Church were content to say that the difference is unknowable, because it has not been revealed: safety lies in adhering to the language of Scripture. St Augustine, believing that in the structure of the human "mind"—the personal life of man—there is a created "image" of the Triune Godhead, attempted to find an image of the difference between divine generation and procession in the difference which exists in the "mind" between the acts of knowing and willing. For the image of the Father, he took what we now call the field of the unconscious or subconscious self, which he called "memory"; for the image of the Son, the conscious act of self-awareness which is a kind of "offspring" of this "memory"; and for the image of the Spirit, the voluntary affirmation of self which he thought to be involved in all self-consciousness, but which cannot be conceived as "generated" in the same way from the "memory".[7] St Thomas Aquinas took over what in Augustine had been a product of speculative meditation as a piece of formal theology: in the *Summa Theologica*, it has become orthodox doctrine that God knows himself in the Son, and loves himself in the Spirit.[8] We shall return to these ideas when we come to consider the doctrine of the Trinity at the end of the Creed.

c. In the original form of the Creed, as it was accepted at the Council of Chalcedon in the year 451, the words "and from the Son" were absent, as they are in the text of St John; and they have never been admitted by the Eastern Orthodox Church. In the West, St Augustine taught that the Spirit must be believed to proceed from the Son no less than from the Father; for in Scripture the Spirit is Spirit of the Son as well as of the Father: Christ himself says "all things that the Father hath are mine", and of the Spirit that "he will receive of mine and show it unto you"—so that he was able to bestow the Spirit upon his disciples and upon the Church.[9] Under Augustine's influence, this doctrine of the "double Procession" spread in the West, and by the beginning of the ninth century had made its way into the Creed by the insertion of the word *Filioque* ("and from the Son") nearly everywhere except at Rome. Charlemagne tried to induce the Roman Church to come into line; but Rome at that time did not want to provoke the rupture with the Eastern Church which was likely to be caused if official countenance were given to a change in the Creed. It is uncertain when the final step was taken—perhaps not before the eleventh century, when the permanent schism between Rome and Constantinople began. The causes of that schism were not really theological, and the credal question was only one of a number of pretexts. But the *Filioque* clause did conflict with traditional Greek theology.

The Eastern doctrine was that the Spirit proceeds from the Father "through the Son". The most revered authorities in the Eastern Church were the Cappadocian Fathers of the fourth century; and it had been their teaching that the Father is the sole source or "cause" of Godhead, and that this is what makes it possible for Christians to maintain the divine unity; that unity would be broken if God the Son were equally with God the Father the source or "cause" of God the Spirit. The Son can be no more than the *means* by which in revelation and redemption the Spirit is given. This is as much as to say that Scripture is to be interpreted in accordance with certain theological presuppositions; for Scripture nowhere says that the unity of the Godhead centres in the Father alone. Karl Barth has strongly asserted the reality and importance of the difference between Eastern and Western doctrine in this matter, on the ground that our beliefs about God in his eternal being can only be derived from what we know of his activity in revelation and redemption. But if revelation and redemption include the outpouring of the Spirit, the Spirit must "proceed" from the Son no less than from the Father, in order that the Son may be the true and perfect revelation of the Father. And Barth supports his assertion by the Augustinian doctrine that the Spirit, which is the bond of union between man and God and between man and man, is this *because* in the eternal being of God the Spirit is that mutual love which exists between Father and Son, and which could not be mutual did it not "proceed" from both.[10]

3. *The Spirit as Light, Life, and Love*

a. According to the New Testament, the Spirit is given to the Church, and through the Church to each individual Church member, who takes the gift to himself in the Sacraments by which he enters and is maintained in the Church's *koinonia*, its communion or fellowship. It was natural for the Church to claim an exclusive possession of the Spirit's gift—to say in effect that outside the Church there is no Spirit. We find Origen using the figure of three concentric circles to illustrate the respective spheres or ranges of activity belonging to the three Persons of the Trinity: the range of the Spirit being that of the innermost circle confined to the "saints", i.e. to those who belong to the Holy Church.[11]

But the early Apologists of the second century, finding it impossible to separate the Spirit who "spake by the prophets" from the *Logos* or Word of God which the prophets claimed to have received, had made no clear distinction between the *Logos* and the Spirit of the pre-existent Christ. They boldly claimed for this *Logos*-Spirit, not only the inspiration of the Hebrew prophets, but all and every enlightenment of the human mind without respect of age or race, and especially the development of Greek philosophy and its trend towards monotheism. Thus they gave to the words of St John's Prologue—"the light that lighteth every man"—an extension beyond what the writer may himself have intended. Truth, wherever it may be apprehended, can only come from the presence of the Spirit of Truth.

b. But the *Logos* in St John is also he "through whom all things were made": the prophetic Word and the creative Word of God are one and the same. And as we have already seen, the Old Testament in its later parts links both the creative Word and the Wisdom by which God created all things with the Spirit. "The Spirit of God hath made me, and the breath of the Almighty giveth me life", says Elihu in the Book of Job—recalling how in the words of Genesis "the Lord God formed man of the dust of the ground, and breathed into his nostrils the breath of life".[12] So in the New Testament the Spirit is called the Life-Giver[13]; and when the risen Christ breathes the Spirit into his disciples, there is indeed a new creation.[14]

No doubt in the New Testament the life which the Spirit gives is salvation-life, "true" life because it is life in fellowship with God. But if grace is the perfecting of nature, we cannot suppose that the gift of the Spirit has nothing to do with life in its natural origin and condition.

(1) Life in its fulfilment, eternal life, is the knowledge of God,[15] which means that personal relationship to God which is obedience inspired by love. To know and love God apart from loving fellowship with our neighbour man is impossible.[16] This loving fellowship with God and with one another is therefore the fulfilment, the *telos* or destined end of man in God's world. But man himself, as we know, is the product of a gradual creative process. As giver of life, then, the Holy Spirit must be conceived as present and working in the cosmic process at all its levels; and the line of creation which leads up to man is marked by the activity of the Spirit as *unifying power*. Unity is at its lowest in the sphere of inanimate matter. Evolution continually transforms the simpler rudimentary unities

into the higher and more complex. In man, organic life is raised to the level at which personal fellowship with God has become possible, where the creature has been endowed with the power of self-determination and so made capable of free response to the divine self-giving.

(2) Moral freedom, however, requires that this response be not automatic, like the "conditioned reflexes" of Pavlov's dogs, but consciously willed—springing from the established unity of personal life. Inspiration, in the most general sense of the word, may be said to denote the confrontation of the mind by the revealing Spirit with the spiritual values of truth, beauty, and goodness, and the spontaneous recognition and appreciation of these values by the receiving mind. The men whom we call inspired are the high points of Spirit-prompted response to God's giving of himself in revelation. They are the exception, not the rule, because a free response could only be uniform and universal if there were no factors interfering with it anywhere; but such factors are actually present, not only in the varying degrees of evolutionary advance, but in the reality and the infective power of sin. Because this power is such that men cannot deliver themselves from it, they can never claim their own response to revelation as an achievement of their own. They must always acknowledge that the response they make is the Spirit speaking in them. From the point of view of God's purposes, these recipients of inspiration are the "chosen": they represent "the purpose of God according to election",[17] of which St Paul speaks. And this principle of election is seen on a wider scale in the choice of Israel as witness of God's saving activity in history, and of the Church as the heir of the promises to Israel, the true Israel "after the Spirit", the "Israel of God".[18]

(3) Between the original meanings of the words "holiness" and "communion" there is an apparent contradiction.[19] At first, the "holy" is separated from and opposed to all that is "common" or profane.[20] In the later Judaism, holiness becomes exclusive, concentrated by isolation of the Holy People from contamination by the world. In Christ, the concentration of holiness in him who personifies the Israel of God, *identifies itself with what is common*, i.e. with the world of sinners; and from the Cross where this identification is to the uttermost, the movement of the Spirit of holiness is the reverse of concentration. "The Holy Ghost said, *Separate* me Barnabas and Saul for the work whereunto I have called them."[21] And with the mission to the Gentiles that work is to become ever more

*in*clusive, "common", just because its aim is community, *koinonia* —the love which in the words of St Thomas Aquinas is essentially "diffusive of itself".[22] Sanctification, making holy, still demands the separation, the setting apart of what is sanctified. The elect *are* set apart; but this separation is not for privilege but for service, "for the work whereunto" the Spirit has "called them"; and that work consists in the *communication*, the sharing of what has been given to them. Inspiration must always include the enabling of the inspired man to convey to others, in whatever form, the vision or the message he has received. The Spirit that spake by the prophets enables us to share in that understanding of the "wonderful works of God"[23] in the sacred history which was theirs.

(4) Because the purpose for which man was created is this Communion of Saints, the appropriate instrument of the Holy Spirit is the fellowship or communion of the Church, through which revelation and redemption are to be communicated to "them that are without". The only way in which the Holy Church can fulfil its task is by presenting its holiness to the world *in the form* of fellowship, communion—the sacrament or effectual sign of the divine love which gives itself.

Here then lies the peculiar sinfulness of disunity in the Church. The sectarian tendency has always appealed to the text "Come out from among them and be ye separate".[24] But to justify by that text separation from any who confess that Jesus is Lord must imply the denial that the Holy Spirit is present wherever that confession is made.[25] And it behoves the Church Catholic not to incur the guilt of a similar denial.

REFERENCES

1. John 3.34.
2. 2 Cor. 3.12–18.
3. Cf. Heb. 1.13f.
4. Tertullian, *Adversus Praxean*, 2, 13.
5. Origen, *In Ev. Johannis*, II. 10f.
6. Gregory of Nazianzus, *Theological Orations* (ed. Mason), V. 10.
7. Augustine, *De Trinitate*, X. 17, 18; XV. 39–42, 48.
8. *Summa Theologica*, I. q.27.
9. Augustine, *Tractatus in Ev. Johannis*, xcix. 6ff.
10. K. Barth, *Church Dogmatics*, I, 1 (E.T. *The Doctrine of the Word of God*), pp. 546ff.
11. Origen, *De Principiis*, I. 3.

12. Job 33.4; Gen. 2.7.
13. John 6.63; 2 Cor. 3.6; cf. Rom. 8.10ff.
14. John 20.22.
15. John 17.3.
16. 1 John 4.7f.
17. Rom. 9.11.
18. Gal. 6.16.
19. See O. C. Quick, *Doctrines of the Creed*, pp. 284ff.
20. "Common" is the word for "unwashed hands" in Mark 7.2
21. Acts 13.2.
22. *Contra Gentiles*, III. 24.
23. Acts 2.11.
24. 2 Cor. 6.17.
25. 1 Cor. 12.3.

CHAPTER 16

One . . . Church

1. *The Church of Israel*

IN Israel, as in other ancient peoples, religion was the affair of the community, and of the individual only as a member of the community. The primitive religious community was the family or group of families in blood-relationship. It was in and by its religion that the social group expressed and maintained its cohesion. Whatever political unity existed between the Twelve Tribes rested upon the common devotion to Jehovah, as the God who by entering into covenant with Israel had made it the people "for his own possession", his "peculiar treasure".[1] The break-up of the nation would naturally mean the break-up of its religion; and this was shown at once upon the split between northern and southern tribes after the reign of Solomon. The prophets saw in the dissolution of Israel's national existence, under the successive hammer-blows of Assyria and Babylon, the punishment of national apostasy from Jehovah; yet they would not believe that Jehovah had finally abandoned the people whom he had chosen. "I am Jehovah: I change not. *Therefore* ye sons of Jacob are not consumed."[2] Not even when Jehovah has been exalted as Creator and Ruler of the world and all nations in it, can it be thought that his covenant with Israel is superseded or his promises to Israel cancelled. The Remnant upon which Isaiah fastens his hope for the future is but the nucleus or seed of a restored and purified nation.[3] Ezekiel looks forward to nothing less than a resurrection of God's people from the dead.[4] Even Jeremiah's prophecy of the New Covenant does not substitute a religion of the individual for the ancient bond between Israel and Jehovah; for Jehovah seals the New Covenant with the same promise which had sealed the Old: "I will be their God, and they shall be my people."[5]

When apocalyptic takes the place of prophecy, the vision is of a new earth as well as a new heaven; and in the new earth the "saints of God" who will "possess the kingdom" are certainly envisaged as an elect community.[6] And when prophecy wakes once more in the fifteenth year of Tiberius Caesar, the "righteous and devout" are still "waiting for the consolation of Israel".[7] The coming Kingdom heralded by John the Baptist is indeed the rule of God, and when it comes men will draw no advantage from having Abraham to their father. But the Mightier One who is to establish that rule will not be without a people ready to obey it—that people which it was the Baptist's task to "make ready".[8]

2. The Purpose of Jesus

Jesus, we know, transformed all current conceptions both of the Kingdom and of the Messiah—including those of the Forerunner himself. But it is really impossible, in view of what happened after his death, to doubt that he led his disciples to recognize in him the Lord's Anointed, that his preaching was a call to men to enter the Kingdom of God not as so many isolated individuals but as the heirs in common of God's promises, and that his choice of the Twelve whom he named Apostles and bound to himself by a New Covenant meant the renewal of Israel. That he should have spoken of building on their faith his Church, his *Ecclesia*, is no more than we might expect.[9] *Ecclesia* was the Septuagint translation of the Hebrew word for the "congregation"—the people gathered together for common action as the people of Jehovah. But Jesus did not "found" a Church. He called the ancient Church which *was* Israel, the nation obedient to the call of God, into new life from the dead.

3. St Paul and the Body of Christ

a. St Paul's use of the word *Ecclesia* makes it plain that its first meaning for him was the meaning of its Hebrew original—the "congregation" or gathering together in one place of the people of God. In the Jewish Dispersion, the meeting of faithful Israelites in each local synagogue or place of assembly represented the spiritual unity of the scattered nation. In just the same way for St Paul the missionary the word "Church", whether singular or plural, means first the visible congregation of believers in a particular place: indeed this meaning is almost the only one to be found until we come to the later Epistles. But the local "Churches" are not simply parts of a larger aggregate: the Church in Corinth *is* the Church of God, united "with all that call upon the name of our Lord Jesus Christ in every place".[10] And *the* Church, in which "God has set apostles, prophets, teachers", and so on,[11] is not the particular Church of Corinth by itself; nor was *the* Church which Paul had once persecuted[12] any one local collection of Christians. There is a whole, a universal Church of which each individual believer is a part, and that whole is what St Paul calls the Body of Christ.

b. In studying the use and meaning of the word "body" in Pauline theology,[13] we have to remember that St Paul, though he wrote in Greek, *thought* (at least for the most part) as a Hebrew. The Greek antitheses between body and soul, matter and spirit, are foreign to Hebrew thinking, in which man does not "have" a body but *is* a body: the living body *is* the man in his outward manifestation. In St Paul's Greek, "body" and "flesh" represent the same Hebrew word, which denotes human nature as such, what is common to all men and makes them one—mankind "in the solidarity of creation". So the body is not viewed as a principle of differentiation, that which individualizes, separates one man from another.

There is, however, a distinction in St Paul's use of the two words. "Flesh" generally denotes human nature in its *unlikeness* to God, its remoteness from him and its contrast to him. God forbore to punish the sin of Israel, says the Psalmist, "for he remembered that they were but flesh".[14] So for St Paul to live "according to the flesh" is to live without God.[15] But he never speaks of living "according to the body": he uses this word rather for human nature as made for God and made in his image. "The body is for the Lord, and the Lord for the body."[16] Yet there is a "body of flesh", a "body of sin", "deeds of the body" which are sinful, and even a "body of death".[17] For human nature is fallen, and the "body of flesh" has been made captive to sin and death. But Christ has taken this same "body of flesh", and in complete identification with it has "died to sin"—"put off" on the Cross that flesh which apart from God is sinful and subject to death.[18] And Christians must have died the same death: they must have been crucified together with Christ; and that is possible for them because the Church, in which they have been baptized "into Christ" and his death,[19] *is* none other than the Body of Christ, the risen Body which has passed through death.

c. We are so familiar with the use of the word "body" in the sense of a corporation, a "body politic", that we are hardly conscious of its being a metaphor. But the metaphorical use was not a familiar one either to St Paul or to his readers. Similarly, we use the word "member" in social contexts where its metaphorical character is quite forgotten. But St Paul did not speak of the "body of Christians": he spoke of the Body of Christ. Christ's risen body is a real body, not a metaphorical one—though of course it is a "spiritual body" in the sense in which that phrase is used in the fifteenth chapter of 1 Cor.[20] Accordingly, when St Paul tells the Corinthians that they (i.e. their bodies) are "members of Christ", he means that they are limbs or organs of this Resurrection-Body; and since that Body is not metaphorical, its members, though not actual arms and legs, are what they are in a sense quite different from that in which the elected candidate becomes a Member of Parliament. St Paul uses the simile (not metaphor) of the natural human body, in which the many members have their differing functions, in order to explain, not how the many can be one in Christ, but how the one Christ can and must be many without ceasing to be one. "As the body is one, and hath many members . . . so also is Christ." The "one body" of the twelfth chapter of 1 Cor. is the same Body in which Christians share in the Eucharist, provided that they discern its meaning as the Body in which Christ died "for them".[21]

d. Indeed, the words of Christ at the Last Supper may well have been the chief source of St Paul's conception of the Church's unity and its real identity with Christ. But he had also behind him the Hebrew way of thinking and speaking of the people of God as a single person. Israel is both the patriarch and all his children: the "I" of the Psalms hovers continually between individual and community: the Servant of Second Isaiah stands for the Remnant—which itself stands for the whole people. So, now that Israel's destiny has fulfilled itself in the one person of the Messiah, the Church "stands for" the Messiah risen from the dead. And St Paul has known this from the moment in which he heard the risen Christ saying to him, "Saul, Saul, why persecutest thou *me?*"[22]

e. The unity of the Church, then, is not made by and does not depend upon anything in its outward organization—though the ordering of its common life and worship must be such as to express the unity which it already possesses as the Body of Christ. It is a *given* unity, because it derives from the one Gift which Christ bequeathed to it—the presence and power of the Spirit in whom all its members share, and who gives to each his part in serving the Fellowship—the *Koinonia*. And this gift of the Spirit, we remember, is what assures the Church that the New Age has begun, that its citizenship is in heaven. "There is one body, and one Spirit, even as ye are called in one *hope* of your calling."[23] The Christian hope is grounded in the Church's possession of the "firstfruits" of the Spirit—just as Christ is the firstfruit of the Resurrection in the Last Day.²⁴ So, though we have already received the Spirit of adoption, we must still *wait* for its fulfilment in the "redemption", the final deliverance of our body from death.²⁵

4. *The Church and the Kingdom of God*

a. This raises the question of the relation between the Church and the Kingdom of God, which was the central theme of the preaching of Jesus, and is named in St Matthew's Gospel alone three times as often as in the Acts and all the Epistles. Roman Catholic doctrine identifies the Church with the Kingdom of God—or at least claims that the Kingdom is realized, manifested in the Church. Now the Kingdom of God in the Bible is the rule of God and not the sphere in which it is exercised or accepted—the people subject to it. That the Lord *is* King, that his rule over the world does not depend upon men's recognition of it and obedience to it, is the unshakable faith of the Old Testament. So when Jesus preaches that the Kingdom is at hand, and teaches his disciples to pray for its coming, he cannot mean that the rule has not yet begun. He can only mean that it is about to be *seen*, manifested as a present reality. We know that he appealed to the manifest victory over the powers of evil in his own casting-out of devils as sign of the Kingdom's coming. But such evidence was not irresistible: there were other exorcists who could claim similar results:²⁶ the manifestation remains incomplete. The apocalyptic vision of a time when God's Kingdom should "*appear* in his whole creation"²⁷ has not yet been realized. Even the resurrection of Jesus became convincing proof to the Apostles that the Kingdom was indeed come "with power", only when the power of the Spirit had come upon them.²⁸ They gave their witness; but it was refused, and the refusal threw them back again upon the future. There could be no final and complete manifestation of the rule of God till the time of the "restitution of all things", when the risen and ascended Christ should himself be "revealed" in majesty.²⁹ In the meantime, the Church is "saved in hope": it hopes for what it sees not, and with patience waits for it.³⁰ In five out of twelve scattered references to the Kingdom of God in St Paul's Epistles, it is spoken of as an "inheritance" into which Christians have yet to enter.

b. But it cannot be *only* a matter of waiting, either for the Church or for the individual believer. In the sixth chapter of the Epistle to the Romans, St Paul is meeting the objection that his doctrine of justification by faith seems to leave us free to stay as we are, to "continue in sin that grace may abound". His appeal is to the significance of baptism, in which we have all shared in the death of Christ, in order that by virtue of his resurrection we might walk in newness of life. If we "reckon ourselves" dead to sin, if that is what our baptism *means* to us, we must see to it that the rule, the sovereignty in our outward earthly existence (our "mortal bodies") belongs not to sin but to God: we must present ourselves to God as men who have been brought from death to life.[31] We must become that which by our baptism we are. If we are risen together with Christ, our minds must be set where he is, and our earthly passions must be done to death.[32] In short, the Christian life must be a process of change, of growth into Christ, by which his members are transformed into the likeness of that image of God which is set before us in him.[33]

c. And that will be true of the Church as a whole as much as of each individual member of it. Biblical theologians have become a little too fond of telling us that the Church of the New Testament is an "eschatological entity", and assuming that we all know what that means. We know, of course, that the Greek word *eschatos* means "ultimate", "last". We do not always notice that its use in the New Testament with reference to what we call the Last Things is much less common than we might have expected. It does not occur in that reference in the Synoptic Gospels, or in St Paul's Epistles except for the "last trumpet" in 1 Cor. 15. Its home is in the Johannine writings—which is surprising, when we remember that these writings are generally supposed to present the Christian faith as a present possession of eternal life rather than as a hope for the future. *Eschatos* properly denotes the point of time or space at which a period or a line comes to a finish, a termination. St Augustine was fond of pointing out that the Latin *finis*, which can mean an "end" in this sense, can also mean an "end" in the sense of the Greek *telos*—the fulfilment or accomplishment of purpose: there is a *finis qui consumit*—an end which is a consumption, a termination; but there is also a *finis qui consummat*—an end which is a consummation, a completion. The last word of the crucified Saviour in St John's Gospel is *tetelestai*—"It is fulfilled." The sacrifice of the Cross was the summing-up, the perfecting of the life offered in service to God; and it was at the same time the manifestation, the acting out of God's purpose of salvation. It was the final assurance that the Lord is King, that he rules over the whole process of history, and that the "end" of that process is the fulfilment of the purpose for which the world was made.

But this *telos*-end is not a date in time or the end of time: it is that whereby the historical process is given its meaning, its dark places are illuminated, and God's creation shown to be good. The *telos* for the individual, what gives meaning to his life, is the realization of his true being as a child of God. The *telos* for the Church, what gives meaning to its existence, is the "summing-up" of all things in Christ, the gathering of all mankind into the One Body.[34] And that, plainly, cannot be the same thing as a moment in history at which all men living at that moment should be within the Church; for the family of God is not limited to those who at any one moment compose the population of the world, and even if the preaching of the Gospel should one day succeed in converting the whole world to Christ, that would not by itself mean that God's purpose was accomplished.

Yet the Church, no less than the individual, has its existence in time, and prays that God's Kingdom may come on earth as it is in heaven. The work of Christ, in one sense "finished" on Calvary, in another began there and then and goes on unceasingly so long as the world shall endure. The Church exists to represent Christ both in his finished and in his continuing work. So, as for each member of Christ fulfilment can only be reached through change and growth, the Body of Christ must itself have its increase—an increase like that of the lad of Nazareth, in wisdom and stature and in favour with God and man.[35] The increase of the Body must be the building up of itself in love.[36]

REFERENCES

1. Ex. 19.5; 1 Pet. 2.9.
2. Mal. 3.6.
3. Isa. 6.13.
4. Ezek. 37.12f.
5. Jer. 31.33.
6. Dan. 7 and Enoch 62.
7. Luke 3.1; 2.25.
8. Luke 1.17; 3.16f.
9. Matt. 16.18.

10. 1 Cor. 1.2.
11. 1 Cor. 12.28.
12. Phil. 3.6.
13. The following paragraphs are much indebted to J. A. T. Robinson's *The Body* (Studies in Biblical Theology).
14. Ps. 78.39.
15. Rom. 8.1–15.
16. 1 Cor. 6.13.
17. Col. 2.11; Rom. 6.6; 8.13; 7.24.
18. Rom. 8.3; 6.10; Col. 2.11.
19. Rom. 6.3.
20. 1 Cor. 15.44.
21. 1 Cor. 12.12; 10.16; 11.24,29.
22. Acts 9.4; 22.7; 26.14.
23. Eph. 4.4.
24. Rom. 8.23; 1 Cor. 15.20.
25. Rom. 8.15,23.
26. Matt. 12.28,27.
27. Ascension of Moses, c. 10 (*Apocrypha and Pseudepigrapha of the Old Testament*, ed. Charles).
28. Mark 9.1; Acts 1.8.
29. Acts 3.21; 2 Thess. 1.7.
30. Rom. 8.24f.
31. Rom. 6.11ff.
32. Col. 3.1–5.
33. 2 Cor. 3.18.
34. Eph. 1.9f.; cf. the *telos* in 1 Cor. 15.24.
35. Luke 2.52.
36. Eph. 4.16.

CHAPTER 17

Catholic and Apostolic

1. The meaning of the words

a. The "one Catholic and Apostolic Church" of which the Creed speaks was not, in the minds of those who formed the Creed, an ideal. It was nothing so vague or mysterious as an "eschatological concept", but an actually existing society. It could properly be called "holy", as it is in the Apostles' Creed, in the same way that St Paul was able to include all the members of the Church at Corinth under the designation of "saints",[1] despite their manifest and various shortcomings in what we understand by "saintliness". Holiness belongs to the calling of the Church and its members, not to their achieved character or habitual conduct. It and they are set apart, "separated" for God's service.

But when we speak of the Church as one, Catholic, and Apostolic, do we mean in the same way that the Church is *called* to be these things, but that its unity, its Catholic and Apostolic character, have yet to be realized or restored? Do we believe in the Holy Catholic Church, and regret that it does not—at present—exist? Or do we mean that this Church in which we ourselves live *is* all these things already and unalterably? In a divided Christendom, it is possible for us to make that claim only by putting our own interpretation on the words of the Creed. We may say, for example, either that unity involves, or that it does not involve, unity of outward order and obedience. And similarly we may (and we do) interpret "Catholic" and "Apostolic" as best suits our own special position— the particular "Church" to which we belong.

b. There is not much doubt, however, about the original meaning of these words as the Creed uses them. "Catholic" meant simply "universal". The Church claimed to be universal both as spread over all the world, and as embracing in its membership all sorts and conditions of men. The Church, it was believed, is catholic (1) because it is what it is wherever it is, because the "Churches" of Jerusalem, Antioch, Alexandria, or Rome are equally and alike *the* Church of Christ; and (2) because (in St Paul's words) there is in

Christ neither Jew nor Greek, bond nor free, male nor female: because in Christ Jesus all are one—one not as an abstract unity but as a concrete *person*.[2] The Church, that is, knows no limits or barriers of race, class, or sex. "Apostolic", on the other hand, was an adjective at first applied to particular local Churches whose tradition claimed that they had been founded by an Apostle or Apostles, such as Jerusalem, Ephesus, or Rome—there were of course many others. As applied to the Church Catholic, the word simply recalled the fact that the Apostles of Christ were the original nucleus round which the Church had gathered in the beginning. *They* were not of course its founders. But when the Church Catholic was called Apostolic, what was meant was that the Church as it now exists is the *same* as the Church of whose birth and growth the Acts of the Apostles told the story.

c. Thus the words "Catholic" and "Apostolic" signified a double continuity—a continuity in two dimensions, both in space and in time. It is one and the same Church that links together men whose lives are set in different countries, in different kinds of human society, in different civilizations, in different ages. From the second century onwards an increasing stress was laid, for evidence and expression of this continuity, on the Episcopate. In every local Church, the Bishop came to be regarded as the effectual sign of unity and Apostolicity. His rule was the check upon centrifugal and schismatic tendencies, and his teaching authority was held to rest upon the unbroken chain of succession from the Apostles or "apostolic men" who founded the Church over which he presided —just like the authority of the head of a family or an hereditary monarch. It was less easy to show how the Episcopate represents or effects the unity of the *Catholic* Church, the Church universal. Cyprian, Bishop of Carthage in the third century, held that an equal status belongs to all Bishops, that all share alike in the episcopal authority;[3] but such a theory could provide no guarantee against disunion between one local Church and another. Some further safeguard of unity was needed; and it was sought, first in the development and use of the Ecumenical or General Council, in which decisions by the majority must (in theory) be accepted by all, and later in the Papacy—the supreme authority of the Bishop of Rome. The superior advantages of the Papacy as an institution for this purpose are plain enough. If we want *any* outward expression of the unity of the Church universal, to which we can look for the effective preservation of that unity, nothing can provide it so well as the single individual who will stand as the Vicar of Christ.

2. *The Church's task*

a. The Papacy, however, has proved no more successful than the Council of Bishops in effecting that which it signifies—in maintaining the real unity of the Church either in faith or in order. And the only criterion by which we can judge whether any of the separated Churches is true to its nature as Catholic and Apostolic is to ask how it is fulfilling its proper *task* as the Body of Christ. What then is the purpose of the existence of Christ's Body in the world? What is the work which the Holy Spirit carries on through it?

The purpose of the Body in which the Son of God took flesh in the womb of Mary was to be the effectual sign, the expression and the instrument, of God's saving grace. If the Church is rightly conceived as the Body of Christ's resurrection, its purpose will be the same, though on a different plane. In Jesus Christ, through a particular human life God expressed and conveyed his love to men, and man in the person of the Son of Man expressed and conveyed his response to God's love. In the Church, there is expressed and conveyed what could not be expressed or conveyed till the Son of Man was glorified through Cross and Resurrection—namely, man's response to the love of God, working itself out as the fulfilment of Christ's new commandment that we should love one another, as the life of the people of God united in mutual service and in common worship of the divine King.

The Church then will be the effectual sign, the sacrament, of the Kingdom of God, "the witness to the world of its true nature, and the pledge and instrument of its destiny".[4] Its task will be "to represent the ultimate meaning and purpose of all human society, and to be the living means whereby all human society is incorporated into the fellowship which it represents".[5] It is never a perfect witness or a perfect instrument, because it is always made up of imperfect human beings. When it prays "Thy kingdom come", it must always pray also "Give us this day our daily bread", and "Forgive us our trespasses". But even in the confession of its constant need for sustenance, both physical and spiritual, and for the forgiveness of its sins, the Church is witnessing, representing to the world men's universal need of God, and the way in which that need is met.

b. The Anglican Article XIX *Of the Church* defines the "visible Church of Christ" as "a congregation of faithful men" (i.e. believers) "in which the pure word of God is preached and the sacraments be duly administered according to Christ's ordinance". This definition reproduces fairly closely the one given in the Lutheran Confession of Augsburg drawn up twenty years earlier. With the Sacraments and their "due administration" we shall be concerned presently. Here we ask, What is the preaching of the pure word of God?

(1) If we want to know *how* the Church effects that which it signifies, *how* the Spirit acts through the Body of Christ, we should look first to the manner in which Christ himself in Incarnation and Atonement was the effectual sign of God's self-giving to men. In St John's prologue, the Word that has become flesh is the Word that was in the beginning—God in his communication of himself, from which the created world has its being, its light, and its life. In the rest of the Gospel, the Word is invariably the word that Christ *speaks*—though that "word" is by no means confined to the actual discourses which the Evangelist records: the works that he does bear witness of him.[6] The Word stands for the whole self-communication of Christ to as many as receive him, for the disclosure in act as well as in speech of the meaning of his mission. "I have given unto them the words which thou gavest me, and they have received them, and have known that I came out from thee; and they have believed that thou didst send me."[7] The word that Christ has given to his disciples, the word in which they must "continue" if they would be his disciples indeed,[8] is the revelation of God, offering the knowledge of himself to men in terms which they can understand if they will. "He that hath ears to hear, let him hear."

(2) When the writer of Acts has occasion to mark the progress of the Christian Church, what he says is that "the word of the Lord grew and multiplied", "the word of the Lord grew mightily and prevailed".[9] That God's word is powerful, that (in the homely phrase) what God says, goes, had been the faith of the prophets. "Is not my word like a fire? saith the Lord; and like a hammer that breaketh the rock in pieces?"[10] Or, in gentler imagery: "As the rain cometh down, and the snow from heaven, and returneth not thither, but watereth the earth, and maketh it bring forth and bud, that it may give seed to the sower, and bread to the eater: so shall my word be that goeth forth out of my mouth: it shall not

return unto me void, but it shall accomplish that which I please, and it shall prosper in the thing whereto I sent it."¹¹ But to speak of the word as "growing", "increasing", was possible only for one who could almost identify the word with the Church which proclaimed it. The Church can *grow*, can have increasing effect in and upon the world, only as it is the bearer of the Word of power. The definition of the Church in the English Reformers' Article implies, in its historical context, that a congregation of believers is the Church inasmuch as it hears the Bible faithfully expounded, and receives the Sacraments with an instructed understanding of the Biblical truths which they express. But if we have anything to learn in these days from Karl Barth, it is that the proclamation of the Word is not a part but the *whole* of the Church's business: that whether the Church is preaching to the heathen, or instructing the faithful, or celebrating the Sacraments, or giving glory to God in common worship, it is always and everywhere proclaiming the one Word of the Gospel.

(3) This Word itself, the Gospel of Christ crucified and risen to reconcile the world to God, cannot alter. But its embodiment in the Church must live and grow, as the Church lives and grows in the changing world of time—as we see it living and growing in that first youth of its own of which the New Testament tells the story. The Bible and the Sacraments are with it to keep it true to itself; but the Church can never be exempt from the necessity of making out their meaning afresh. Bible and Sacraments are the treasure of the Church. The Word is for the world, and out of its treasure the Church must bring forth things new as well as old.

We have become more than a little allergic to the reiterated demand for a "restatement of Christianity in terms of modern thought"; and we find it convenient to forget that this is what has been happening all the time—except in days when the Church has been somnolent. If we change the form of the phrase, and say that the Church must speak so as to be understood, it sounds less objectionable, though no doubt more difficult now than ever before to carry out in practice. The Church may, perhaps must, hold a different language within her own house, when she is instructing her children, to that which she holds when she speaks to defend and commend her faith to the unbelieving world. What cannot be tolerated is that the two languages should mean different things—that there should be two different Gospels. For the Church's children are not, or certainly ought not to be, shut up in a refrigerator from the disintegrating influences of the temperature outside. The children of light are not meant to be less wise in their generation than the children of this world; nor are the children of this world meant to become children of light by closing their eyes to the Light that lighteth every man.

3. The Authority of the Church

This brings us to the question of the Church's authority in matters of faith and conduct. There is a story of a Roman Catholic theologian who said that a certain Anglican held all the same doctrines as he did himself, but for the irrelevant reason that he believed them to be true. Whether that story is or is not fair to the Roman position, it indicates a theory of the Church's authority which is hard indeed to reconcile with the method of Jesus, who challenged the minds of men with his parables, and would have them judge even of themselves what is right.[12] The only ultimate authority is the authority of the Word which is truth, and which calls for acceptance *because* it is true.

The authority of the Church is of a different kind. It rests upon the given fact of a certain quality of life, ethical and spiritual, which has been so closely and so commonly associated with faith in Christ that only prejudice can refuse to admit that the life is product of the faith. This fact cannot be countered by pointing to the cases, equally conspicuous if not demonstrably more numerous, in which Christian belief has shown no such fruits; for all that is so proved is what we knew already, that men's lives are often at variance with their professed beliefs—which is as true of atheist as of Christian. On the other hand, we can freely allow that in the accounts which the Saints have given of their experience it is not easy to separate the element of objective fact from that of subjective interpretation: the genuineness (say) of Augustine's or Wesley's Christian experience does not validate the theology of either. The doctrines of the Church, from St Paul onwards, have been the human interpretations of an experience in which the souls of men have been confronted with the Word of God in Christ. The moral authority of the Church is sufficient to lend a weight to these interpretations which it would be unreasonable to deny or depreciate. But there is an immense difference between a claim for respectful consideration of the forms in which the Church has sought to make its faith articulate, and a demand for the acceptance of faith and forms alike, *because* it is the Church that teaches them. For that assumes, either that the forms are as unalterable as the faith, or—if any change in the forms is envisaged as possible—that the mind and understanding of no individual member of the Church as such can or ought to contribute in any way towards it: that we must all believe just what we are told until we are told to believe otherwise.

The claim of infallibility, explicit or implicit, is by no means confined to the great Church which has erected the claim into a dogma. But wherever and however it is made, it must be held to weaken rather than to strengthen the real authority of the Church. "I am the Lord, that is my Name; and my glory will I not give to another, neither my praise to graven images."[13] When any man comes to believe, however sincerely, that he or any other man is set in the place of God, he is falling victim to the primal temptation of idolatry.

Note on the Communion of Saints

Between the "Holy Catholic Church" and the "Forgiveness of sins", the Apostles' Creed inserts the "Communion of Saints". This clause was not part of the Old Roman Creed, and it was never adopted in the Eastern Church.[14] The first evidence of its use comes from the end of the fourth century, and it probably originated in Gaul where it had its greatest vogue. It may naturally be connected with the intensive development of the cult of saints and martyrs which was a characteristic feature of the period. Its insertion in the Creed shows that at that time the "Holy Catholic Church" was taken to mean the visible Church on earth. A creed which contained the clause was expounded, about A.D. 400, by Nicetas the Bishop of Remesiana in Dacia. He says that since the Church includes "patriarchs, prophets, martyrs, and all other righteous men who have lived or are now alive or shall live in time to come", as well as "the angels and the heavenly virtues and powers", we believe that "in this Church we shall attain to the Communion of Saints". He thinks of the Communion of Saints, that is, as an "eschatological concept". But most other expositors treated it as declaring our present enjoyment of fellowship with departed Saints; and this has remained the way in which it has most generally been understood. Not always, however; for by the eleventh century it was also being interpreted in reference to the Sacraments. This was possible, since the Latin *sanctorum* could be neuter as well as masculine, and the meaning could be "communion or participation in hóly things". No doubt this interpretation arose from a feeling that the Sacraments ought to have a place in the Creed, whereas the "Communion of Saints" might seem virtually equivalent to the "Holy Catholic Church". St Thomas Aquinas tried to give a place to both meanings, by explaining the *communio sanctorum* as the sharing of all the faithful in those common benefits, especially the Sacraments, which the saints enjoy.

It is most unlikely, nevertheless, that the words originally had any such reference. As we use the clause today, we naturally take it as a reminder that the Church is a much greater thing than the company of believers on earth at any one time. Of the ways in which it is possible for the Church on earth to have communion with the departed, the Creed says nothing. We are free to think of that as we will—so long as we are not led to imagine that our communion with the Saints in Paradise is in some way easier or more immediate than our communion with Christ. For it is "in Christ" and only "in Christ" that we and they are one. There can be no doubt that the cult of Saints and the transference of prayer to them has gone with a loosening of faith in Christ as our brother man and a growing fear of his divinity as our stern Judge. The invocation of Saints becomes a doubtfully valid practice when it implies that we can approach Christ or approach him more effectively "through" them. For there is no line of communication between us and the departed that does not pass through Christ.

REFERENCES

1. 1 Cor. 1.2; 6.1; 2 Cor. 1.1; etc.
2. Gal. 3.28 (R.V.).
3. Cyprian, *De Catholicae Ecclesiae Unitate*, 5.
4. J. A. T. Robinson, *The Body* (Studies in Biblical Theology), p. 83.
5. O. C. Quick, *The Christian Sacraments*, p. 105.
6. John 10.25.
7. John 17.8.
8. John 8.31.
9. Acts 12.24; 19.20.
10. Jer. 23.29.
11. Isa. 55.11.
12. Luke 12.57.
13. Isa. 42.8.
14. For the history, see Kelly, *Early Christian Creeds*, pp. 388ff.

CHAPTER 18

I acknowledge one Baptism
for the remission of sins

WE have said that the purpose of the Church is to embody the
Gospel, to be the outward and visible sign of the Word which
it preaches. As the Body of Christ, the Church is the sacramental
expression of the Word Incarnate who is risen and alive for evermore. It is in line with this purpose that there should be outward
and visible signs of acceptance of the Gospel, of becoming and
remaining a member of Christ. The Sacraments of the Church
bring the Word home to the individual, and are a constant reminder
that he cannot stand by himself, that it is in the fellowship of the
people of God that the Holy Spirit is given to him.

Baptism is the only sacrament mentioned in the Creed; and the
mention of it is peculiar to Eastern Creeds. In the West, however,
the Forgiveness of Sins was no doubt always understood as the
inward and spiritual grace of which Baptism is the outward sign.
It seems strange, when we remember how central was the place of
the Eucharist in the life of every Christian in the early centuries,
that our Creeds should make no mention of the Sacrament by
which the membership of Christ, conferred in baptism, receives its
perpetual renewal. A doctrine of the Sacrament by which the
individual is once for all enrolled in the people of God, enters into
the life of Christ's Body, must be incomplete apart from a doctrine
of the Sacrament by which that life is constantly sustained. We shall
therefore give separate consideration to the Eucharist when we
have dealt with the Creed's reference to Baptism.

1. Baptism in the Early Church

a. Acts tells us that the outward and visible sign of baptism was
from the first the way in which the Apostles called their hearers to
signify their obedience to the Word, their confession that in Jesus
the Messiah has indeed come.[1] That was the first though not the
only difference between this baptism and the baptism of repentance

unto the remission of sins, to which John had called the people in the wilderness of Judaea.

Washing with water, all through the Old Testament, is the simplest and most direct of symbols for the removal of religious defilement. In Tabernacle and Temple stood the great laver or "sea" to hold the water in which the priests' ritual purifications were performed.[2] And these ritual washings gave the prophets a natural form of expression for the cleansing of Israel's sin by repentance and amendment. "Wash you, make you clean; put away the evil of your doings from before mine eyes." "O Jerusalem, wash thine heart from wickedness, that thou mayest be saved." "Then will I sprinkle clean water upon you, and ye shall be clean: from all your filthiness, and from all your idols, will I cleanse you."[3] If, as seems probable, a water baptism had already become a part of the ritual reception of heathen proselytes into Judaism, it would be entirely appropriate that John should have used a like ritual in order to express the need of cleansing from the defilement of sin, even for the children of Abraham, if they would be ready to stand before God's judgement in his Kingdom. In any case, the last of the prophets will not have forgotten the words by which that need had been expressed by Isaiah, Jeremiah, and Ezekiel.

b. Firmly fixed at the beginning of the Gospel story is the acceptance by Jesus of this sacrament of repentance and cleansing. It must have happened, for the Christian tradition could never have invented an action of the Christ which (as Matthew saw) called so loudly for explanation.[4] We may best understand it as the deliberate act of one who could not and would not separate himself, as the Pharisees did, from the people of unclean lips among whom he dwelt—one upon whose heart the sins of his own people lay as heavily as if they were his own. The voice and the vision which greeted the action told him that in so doing he had received his anointing to a Messiahship which would be that of the Servant in whom the Lord was well pleased and upon whom the Spirit was bestowed.[5] We cannot tell whether the words from one of the Servant Songs of the Second Isaiah carried with them for him who heard them the implication of another—that it was to be the Servant's task to make many righteous by bearing their iniquities.[6] But we can be fairly sure that when Jesus spoke on a later day of the baptism he had yet to be baptized with, he must have thought of that past baptism in Jordan as the foreshadowing of the time now approaching, when he was to fulfil the work of the Servant by giving his life a ransom for many; and that his call to his disciples to take up their cross and follow him was in effect the same as his promise to the sons of Zebedee that they should share his baptism.[7]

c. If that be so, it follows that whether the charge to teach all nations, baptizing them into the name of Father, Son, and Holy Spirit, was or was not given by the risen Jesus in those words,[8] the Apostles were not departing from their Master's intention when they made baptism into the name of Jesus the sacrament of discipleship. Christian baptism was still a baptism of repentance, like the baptism of John: it demanded and implied a change of heart. The convert must confess that he has no claim of his own upon God's favour, no rights of membership in God's people. He must confess that he can be cleansed from the defilement of sin only by God's free act of forgiveness.

It was St Paul who firmly linked the forgiveness of sins in baptism with the death and resurrection of Christ, and taught that to accept Jesus as Lord means to pass with Jesus through death and resurrection, to be crucified with Christ and to rise again with him from the dead. In St Paul's language, therefore, baptism as the sacrament of conversion is an "imitation of Christ"—a death to sin and a rising again unto righteousness. "Know ye not", he says —implying that this is something which ought to be familiar to every baptized Christian—"Know ye not that so many of us as were baptized into Jesus Christ were baptized into his death? Therefore we are buried with him by baptism into death, that like as Christ was raised from the dead by the glory of the Father, even so we also should walk in newness of life.'"[9] And the power of the new life is the Spirit of God who raised up Jesus from the dead.[10] For baptism into Christ carries with it the same descent of the Holy Spirit upon the baptized which had marked the baptism of Jesus as the anointing of the Servant-Messiah. To receive Christian baptism was to share in the baptism of the Christ by water and the Spirit.[11]

Thus what happens to the Christian convert in baptism is a self-identification of the sinner with Christ—his acceptance of the Cross which Jesus had held out to those who would follow him, in the faith which was the faith of Jesus that the Cross is the way of life. And so to be identified with Christ was to share through the life-giving Spirit in that blessed relation to God in which Christ himself stood—to win the right to call the Father of Jesus our Father, and at the same time to be united in fellowship as a member of God's family with the whole brotherhood of Christian people.[12]

In the Catechetical Lectures of Cyril of Jerusalem we have a vivid illustration of the teaching given to catechumens of the fourth century before and after their baptism. They are assured that by this sacramental sharing in Christ's death and resurrection they receive at once a real cleansing from sin and a real adoption into divine sonship. On entering the baptistery, they strip naked, as Christ was stripped for the Cross, to signify the putting off of the old man; they go down into the water and rise from it, as Christ was buried and rose again—the triple immersion symbolizing the three days and nights of Christ in the tomb; like Christ at his own baptism, they receive the chrism of the Holy Spirit which gives them the right to call themselves Christians and the power to fight and conquer the temptations of the devil, as Christ conquered them in the wilderness; and the Father's voice pronounces over each of them: "This *has become* my son." It is all an "imitation", a figurative reproduction, of the work of Christ for their salvation.[13] Baptism is still as it was for St Paul above all else identification with Christ. The only point of Pauline doctrine left to be assumed is that to be identified with Christ is to be incorporated in his Body the Church.

d. For St Paul, as for the writer of Acts, it went without saying that baptism was admission to the Church, being received into the congregation of Christ's flock; but, as we have already seen, that was the same thing as being made a member of Christ. The Jerusalem crowds, whom St Peter called to repent and be baptized, were being called to take up their true inheritance as children of the covenant which God made with Abraham.[14] It was the Spirit, flowing over from the risen Messiah into his people, that made the difference between the baptism of John and baptism into Christ.[15] The Church was the new creation of the Spirit. The outward and visible sign in baptism was the cleansing of the body with water: the thing signified was the renewal by the Spirit of God of a people for his own possession—the people of the New Covenant, whose iniquity was forgiven and their sin no more remembered.[16]

This re-creation of a people of God who are to walk in newness of life is the essential significance of Christian baptism in the New Testament. The Spirit is the power of the risen Christ: "He, being by the right hand of God exalted, and having received of the Father the promise of the Holy Ghost, hath shed forth this which ye now see and hear."[17] And the power of Christ's resurrection extends itself through baptism to all who enter the life of the Church, which is the sacrament of the Resurrection Body.

The thought of the *newness* of this resurrection life leads in the First Epistle of Peter to the description of baptism as a new birth. The baptized are new-born babes, whom God has "begotten again unto a living hope by the resurrection of Christ from the dead".[18] And this links St Paul's account of baptism as a sharing in Christ's death and resurrection with the teaching of the Fourth Gospel in the discourse with Nicodemus. The child of man who would claim the right, which the acceptance of Christ confers upon him, to become the child of God, must be born again of water and the Spirit.[19] Because it is indeed life from the dead, the beginning of the Christian life must be a new birth.

2. *The change to Infant Baptism*

a. So far, we have been setting out the doctrine of Baptism as we find it in the New Testament. All its elements are given their place in the Prayer Book service for the Ministration of Public Baptism of Infants, and it is summarized in the prayer of thanksgiving spoken by the Priest at the end of that service. But it was plainly developed while at least the great majority of the recipients of baptism were adults. Its theology was a theology of travelling missionaries, not of diocesan bishops. Neither the New Testament nor the evidence available from the second century enables us to say how quickly or how generally the Church moved to meet the natural desire of Christian parents to have their babies christened. By the time of Tertullian, about the beginning of the third century, infant baptism was common enough in North Africa for him to express his disapproval of it, and for Cyprian the Bishop of Carthage a little later to defend it.[20] By the time of St Augustine it had become the irrefutable proof that the Pelagian revolt against the doctrine of original sin was heresy. For the Church had *one* baptism for infants and adults, and the pattern of the early liturgies had not obscured its character as grounded upon the confession and remission of sin—putting off the old man and putting on the new, through a death and a resurrection. But the liturgies had also given a distinct place, within the complex baptismal rite, to a representation of the gift of the Spirit in the ceremonies of anointing and laying-on of hands. Although the New Testament says nothing of

an anointing with oil in connection with the administration of
baptism, the chrism was an obviously appropriate symbol for incorporation in Christ, and in Eastern and Western Churches alike it
remained part of the baptismal ritual. Twice in the Acts we read
of the Holy Spirit's descending upon persons previously baptized,
when Apostles had laid their hands upon them.[21] Yet the Eastern
Church found the laying-on of hands less significant than the
chrism, and eventually ceased to practise it at all. In the West it
became detached from Baptism and was reserved to the Bishop.
The result might well have been to diminish the significance
attached to Baptism, by associating the gift of the Spirit with Confirmation alone. But this did not happen. St Thomas Aquinas was
constant in his teaching that baptism is our re-birth into the life of
the Spirit (*in vitam spiritualem*), and gives full membership in the
Church. In Confirmation, we receive a further strengthening by
the Spirit, an "increase of grace".[22]

b. The English Reformers saw nothing wrong with this medieval
doctrine. But they did their best to safeguard the principle of Justification by Faith, by stressing the responsibility of the godparents
for the Christian upbringing and instruction of the child, in order
that its baptism might be (in the words of Article XXVII) "rightly
received". At the same time the Prayer Book service of Confirmation was framed so as to emphasize the requirement of conscious
and intelligent acceptance by the candidate of the faith professed
on his behalf by his sponsors at his baptism. Having come to years
of discretion, he must "ratify and confirm" the pledge then given
for him, in order that his baptism may be "confirmed", and he
himself "confirmed", strengthened by the Spirit for Christian life
and service. As Jeremy Taylor said, "We put our seal to the profession, and God puts his seal to the promise".[23]

3. The Contemporary Problem

The increasingly grave disquiet which has been felt in recent
years with regard to the existing practice of infant baptism is due
not to the separation of Baptism from Confirmation but to the
persistent survival in our de-Christianized society of the custom of
bringing babies to Church to be "christened"—although the parents
may have no serious desire or intention that they shall be Christianly
brought up, and there may be little or no prospect of the sponsors
being in a position to take their duties seriously, even if they were

disposed to do so. With the pastoral problem as such we are not here concerned. But we are bound to face the question: What theological justification can there be for administering the outward sign of rebirth into the life of the Spirit to infants for whom we may have little expectation, and far less assurance, that it will be made possible for them to "become what they are"?

a. It should be clear, to begin with, that right and wrong in such a matter cannot be made to depend upon what in any case is a question of degree. The Church, after all, has never been in a position to judge the motives even of the adult candidate for baptism; and the same must hold for the motives of parents and sponsors. In no particular instance can we be sure how much or how little they will do to fulfil their undertaking: we can only do our best, as in the similar case of those who ask to be married in Church, to make them understand the meaning of their solemn pledge. The Church may rightly put to parents who seek Christian baptism for their children the question which St Augustine used to put to the heathen peasants of North Africa who sought it for themselves: "What is it you really want?"[24] But to refuse what is asked unless that question can at once receive a satisfactory answer may be to shut up the Kingdom of Heaven against men.

b. We must be able to say what we mean by the outward form and matter of the Sacrament. If there is *one* Baptism for infants and adults, we must avoid the suggestion that the mystical washing away of sin means one thing for the adult and quite another for the infant. We still lack a form of Service which will make it clear that the adult no more than the child is released in baptism simply from the *guilt* of sinful actions. The notion that Baptism could do nothing more than remit the penalty incurred for pre-baptismal offences began very early to work havoc with the theology as well as with the practice of the Church. The sin from which the Sacrament gives cleansing is the general infection into which human nature has fallen by its separation from God. Apart from God, human beings are the product of an environment which is always more or less tainted; the most favoured child of nature breathes an air which is thick with the mists of ignorance and false values. Every decent mother will rebel against the bare statement that her child was conceived and born in sin; but no honest mother will pretend that there is nothing but what is wholesome in the subtle influences which have shaped and coloured the growing body and soul of her child from the very moment of its conception. When she asks for baptism for her baby, she is simply confessing that there can be no protection for it from the noxious soilings of our sinful world, *unless* there be somewhere available a power greater than all the powers of evil to which that world is subject—*unless* that power be sufficient, not only to begin but to continue its work of cleansing and health-giving, not only to neutralize evil influences from without but to enter the growing soul and break the chains of stunting habit which its own actions would otherwise bind upon itself. Natural birth plants the child irrevocably in the organic life of a human society: beginning in the family, it passes into the social textures of school, work, and citizenship. It cannot and is not meant to escape the influences of a communal existence—influences by no means all evil, still less totally corrupt. But if there be no check upon its domination by them, the Earthly City will enslave it; and that is why it can only have freedom by enfranchisement in the City of God.

c. Baptism no more than the Eucharist is to be treated as though it were simply an operation for the benefit of the individual. Both Sacraments are actions of the Church; in both it is the Body of Christ that is being built up and nourished for presentation to God. At every baptism Christ's claim upon the soul of Everyman is being asserted and acknowledged; and the Church in taking to herself a new member cannot offer it for dedication to her Master's service without at the same time and in the same act dedicating herself anew. The signing of the baby with the sign of the Cross represents an allegiance that is corporate *before* it is individual. That is why, in the rubric prefixed to the Prayer Book Order for the Ministration of Public Baptism of Infants, it is said to be "most convenient" that Baptism should be administered "when the most number of people come together; as well for that the Congregation there present may testify the receiving of them that be newly baptized into the number of Christ's Church; as also because in the Baptism of Infants every man present may be put in remembrance of his own profession made to God in his Baptism".

d. But when we have said that Baptism is the action of the Church, we must add that this action can be no more than the medium through which God does what he alone can do. It is no more within the Church's power to create a child of God than it is within the power of a man and a woman to create another living soul. It is indeed the peculiar virtue of Infant Baptism to force us back upon the confession that God is the only giver of the *vita spiritualis*, as he is the only Giver of natural life. As he acts through the natural love of man and woman to bring a soul into being, so he acts through the charity which the Spirit imparts to the Church to translate the soul into the Kingdom of his Beloved Son. In its rebirth as in its birth, the soul lies passive in womb and cradle.

Finally, the nature of sacramental grace is misconceived if its reality is measured by its observable effects in those to whom it is given. St Paul would never have admitted that the failure of his converts in Galatia or Corinth to bring forth the fruits of the Spirit, any more than their failure to speak with tongues or prophesy, meant that they had not received the Spirit in their baptism. But what is given in baptism is not holiness (in the sense of "saintliness") but Holy Spirit. Evidently, the grace of all baptism, whether infant or adult, is initiatory: it is God's promise that he will not take his Holy Spirit from us. But if there is to be any meaning in the prayers which the Church offers on behalf of the baptized, they must be offered in faith; and if we offer them in faith, we may believe that we *have received* that for which we ask in Christ's Name.[25]

REFERENCES

1. Acts 2.37–41.
2. Ex. 30.17ff.; 2 Chron. 4.2ff.
3. Isa. 1.16; Jer. 4.14; Ezek. 36.25.
4. Mark 1.4–11; Matt. 3.13–15.
5. Mark 1.10f.; Ps. 2.7; Isa. 42.1.
6. Isa. 53.11.
7. Luke 12.50; Mark 10.45; 8.34; 10.39.
8. Matt. 28.19; cf. p. 3.
9. Rom. 6.3ff.
10. Rom. 8.9ff.
11. Acts 2.33,38.
12. Rom. 8.14ff.
13. Cyril of Jerusalem, *Catecheses*, iii and xix–xxi.
14. Acts 3.25.
15. Mark 1.8.
16. 1 Pet. 2.9 (Ex. 19.6); Jer. 31.34.
17. Acts. 2.33.
18. 1 Pet. 1.3; 2.2; 3.21.
19. John 1.12; 3.5.

20. Tertullian, *De Baptismo*, 18; Cyprian, *Ep.* lxiv.
21. Acts 8.17; 19.6.
22. *Summa Theologica*, III, q. 69, a. 5; q. 73, a. 1,2,5,7.
23. *Jeremy Taylor's Whole Works*, (1862), Vol. V, p. 656.
24. Augustine, *Enarrationes in Psalmos*, cxxxiv. 22.
25. Mark 11.24.

CHAPTER 19

The Eucharist

THE Christian doctrine of the Eucharist must begin with what Christ did on the night in which he was betrayed, and with what the New Testament can tell us of how it was understood by the first Christians.

1. The Last Supper

a. The Marcan tradition represents Jesus as having eaten the Passover with his disciples on the eve of his crucifixion, whereas the Fourth Gospel clearly places the crucifixion on the morning before the Passover was sacrificed.[1] The prevalent opinion of modern scholars has been that the arrest and trial of Jesus are unlikely to have been carried out on the night of the Passover itself. But the arguments generally used to support this judgement have been shown by Professor Jeremias of Göttingen to be a good deal weaker than was supposed, and in any case inconclusive.[2] Now it was part of the Passover ritual that the head of the family should expound the "meaning of the service" in accordance with the command in the Book of Exodus[3]; and if the Last Supper was in fact the Passover, Jesus must have given this liturgical exposition before distributing the bread to his disciples. Moreover, the bread and the wine themselves belonged to the liturgy: they were sacramental food and drink *before* the new meaning had been given to them by Jesus in his "words of institution". But even if the meal were not the Passover, it is undisputed that Jesus was crucified at the time of the feast, and Passover thoughts cannot have been absent from his mind as he looked forward to his approaching death. His recorded words at the Supper are therefore to be understood in relation to their Paschal background.

"The deliverance of Israel from the Egyptian bondage was to the Jew what the resurrection of Jesus was to the Christian. Its commemoration year by year taught successive generations that God can deliver his own from death, and can transport them out of a helpless bondage into a life of freedom and strength."[4] In the time of Christ, the Passover had become the great festival of Messianic hope: it was both the thankful remembrance, the *eucharistia*, of what God had done in the beginning of the nation's life, and the confident prayer that he also would "remember" his mercies to Israel and fulfil his promise of restoration. The sharing, the communion, in the Passover meal was thus for all Jews the sacrament of their share in the coming Kingdom of the Messiah.

b. Jesus too, we know, was looking forward to the day when the Paschal feast would have its fulfilment in the Kingdom of God.[5] But he had already taught his disciples that the price of the Messianic redemption is the death of the Messiah.[6] The deliverance of God's people, now as at the first Exodus, must be through sacrifice; and the sacrifice would be performed, not by the substitution of a lamb for Israel's firstborn,[7] but by the willing self-offering of the firstborn of the new Israel to death at the hands of the oppressors. He would die, alone, on behalf of his people. Yet he would call them to make his sacrifice their own by the solemn sharing in the broken bread and the wine outpoured which showed forth his death, in order that they might share also in his victory, eat and drink at his table in his kingdom.[8] The words "This is my body. . . . This is my blood" make this sharing a sharing with the Messiah himself in his Paschal sacrifice: they bind the partakers into a communion, not only with the benefits of his death, but with him who dies. And what the old Israel had done for a memorial of God's great salvation, wrought long ago and to be wrought one day again, the new Israel should do in remembrance of the Saviour himself, showing forth before God and recalling to themselves their sharing in the Lord's death, until he come.[9]

2. *St Paul*

"Until he come"—the words are St Paul's, but there is reason to think that they stand for something that had marked the character of the Church's Eucharist from the beginning. The story of the two disciples at Emmaus suggests that the breaking of bread on the first day of the week, the day of the resurrection, must always have taken place in an atmosphere of trembling yet joyful anticipation. We may perhaps see a trace of this in the "gladness", the *agalliasis* or exultancy with which according to Acts the first members of the Pentecostal Church were accustomed to celebrate the breaking of bread.[10] For the Lord was at hand: he had eaten and drunk with his disciples after he was risen;[11] and one day—any day—his presence with them at the table might become a visible presence once again. *Marana-tha*—Lord, come!—may well have been from the first the Church's Eucharistic prayer.[12] In 1 Cor. 11, St Paul is not rebuking the Corinthians for partaking of their Eucharistic food with gladness, exulting because by the resurrection of Christ the day of redemption has drawn near. He is reminding them that it was *because* Christ gave his Body and Blood for us that he is alive and will come again. It is only in the humble self-knowledge of forgiven sinners, "bought at a price",[13] that we can worthily eat the bread and drink the cup of the Lord. The bread and cup are holy things: the Body which the faithful communicant must "discern" in them is the Body which for our sins has passed through death in order that we may share in its risen life; and the lesson is the same as that which is drawn in Rom. 6 from the baptism into Christ which is a baptism into his death.

In 1 Cor. 10, it is the meaning of the Eucharist as an actual sharing in the Messiah's sacrifice that St Paul is urging upon those who see no incompatibility between it and the good-fellowship (*koinonia*) of heathen club-dinners in honour of this god or that. The sharing of the many in the one loaf means that they are one body—and that not merely by symbolizing the fellowship which exists between them. The argument would lose its point if the "one body" here stood for no more than the outward unity of the Church; for what is being set against *koinonia* with demons is *koinonia* with Christ. The one body of which the communicants in the Eucharist are affirming their membership is the living Body of Christ. Because they are members of Christ, the spiritual worship of Christians is the offering of their bodies, their whole personal being, as a living sacrifice, holy and acceptable unto God.[14]

3. *St John*

The sixth chapter of St John's Gospel, as most commentators agree, is not in any narrow sense a "discourse on the Eucharist". The subject of the whole chapter is simply the gift of eternal life, and the "sign" of the gift is the feeding of the Five Thousand. There can be no final victory over death unless life be nourished by a heavenly food; and the Bread of God which comes down from heaven is nothing but the Christ who gives life to those who can *believe.*[15] To believe in Christ *is* to be fed with the meat that abideth unto eternal life.[16] Augustine's famous comment *Crede, et manducasti*—"Believe, and thou hast eaten"—had in the context of his exposition no reference to the Eucharist.[17] That reference only becomes plain in vv. 51ff.—"The bread that I will give is my flesh for the life of the world"—and in the following explicit coupling of the eating of the flesh of the Son of Man with the drinking of his blood. The important question turns upon the interpretation of the saying in v. 63: "It is the Spirit that quickeneth; the flesh profiteth nothing." But it is most unlikely that this saying conveyed in the mind of the Evangelist a depreciation of the Church's Sacrament as having no more than a symbolic value. No "sign" in the Fourth Gospel is a "mere" symbol. The "murmurings" among the disciples at the "hard saying" about eating the flesh and drinking the blood of their Master are not due simply to crude misunderstanding—any more than the previous "murmurings" of the Jews at the claim of Jesus to be the Bread that comes down from heaven.[18] In both cases the "offence" comes from the difficulty of *believing* that what seems to be of the earth earthy can have such power. That the gift of eternal life can be conveyed by anything that we put into our mouths is as hard to believe as that the son of Joseph has come down from heaven; and in both cases what is lacking is not a more intelligent understanding of what Jesus has said, but *faith*—that faith in Christ himself which can only be given to men by the Father who sent him.[19] And the offence will not be less when the bodily presence of the Incarnate Word has been withdrawn, and the Ascension is followed by the new age of the Spirit.[20] It is indeed the Spirit that gives life, but he will give it in the Church through the holy food of the Eucharist, as it was given through the flesh, the common humanity in which Christ has spoken the words that are Spirit and life.

If this interpretation of vv. 60–65 is accepted, it follows that the "hard sayings" of vv. 53–58 simply translate into terms of the Eucharist in the Church what has been said about the true Bread that comes down from heaven. In the mind of the Evangelist, the Eucharist is for Christians the "sign" of the gift of eternal life, just as the miracle of the loaves and fishes should have been for those who saw it by the sea of Galilee. And it is quite plain that the Eucharist is here presented in one aspect only—that of union with Christ by faith, believing reception of the Incarnate Word. "He that eateth my flesh and drinketh my blood abideth in me and I in him."[21] The Eucharist is simply the sacrament of union with Christ—a union which because it *is* eternal life must carry with it the assurance of its fulfilment "in the last day".[22]

The meaning of this mutual indwelling of Christ and his Church is developed at length in the Last Discourses in the Upper Room, especially in the allegory of the Vine and the Branches, with its double reference to the Vine of Israel which God has planted, and to the fruit of the vine in the Eucharistic cup—the fruit which is love. To abide in the love of Christ is to abide in the love of one another.[23] The whole series of discourses can be read as an exposition of the Eucharist, the New Covenant and the New Commandment, both sealed in the blood of sacrifice.

4. *Communion in Sacrifice*

There can be no doubt that the dominant significance of the Eucharist in the New Testament is *communion*. It is the action whereby the Church celebrates and renews its *koinonia* with its Lord, crucified and risen—risen because crucified. The Eucharist is the continual reaffirmation of baptism, the dying and rising again with Christ which makes the Church what it is—the Body of the Resurrection. But that Body is the Body offered on the Cross which still bears the print of the nails. The sacrificial interpretation of Christ's death, which lies behind every reference in the New Testament to the "blood" of Christ, is derived from and (as we have already suggested) dependent upon the tradition of Christ's own words at the Last Supper. Yet no New Testament writer calls the Eucharist a sacrifice in so many words; and the Epistle to the Hebrews, which is expressly concerned with the understanding of Christ's death as the true sacrifice, the offering of himself which makes him a priest for ever, has no clear allusion to the Church's Eucharist.[24]

But when we leave the New Testament, we find in Christian writers from Clement of Rome (at the end of the first century) onwards a constant and unvarying application to the Eucharist of sacrificial language. It is not only a perpetual memorial of Christ's sacrifice, a re-calling before God or re-presentation in time of the offering which is now eternal in the heavens. It is also, and indeed in the first place, an offering made by the Church. The Church, believing that in the Eucharist the heavenly High Priest is ever present to enact for his people on earth the reality of his eternal self-offering, assimilated the action and the liturgy which expressed it to the Old Testament sacrifices, in which the worshippers must bring their own offering to the priest, that he may present it on their behalf to God. At first, this was simply and clearly signified by liturgical practice. Each member of the congregation brought with him his own contribution to the Eucharistic elements, to be presented by the deacons to the presiding bishop and laid on the altar-table. Thus, in the united oblations of all her members, the Church offers herself. Her offering here and now is taken up by the consecration of the elements into the Son of God's heavenly presentation, to the Father whose will he came on earth to do, of the Body which is his risen humanity; and the accepted sacrifice is given back, like the ancient "peace-offering" under the Old Covenant, to the offering Church, that she may realize by partici-pation and incorporation in her Redeemer, her atonement with God.

This is in fact the Eucharistic theology of St Augustine. When he comes, in the Tenth Book of the *City of God*, to point the difference between the sacrificial cults of paganism and Christian worship, he defines the "true sacrifice" as "every work done to the end of our union with God in holy fellowship". The Christian man himself, "consecrated in God's name and devoted to God, is a sacrifice inasmuch as he dies to the world that he may live to God". And "the whole City of the redeemed, the congregation and fellow-ship of the saints, is the universal sacrifice offered to God through the great High Priest, who offered himself in his suffering for us, that we might be the Body of so great a Head. . . . That is the sacrifice of Christian people—the many become one Body in Christ." And in the sacrament of the altar "it is made plain to the Church that in that which she offers she is offered herself".[25] In this theo-logy, offertory is inseparable from communion. "If you are the Body of Christ and his members, it is the sacrament of yourselves that is laid upon the altar, the sacrament of yourselves that you receive." "If you have rightly received, you are yourselves that which you have received." "Be what you receive, and receive what you are."[26]

5. *Disintegration*

It was the separation of offertory from communion that destroyed the integral unity and the true significance of the Eucharistic action. Dom Gregory Dix has shown how this happened in the

Eastern Church of the fourth century, in the Liturgy of Cyril of Jerusalem.[27] The invocation of the Holy Spirit, to transform the material elements of the Church's offering into the Body and Blood of Christ, "completes" (the word is Cyril's) the spiritual sacrifice; and the presence of the sacred Victim on the altar is enough *by itself* to give power to the Church's intercessions for the living and the dead. The sacrifice *has been offered* and pleaded. Communion has become an appendage; and the non-communicant worshipper will naturally think of it as an easily detachable appendage, the loss of which need not deprive him of his part in the Church's Eucharist.

No doubt, one reason for the growing infrequency of lay communion from the fourth century onwards, when Christianity had become the established religion of the Empire, was the fear of "unworthy" communion. It was easier now for the Church to baptize all nations than to teach them to observe all things whatsoever Christ had commanded. In discouraging from communion not only open and notorious sinners but all who could not or would not take seriously the need for penitent self-preparation for reception of the Sacrament, the Church's pastors may well have been doing what they could to uphold the moral obligations of the Christian calling. Yet we may doubt whether the remedy was not worse than the disease. If Christ came into the world to save sinners, if apart from Christ we can do nothing, and if the grace of Christ is given through the receiving of his Body and Blood, can it be right to fence off the means of grace from those who need it most, or to suggest that we must be worthy of the gift *before* we can receive it?

6. *Eucharist and Atonement*

The fundamental question is that of the relation between the Eucharistic sacrifice and the sacrifice of Christ. We are accustomed to say that the Eucharist is neither a mere commemoration of Christ's sacrifice nor a repetition of it, but its re-presentation—the making present, in the Church's supreme act of worship, of the one perfect and sufficient sacrifice. But if *all* that happens in the Eucharist is the representation of what Christ has done for us once and for all, why should not the Liturgy come to an end with the consecration? Our offerings of bread and wine have become the Body and Blood of the Lamb, standing as it had been slain. The Lord who was dead and is alive for evermore is present with us, and our prayers for ourselves, for the world, and for the living and the dead, may ascend in union with the intercession of our heavenly High Priest, sure of acceptance. What more is needed?

For answer, we have only to go back to the Last Supper. What Christ declared to be his Body and Blood was bread and wine, distributed to those who sat at table with him. What was to be done in remembrance of him was to eat and drink; and what that action signified was more than the appropriation of "the spiritual principle of his living manhood":[28] it was atonement with God through incorporation in the self-offering of the Son of God, made man and crucified for us. For their sakes he sanctified himself; but it was in order that they also might be sanctified in truth—really and truly partakers in his sacrifice.[29]

The Eucharist, performed in accordance with Christ's ordinance, is the safeguard against all crudely substitutionary theories of Atonement. In a sense, no doubt, it is true that Christ died "in our stead"; for if he had not died, the life which his death won for us could not have been ours. But the death from which he delivered us was a death which was not and could not be his: if eternal death be the punishment of sin, Christ did not and could not undergo it instead of us. When the Reformers insisted on the sufficiency of the sacrifice which Christ offered once for all, it is clear that they had not escaped from the defects of the medieval idea of a propitiation for sin which has all its efficacy (as it were) outside the sinner—so that he need do no more than look on at the representation of the sacrificial death of Christ. Without a deeper understanding of what St Paul meant when he said that "if one died for all, then all have died",[30] the efforts made by Reformers, Protestant and Catholic alike, to restore the communion of the laity to its proper place in Christian worship, could have little lasting effect. If the Eucharist is to fulfil the purpose of its institution, it must be *more* than "a perpetual memorial of the sacrifice of the death of Christ". The "benefits that we receive thereby" are not merely recalled to mind in the Sacrament: they are conferred upon us inasmuch as by the receiving of Christ's Body and Blood we are strengthened by grace to make his sacrifice our own.

7. *The Presence*

It was only when the Eucharist became disintegrated by its celebration without general communion of the worshipping Church that

Christians were moved to ask *how* Christ is present in the consecrated elements, before and apart from communion. It was natural
to take for granted that even though the presence of Christ be
given in order that he may be received, he cannot be received until
he is present—or at least that consecration must in some way focus
his presence in the Eucharistic elements through which he is to be
received. Roman Catholic doctrine answered the question How?—
for those who were trained in scholastic philosophy—by the meta-
physical theory of Transubstantiation. Richard Hooker, the
theologian of the English Reformation, desired very wisely that
"men would more give themselves to meditate with silence what
we have by the Sacrament, and less to dispute of the manner how".
Unfortunately, he broke his own good rule by declaring outright
that "the real presence of Christ's most blessed Body and Blood is
not to be sought for in the Sacrament" (i.e. in the consecrated
elements) "but in the worthy receiver of the Sacrament".[31] That
is the doctrine of Receptionism, which makes the sacramental sign
"effectual" only through the "worthiness" of its recipients; and this
doctrine overthrows the nature of a sacrament at least as certainly
as it is overthrown by the metaphysics of Transubstantiation. When
Christ offered himself to his own people in the flesh, only those who
believed received him. But he was not the less really present to
those who did not believe.

Nevertheless, it is a question whether the nature of the Eucharistic
sacrament is not overthrown as certainly by the usage of High Mass,
where the elements are consecrated for a worship severed from
communion, as it is by a doctrine that Christ is present in the
Eucharist only to the "worthy receiver". We can at any rate welcome the recent movement of return to St Augustine's teaching,
that the Eucharist is the Church's offering of herself, inasmuch as
by the receiving of Christ's Body and Blood she becomes that which
she receives and is made one with the sacrifice of Christ once offered
upon the Cross. The spread of the "Parish Communion" at least
shows that we are moving in the right direction.

REFERENCES

1. Mark 14.12ff.; John 18.28.
2. Jeremias, *The Eucharistic Words of Jesus.*
3. Ex. 12.26.
4. R. H. Kennett, *The Last Supper*, pp. 31, 33.

5. Luke 22.15ff.
6. Mark 10.45.
7. Ex. 12 and 13.
8. Luke 22.30.
9. 1 Cor. 11.23–26.
10. Acts 2.46.
11. Phil. 4.5; Acts 10.41.
12. 1 Cor. 16.22; Rev. 22.20; *Didache*, 10.6.
13. 1 Cor. 6.20.
14. Rom. 12.1.
15. John 6.49f.,33ff.
16. Ibid., 27ff.
17. Augustine, *Tractatus in Joannis Evangelium*, xxv. 12.
18. John 6.60f.,41f.
19. Ibid., 44f.,65.
20. Ibid., 61ff.
21. Ibid., 56.
22. Ibid., 39f.
23. John 15.1–17.
24. The reference to the Eucharist (if there is one) in 13.10 is very
    obscure.
25. Augustine, *De Civitate Dei*, X. 6.
26. *Serm.* 272; 227.
27. Dix, *The Shape of the Liturgy*, pp. 196ff., especially p. 203.
28. Gore, *The Body of Christ*, p. 49.
29. John 17.19.
30. 2 Cor. 5.14.
31. Hooker, *Laws of Ecclesiastical Polity*, V. 67.

CHAPTER 20

And he shall come again with glory to judge both the quick and the dead

WE left this clause, which concludes the Second Article of the Creed, to be considered where it naturally belongs—together with the Creed's final profession of the Christian hope: the Resurrection of the dead and the Life of the world to come. In traditional doctrine, the "Last Things" are Death, Judgement, Heaven, and Hell. The Creed is silent about Hell, and though it recognizes the reality of Death it declares that Death is *not* a "last" word. But it does uncompromisingly assert not only that there is a Judgement to come but that this Judgement is the purpose for which Christ will come again in glory: that the presence for so long hidden will one day be hidden no longer, and that the "revelation" of the Christ to which the first Christians so eagerly looked forward will be the confrontation of all mankind with the righteousness of God.

A. THE SECOND COMING

1. *The Christian Hope*

In speaking of the Eucharist, we suggested that the words of St Paul in 1 Cor. 11—"we do proclaim the Lord's death, until he come"—point to a connection between its celebration in the earliest days and the appearances of the risen Christ. When the first Christians met "to remember him" in the breaking of bread, they were looking forward in eager and exultant anticipation to his visible presence among them once again.

In the paper on "Eschatology and History", printed as an appendix to his well-known book *The Apostolic Preaching and its Developments*, Professor C. H. Dodd wrote as follows: "The true nature of the *geminus adventus* of the Lord can best be studied in the Sacrament of the Eucharist, in which the spiritual consciousness of the Church is most intense. The Eucharist was from the beginning an eschatological sacrament, an anticipation of that heavenly banquet which was the august and mysterious symbol of the perfection of life in the Age to come. Its eschatological character is most clearly and emphatically preserved in the Eastern liturgies, though the Western liturgies (Roman and Anglican) have not altogether missed it. It was also, from a very early date—at least from the time when Paul 'received' the tradition which he 'delivered' to the Corinthians in A.D. 50—a commemoration of the death of the Lord 'under Pontius Pilate', i.e. of the historical facts in which the Church saw a 'realized eschatology'. It is the focus of what Dr Webb has called . . . the 'memory' of the community, by which the events of the past are attested as realities essential to its life. At the same time it has been, again from the time of Paul at latest, and we may suppose from those early days in which 'he was known to them in the breaking of bread', a sacrament of the very presence of Christ in and with his people. Past, present, and future are indissolubly united in the sacrament. It may be regarded as a dramatization of the advent of the Lord, which is *at once* his remembered coming in humiliation and his desired coming in glory, both realized in his true presence in the Sacrament."

The question is whether Dodd's word "realized", here as in his whole theory of the "realized eschatology" of the New Testament, does not subtract too much from the "real" futurity of the "desired" coming in glory.

"This same Jesus, which is taken up from you into heaven, shall so come in like manner as ye have seen him go into heaven" (Acts 1.11).
"The times of refreshing shall come from the face of the Lord, and he shall send Jesus, the Christ fore-ordained to you, whom the heaven must receive until the times of the restitution of all things" (Acts 3.19f.).
"To wait for his Son from heaven, whom he raised from the dead, even Jesus which delivered us from the wrath to come" (1 Thess. 1.10).
"Waiting for the revelation of our Lord Jesus Christ" (1 Cor. 1.7).
"Our citizenship is in heaven, from whence also we wait for the Saviour, the Lord Jesus Christ" (Phil. 3.20).
"Unto them that wait for him shall he appear a second time apart from sin unto salvation" (Heb. 9. 28).
"Be patient, therefore, brethren, until the coming of the Lord" (Jas. 5.7).

"Hope to the end for the grace that is to be brought to you at the revelation of Jesus Christ" (1 Pet. 1.13).
"When he shall appear, we shall be like him, for we shall see him as he is. And every one that hath this hope set upon him purifieth himself, as he is pure" (1 John 3.2).

These passages, taken from six different writers of the New Testament, make it abundantly clear that for all of them alike the Christian life on earth was a life of *hope* as well as of faith; and that the object of this hope, the event to which they looked forward, was the *Apocalypse* or revelation, the *Parousia* or coming, of Jesus Christ. "By hope", says St Paul, "we were saved; but hope that is seen is not hope, for who hopes for what he sees? If we hope for that which we do not see, we are waiting for it in patience."[1]

2. Last Things in the Bible

The Bible begins and ends with imaginative pictures of the Beginning and the End—the First and the Last Things. Both these pictures are drawn from the standpoint of a faith that is grounded in present experience: they are (what the mathematician calls) extrapolations of that faith. The story of Creation and Fall tells how things must have come to be, since they are what we believe them to be. The story of the New Jerusalem coming down from heaven tells how things will surely be one day, since they *are* what we believe them to be. The two stories taken together tell us how we may best imagine the unknowable Beginning and the unknowable End, in order to think rightly of our present condition. Both stories have much in common with the "myths" which Plato told when philosophic argument could take him no further. They are neither true nor false, but they are "likely tales", tales like the truth—because the truth gathered from our present experience demands some such frame as that with which they furnish it.

The truth of present experience for the Biblical writers was the Kingdom, the Rule of God. Prophets and Apostles alike know that "the Lord is King"—and that, not in spite of what they see happening in the world, but *because* of it. The story they tell of the coming Kingdom is not a compensation for its present failure, but a corollary of its present reality. As the prophets see, in the death of the sinful kingdoms of Israel and Judah at the hands of Assyria and Babylon, not a disproof but a vindication of the sovereignty of Jehovah, so St Paul finds the righteousness of God supremely triumphant in the Cross of Jesus, the sinless King of the Jews. In the prophets' story, God's unrevoked choice of Israel to be the place in which his sovereignty shall be revealed is pictured in the figure of the anointed Son of David who will rule in righteousness by the Spirit of the Lord. In the Apostles' story, the same figure is central—but with the difference that while for the prophets he had been only one that should come, for the Apostles he is one who has come already. Their story is more securely grounded than that of the prophets in present experience, because it tells of one whose presence and power is known: Jesus is already designated as Son of God in power by the resurrection from the dead.[2] The New Testament story takes its pattern from apocalyptic rather than from prophecy. But the heavenly Messiah of apocalyptic and his supernatural setting belonged to the *future* no less than the prince in David's line whom the prophets foretold. Neither prophet nor apocalyptist thought, as we profess to think, of a "beyond history", or of "supra-temporal events": they did not deal in inconceivabilities. Their New Age was a *coming* age, not a form of timeless being. For the Pentecostal Church, that New Age had already begun; for he that was to come had come. To proclaim the Kingdom of God was to proclaim the advent of the King as what has actually taken place. What room then was left for any picture of the future? Why did the Church live in hope?

3. *Presence and Coming*

If we are right in thinking that the Apostles would not have recognized in Jesus the coming Messiah, if he himself had never put the thought into their minds—for he was too different from any Messiah they had dreamt of—we may say also that the reason they still looked forward to a future "coming" was that in this too he had led the way. How much of the apocalyptic descriptions of the future coming of the Son of Man belongs to the authentic sayings of Jesus may be disputed; but there is little ground for doubting the authenticity of his words at the Last Supper: "I will drink no more of the fruit of the vine, until that day when I drink it new in the kingdom of God."[3] It was those words that made the Eucharist an "anticipation of the heavenly banquet"—"until he come". Jesus himself had bequeathed to his disciples the hope of his appearing again; and that hope was to remain alive, not only in

those who loved him because they had seen him, but in those many
more who learnt to love him whom they had never seen.

Canon J. E. Fison, in his book, *The Christian Hope*, has urged
that it is only when we understand the first advent of Christ "in
terms of love" that we realize the *necessity* of the Second Advent.
The theme of his book is the double sense of the Greek *parousia*—
"presence" and "coming".[5] The intellectual problem for the New
Testament writers, he says, "was how to express at one and the
same time the Christian conviction, both that in Christ the End
had already arrived, and also that it was in some equally vivid way
to be imminently expected in the future. But what is intellectually
obscure and incomprehensible for logical reasoning becomes mystic-
ally clear and unmistakable in the relationship of love; for whereas
in logic if you now possess something it is unreasonable to go on
hoping for it, in love that is exactly what you must do. The extent
of your present possession is the measure of your future expectation.
. . . It is the present reality of love which guarantees the future, for
love is inexhaustible, and its presence necessitates its *parousia*."[6]

Yet we may ask whether this is quite enough to explain the
Christian hope. Certainly, that hope is more than the natural
reluctance of any intense personal affection to believe it possible that
"I shall never see him again". But it is also more than a confidence
that the love already given is of such a quality as to promise that
more of the same love will be bestowed in the future. For there is a
difference between the knowledge of the Lord present all the days
with those who have never seen him, and the knowledge to which they
look forward "at his appearing".[7] It is the difference of which
St Paul speaks at the end of his hymn of love. "When that which
is perfect shall come, then that which is in part shall be done away.
For now we see through a glass, darkly, but then face to face: now
I know in part, but then shall I know even as also I am known."[8]
Faith is not sight. Even for St Thomas Aquinas the presence of
Christ in the Eucharist was a "veiled" presence, not a permanent
substitute for the vision of Christ's glory.[9] It is because God was
made man that it is possible for us men to meet God "face to
face". The story of the Second Coming does not tell us *how* that
possibility will be realized. But the Church's belief that Christ will
come again in glory is the faith that *in* that same Jesus who was
born and died and rose again and ascended into heaven we may
hope "in the end" to see the glory of God.

B. THE JUDGEMENT OF QUICK AND DEAD

a. The hope of the early Church was to see the Lord again. It was the eager confidence in a final reunion of lover and beloved. None of the passages quoted above to illustrate this hope connect it with the expectation of *judgement*. In all parts of the New Testament we find expressions of the certainty that the coming Day of God will be a Day of Judgement; and in two places in Acts it is said that Jesus has been appointed by God to judge the world, the quick and the dead.[10] Elsewhere the traces of this belief are surprisingly few. St Paul says once that "we must all appear before the judgement seat of Christ";[11] but the only other unambiguous reference in the Epistles is in 2 Tim. 4.1. The scarcity of these allusions becomes the more striking when we recall the great picture of the judgement by the Son of Man in the twenty-fifth chapter of St Matthew's Gospel.

The setting of that picture corresponds closely enough to that which we find in the *Similitudes of Enoch*, where judgement is committed to the Son of Man who sits as in Matt. 25 on the throne of his glory.[12] In Dan. 7, on the other hand, the Judge is not the Son of Man but the Ancient of Days. It is true that the ideal king of Israel is a righteous judge;[13] and the Servant of God in Isaiah 42 is to "bring forth judgement". But all through the Old Testament it is God himself who is the Judge of all the earth;[14] and his judgement is not postponed to the end of history but is continually taking effect. "The Lord is known by the judgements which he executes." "His judgements are in all the earth."[15] The mighty acts of God are indeed always acts of judgement.

We must remember that (as was said when we were considering justification) the judgement of God is not a judicial enquiry or pronouncement but an *act*—the *doing* of justice, the righting of wrong. So, whether it is the prophet of the return from Babylon who sees therein the "drawing near" of righteousness and salvation,[16] or the apocalyptist who dreams of a day when *all* wrongs will finally be righted, what is being asserted is faith in the ultimate supremacy of good over evil—which is the Judgement of God. And naturally enough this judgement is pictured as a Great Divide—the sorting out of sheep from goats, of those who have done good from those who have done evil, and the rewarding of both according to their deeds. For the Hebrew mind sees human character in black and white, and does not concern itself with the shades of grey which are really so much the more numerous. So the Great Divide is easy: the question is simply, Who is on the Lord's side? And "he that is not with me is against me."

b. In the preaching of Jesus, the coming of the Kingdom of God is the coming of Judgement, and that is what gives urgency to the call for decision. In the Epistles as a whole, despite the imminence of the expected *Parousia*, this note of urgency sounds less frequently. The Epistles are addressed to men who have already taken their stand on the Lord's side, and who are therefore already "justified". To be joined with Christ in his death and resurrection is already to have been "righted" by God's judgement; and it is not Paul's way to speak of that judgement as reversible. Similarly in the Fourth Gospel judgement has come into the world with Christ, and this judgement, committed by the Father unto the Son, is not postponed. Those who believe in Christ do not come into judgement: they have already passed from death unto life, whereas those who shrink from the light of Christ, lest their evil deeds be reproved, have already been judged by their refusal.[17] It is John in his Epistle, and not Paul, who speaks of the Christian's "confidence in the day of judgement";[18] but the ground of confidence for both is certainly the Christian's relation to the person of the Judge.

Because the judgement will be the judgement of Christ, for those who *are* in Christ, those who "abide in his love",[19] there can be no fear in the expectation of it. Only in the Epistle to the Hebrews do we find the warning that if we sin wilfully *after* we have received the knowledge of the truth, there remains for us only "a certain fearful looking forward to judgement".[20] But St Matthew preserved in his Gospel for the Church of his time warnings equally severe uttered by Christ himself. "Many shall say to me in that day, Lord, Lord, have we not prophesied in thy name, and in thy name cast out devils, and in thy name done many mighty works? And then will I profess to them, I never knew you."[21] Thus the judgement to come, the judgement of quick and dead in the Last Day, is confrontation with Christ, when "every man's work shall be made manifest, for the day shall show it up".[22]

c. The picture of the Judgement Day in Matt. 25 is a picture of the Great Divide drawn in the lines already familiar in the writings of apocalyptic. The sheep will be separated from the goats: those on the left will depart into eternal punishment, those on the right into eternal life. There is only one innovation on the traditional theme, and that is the criterion by which the division is carried out. It will take *all* by surprise. Sheep and goats alike will ask in amazement, Lord, when saw we thee. . .? It is a warning to all *against* confidence in the day of judgement, against any and every claim to be justified—even to be "justified by faith"! In this life, men may deceive themselves. Some may think that they have believed in Christ, though their life has denied it: others may not imagine themselves to have believed in him, though their life has affirmed it.

But we may not draw the inference that to feed the hungry and clothe the naked will *ensure* to any man his place on the right side in the Great Divide. To ground our thoughts of the judgement to come exclusively on this story may be no wiser than to ground our thoughts of life beyond the grave exclusively upon the story of Dives and Lazarus. Christ will come to judge the quick and the dead. *That* we must believe, if we believe that he came to save the world, and not only those to whom he appeared on earth, or those to whom the word of the Gospel should be preached. But if it is *Christ* who will be the Judge, our whole conception of that judgement must conform itself to what we know of Christ. "God sent not his Son into the world to judge the world, but that the world through him might be saved."[23] If the purpose of Christ's coming had been to render unto all men according to their works, we might echo the disciples' exclamation: "Who then can be saved?"[24] The judgement of God is the offer of forgiveness to sinners, and to stand before the judgement-seat of Christ can be nothing else but to be confronted as a sinner with the aweful holiness of the love of God. On the issue of that dread confrontation the Creed is properly silent. But the question to all must be the same. "Do you plead guilty or not guilty? Are you ready to be judged according to your deeds, or will you see yourself as you are, see yourself as God sees you—and pass through the consuming fire of God's forgiveness?"

REFERENCES

1. Rom. 8.24f.
2. Rom. 1.4.
3. Mark 14.25; Matt. 26.29 adds "with you"—rightly interpreting the saying.
4. Dr J. A. T. Robinson (*Jesus and His Coming*) believes that Jesus spoke of his future "vindication" but *not* of his "coming again", and that the form of the Advent hope which appears in full

bloom so early as in 1 Thess. can be shown to have had other origins. But Robinson himself, who prefers to describe the eschatology of the New Testament as "inaugurated" rather than "realized", admits the implication of a future "consummation" to which Christians must look forward. The life of the Church on earth is to be lived "until . . ."—and why not "until he come"?

5. E.g. in Phil. 1.26 it is Paul's "coming"; in Phil. 2.12 it is his "presence".
6. Fison, *The Christian Hope*, pp. 173, 176.
7. 2 Tim. 4.1,8.
8. 1 Cor. 13.12.
9. Cf. his hymn *Adoro te devote*.
10. Acts 10.42; 17.31.
11. 2 Cor. 5.10; in Rom. 14.10 the better text has "God's judgement-seat".
12. Cf. Enoch 62.2,3,5 with Matt. 25.31.
13. E.g. Jer. 22.15f.
14. Gen. 18.25.
15. Ps. 9.16; 105.7.
16. Isa. 46.13; 51.5.
17. John 9.39; 5.22; 3.19f.
18. 1 John 4.17.
19. John 15.4f.,9f.
20. Heb. 10.26f.
21. Matt. 7.22f.
22. 1 Cor. 3.13
23. John 3.17.
24. Mark 10.26.

CHAPTER 21

And I look for the Resurrection of the dead, And the Life of the world to come

THE story of the End, as it appears all through the New Testament, is no new creation of the Christian Gospel. It was the outcome and expression of Hebrew faith in the Kingdom of the living God. The "coming" of God's Kingdom is the manifest realization of his righteous ordering of the world; and that realization must take effect in a final, a "Last" Judgement, which will sum up and fulfil all the "judgements" of God in the history of mankind. Such a final judgement must be a judgement of *all*, from which the dead can no more be excluded than the living. As Jesus said, the men of ancient Niniveh who repented at the preaching of Jonah will "rise up" (that is, be resurrected) "in the judgement together with this unbelieving generation, and condemn it".[1]

A. THE TEACHING OF THE NEW TESTAMENT

That saying implies a resurrection that is universal, not confined to the righteous: a general resurrection is the postulate of a Last Judgement, if that judgement is really and not only symbolically "to come". There is, however, only one text in the New Testament which states this quite explicitly, and that is a text in the Gospel which is often supposed to substitute a present for a future judgement. "The hour is coming, in which all that are in the graves shall hear the voice of the Son of Man, and shall come forth: they that have done good into the resurrection of life, and they that have done evil into the resurrection of judgement."[2] In one place St Paul says that the God who raised Jesus from the dead will bring to life the mortal bodies of Christians "through the Spirit that dwelleth in them".[3] It is the gift of the Spirit that encourages the hope of resurrection; and one might infer that only those in whom the Spirit is now dwelling will rise again. Elsewhere, however, St Paul seems to speak of the judgement as universal: "everyone" will be requited according to his actions in the body, whether good or evil. Probably, like the writer of the Fourth Gospel, he thinks of the resurrection through the operation of the Spirit as being the only true "resurrection of life".

Two passages are of fundamental importance for the New Testament doctrine of the Resurrection of the dead; and in neither of them is there any reference to judgement. In each of them the doctrine is being asserted and expounded against objections raised by doubters.

(1) *Mark 12, 18–27*. The Sadducees say that there is no resurrection, because they do not find it foretold in the Law of Moses, which they believed to hold everything "necessary to salvation", and because they assume that the story of apocalyptic, of the raising of the dead from their graves in the same bodily form in which they lived and acted, is to be taken *au pied de la lettre*. If men's bodies are to be restored to life, what purpose will those bodies serve? Presumably, the same as that for which they have been given in this present life. But that leads to absurdities when we consider the changing personal relationships for which the divine Law itself prescribes that our bodily functions are to be used. "Whose wife shall she be of the seven? for they all had her to wife."

The answer of Jesus is both defence and counter-attack. a. The "story" which the Sadducees misuse is not a picture of earthly life begun over again, but a profession of faith in the creative power of God. He who made us for this life on earth can remake us for another life in which the changing circumstances of earth, where one generation succeeds another, will have no place. Men will be "as the angels", neither marrying nor being given in marriage. b. And as for the revelation in the Law, the Pentateuch itself to which the Sadducees appeal contains words which assure us that God will never abandon those whose God he has promised to be: the lives of every generation of his people are safe in his hands. The God of Abraham, Isaac, and Jacob is not the God of the dead.

(2) *1 Cor. 15*. St Paul also is confronted by some who say that there is no resurrection. But these doubters are not unbelieving Sadducees, but actually members of a Christian Church. They can hardly have denied, as the Sadducees did, the existence of *any* life after death. Probably they were holding to the Greek conception of an immortality of the soul, conferred by initiation into the Christian "mystery", and giving final release from the body which is the

soul's prison. But to speak of resurrection is to speak of restoration to bodily life; and this to the Corinthian doubters is neither conceivable nor desirable.

St Paul's answer, like that of Christ, is twofold; and there is a remarkable correspondence between the two parts of his answer and the two parts of Christ's answer to the Sadducees.

a. As Christ appealed to the Book of the Law which was God's word for his questioners, so Paul appeals to the Gospel which the Corinthians have themselves "received", by which they "stand", and through which they are saved. The very faith to which the doubters themselves have been converted rests entirely upon the resurrection of Jesus, apart from which there would have been no ground for the Apostolic preaching of him as the Christ who has delivered us from the power of sin. But the resurrection of Jesus was not an escape of soul from body: it was the raising up of one who died and was buried. You cannot at the same time affirm the resurrection of Christ and deny the possibility of resurrection of those for whom he died.

b. In the second part of his answer, St Paul dismisses the presuppositions of the Corinthian "spiritualists", as Christ had dismissed the crude materialism by which the Sadducees would reduce the thought of a resurrection body to absurdities. Christian faith does not divide or oppose body and soul as corruptible and incorruptible parts of a hybrid nature. The *whole* man dies, as the whole Christ died, and the whole man will be raised "in Christ" to life. Like the Sadducees, the Corinthian doubters show that they "have not the knowledge of God" or of the power of his life-giving Spirit. The natural processes of growth are enough to show us that in God's world a living organism can be transmuted from one form of existence into another quite unlike the first. And the same power of God which changes seed into plant can give to the human body he has made a form of existence altogether new. It is indeed true that the perishable "flesh and blood" of our life here on earth cannot enter into the eternal Kingdom of God. We must all pass through the same change through which the flesh and blood of Christ passed. But we may believe that God is able to work in us the miracle which he has wrought in Christ.

(3) There is, however, another passage in which St Paul speaks of death and what follows it in terms which to some New Testament scholars have seemed inconsistent with the Hebrew belief in a

resurrection of the body: they imply rather, it is said, something much nearer to that Greek conception of an immortality of the soul which we have just attributed to the Corinthian doubters. This passage occurs in the fifth chapter of the Second Epistle to the Corinthians—which makes the inconsistency (if there is one) the more surprising. In the previous chapter, St Paul has spoken of the "inner" and the "outer" man—the outer man which "bears about the dying of Christ" and is menaced by decay and dissolution, and the inner man which is being continually renewed by the power of the Spirit. The "earthy tabernacle" may be broken up in death before Christ comes again; but whether that is to befall us or not, we are sure of "the house not made with hands" with which we shall be clothed in heaven, and our natural shrinking from death as a state of "nakedness" may comfort itself with the thought that to die is in truth to "go home" to Christ.

St Paul speaks here, it is true, of a "migration out of the body" for those who may die before Christ comes again. But it is difficult to suppose that he has really abandoned the beliefs he held when he wrote 1 Cor. 15. He knew then that Christians have died and will die before the day when Christ will appear in glory and *all* will be "changed". He thought of them as "asleep", yet asleep "in Christ" —and that is not a very different thought from the "going home" to Christ of which he speaks in the later Epistle. On the other hand, the desire "not to be unclothed, but to be clothed upon" *is* very different from the Greek desire to cast off the encumbrance of the body altogether. And later still in the Epistle to the Philippians he can face his own death as a "departure to be with Christ" and still look forward to the day when the Saviour will come from heaven and change these poor bodies of ours so that they may share the glory of his own—"according to the working of his power to subdue all things to himself".[5] That echoes the words with which he had written in 1 Cor. 15 of Christ's final victory over all the powers of this world, including the "last enemy" which is Death. Resurrection still means for him what it had always meant.

B. THE AFFIRMATIONS OF THE CREED

We have now to consider in the light of this New Testament teaching the two final statements of the Creed. We must ask: (1) What is the significance for us of the belief in a "resurrection of the dead"? (2) What are the grounds of the Christian belief in a life to come? (3) To what kind of life are we led to look forward?

(1) *The Resurrection of the dead.* a. The words of the Creed are those most often used in the New Testament. Nearly all early Creeds, however, had "the resurrection of the flesh" (*sarkos anastasis* or *carnis resurrectio*); and this is the original language of the Apostles' Creed, where "body" was substituted for "flesh" in the English Prayer Book at the Reformation. The New Testament does not speak of a resurrection of the flesh; but the use of the word "flesh" here in the Creeds of the second and third centuries meant a rejection of the Gnostic vilification of the material world as determined as the rejection of Arianism in the fourth century by the term *homo-ousios*. That which God has made, and that which he will clothe with new glory in the End, cannot be evil: the Christian salvation is *not* deliverance from the flesh, but deliverance *of* the flesh from its weakness and fragility as well as of the soul from the power of sin.

It is still important to remind ourselves that there is nothing Christian in the idea that the material creation must be annihilated before God can be "all in all".[6] Indeed, if God is Creator of the material world, and the heavens declare his glory, we must needs believe that his Spirit is not only present but expressed in what is outward and visible. We have no reason to regard a sacramental universe as a *pis-aller* or a temporary expedient. On the contrary, the dualistic separation and opposition of matter and spirit has become for us more difficult to maintain than ever. Our bodies are the means by which we live and act and are known to one another as persons, and a personal existence entirely divorced from material conditions is much less conceivable for us than a transformation of those conditions such as would not involve the abolition of them. The Biblical picture of a new heaven and a new earth, a new creation, speaks to us today more meaningfully than one of the total destruction of space and time and all that is therein.

b. The hope of a resurrection began, we remember, as the hope that in the Day of the Lord, when the cause of righteousness is vindicated, the individual who has died in the service of righteousness will have his share in the vindication. But the New Age itself, to which the resurrection will be the entry, is much more than the rendering of a due reward to all men according to their deeds. It is the establishment of God's Kingdom, the final manifestation of his sovereignty over *all*. The Resurrection therefore is the setting of the individual in his place in the universal community of the people of God; and that is why it can only be represented as taking place in the Last Day, the *Telos* in which the purpose of history is fulfilled.

What then for the individual is the significance of *death*? To speak of resurrection at least implies that death is real: we do not only "seem in the sight of the unwise to die;"[7] for there is nothing in us that is immortal in its own right, nothing at all that death cannot touch. Still, death might have been imagined as a kind of dreamless sleep, of which the sleeper knows nothing till he is awakened: for him, the next moment after death might be resurrection. But the words of St Paul about departing to be with Christ, and Christ's own promise on the Cross to the penitent thief,[8] have encouraged the Church in teaching its members to look forward not only to resurrection but to an "intermediate state", which though really "out of the body" will either be an anticipation of heavenly bliss or a further stage in the preparation of the soul for the life to come. Obviously, this second picture gives a comfort to the individual facing death, and still more to those whom he leaves behind, which must be lacking in the simple expectation of resurrection "in the End". But it is not easy to *combine* with that expectation; for if I can be with Christ without my body, to what purpose will be the new body when the End comes? At any rate, what is affirmed in the Creed is no doctrine of what happens when we die, but the Resurrection of the dead. And that may properly warn us against preoccupation with the "intermediate state" of the individual, rather than with the Day when God's Kingdom will be revealed "in his whole creation".

(2) *The Ground of Belief.* a. Like all else in our "story" of the Last Things, our belief in the Life of the world (or Age) to come must have its ground in what belongs to our present experience. This Christian belief is a different thing from the belief in a natural immortality of the soul which can be held by a non-Christian and even by an atheist. We do not try to prove that the soul cannot cease to exist because of something that is inherent in its nature— as Plato did in the most famous and moving of all his *Dialogues*, the "Last Discourse" of Socrates with his friends in the condemned cell.[9] We believe in the life to come, not because man is what he is, but because God is what he is. That in effect was how Jesus answered the Sadducees. If it is the will of God to be our God, to be the God of each one of us, then God must care for the human beings he has made, and cannot suffer them to perish. So, in the

"logic of hope" which John Baillie sets out in his book *And the Life Everlasting*,[10] the major premise is simply the love of God which we find revealed in Christ—the love which assures us that all the things that matter are safe in God's hands. The minor premise is our conviction that nothing matters more than the human person, that the individual human being embodies a value which is bound up with his *existence*, and must disappear with his disappearance. We may doubt either the creation and preservation of the world by absolute Goodness, or the value of human personality; but unless we doubt one of these two things, we are bound to draw the inference that death cannot separate us from the love of God. And indeed if the major premise be granted, it is not easy to deny the minor; for that which God loves must be precious in his sight.

b. For St Paul, as we saw, the Resurrection was more than a hope for the future. The hope, which he shared with his brother Pharisees, was fortified by the assured fact of the resurrection of Christ; and Christ's resurrection was the demonstration of God's righteousness, the proof that God would not suffer his holy One to see corruption. But if Christ rose again *because* he was obedient unto death, *because* he offered himself as a sacrifice unto God, can we draw from the fact of Christ's resurrection any wider inference than that which St Paul draws, namely, that those who share in Christ's death will share also in his risen life?[11] And do the words of Jesus carry us any further? Is the God of Abraham, Isaac, and Jacob also the God of those who worship idols? In other words, what is our ground for expecting the resurrection of those who are *not* "in Christ"?

The traditional answer has been just the picture of the Great Divide: "they that have done good, unto the resurrection of life, and they that have done evil, unto the resurrection of judgement".[12] But does the "logic of hope" permit the drawing of a line between the persons of the "righteous" and the persons of the "wicked", so that the value-sign is positive for all on this side and negative for all on that? Obviously, *we* can draw no such line: but can—or rather, does—God draw it? Surely, if the Gospel is the good news of God's coming to save men from their sins, and if all men are sinners, we cannot suppose that the love of God is limited by the extent of sinfulness in the sinner. He will have all men to be saved and come to the knowledge of the truth.[13] What we do not and cannot know is whether all men will accept their salvation—if salvation means knowing the truth about themselves as well as

H

about God. But the Resurrection of the dead will bring the possibility of that knowledge to all.

(3) *The Life of the world to come.* Our last question may be put thus: Can we draw from our present experience any inference which could enable us to describe or imagine that life—the life of which we believe that the Last Day will be the beginning? And I think that the answer to this question must be No—and for good reasons.

So long as heaven is conceived as a compensation for the failures and the ills of earth, the picture of it we frame is bound to be eudaemonistic—painted, that is, in the colours of *happiness,* relief from the "miseries of this sinful world".[14] Heaven, we say, will be a state of bliss; and everyone will think of it in terms of those experiences in his own earthly life which have come nearest to giving him complete satisfaction. Such pictures, of course, will vary indefinitely: they may take their key from moments of rest, of activity, of thought, of contemplation; but always we shall be constructing for ourselves our own heaven. This, we say, is what heaven would be for me; and when we hear of another man's dream of it, we say, If it is going to be like that, it is no place for me!—And so long as we are—no doubt unconsciously—prescribing to God the kind of heaven he must provide for us if we are to welcome the prospect of it, we are betraying our unfitness for the only possible heaven, which is a life of which God and not ourselves will be the centre. (Dante made no mistake about that!) For this reason I doubt the value of *any* speculation about the quality of eternal life—e.g. whether its eternity is altogether timeless or retains a certain durational character. The superiority of the traditional conception of the heavenly life as the vision of God seems to lie just here. For to see God as he is must be to lose all interest in ourselves, to desire nothing but to give ourselves to him, as he has given himself to us, and in such ways as he himself will find for us.

REFERENCES

1. Matt. 12.41.
2. John 5.28f.
3. Rom. 8.10f.
4. 2 Cor. 5.10.
5. Phil. 1.23; 3.20f.

6. 1 Cor. 15.28.
7. Wis. 3.2; the writer in fact thinks more as a Greek than as a Hebrew.
8. Phil. 1.23; Luke 23.43.
9. Plato, *Phaedo*, cc. xli–lvi.
10. J. Baillie, *And the Life Everlasting*, c. vi.
11. Rom. 6.5; 8.11.
12. John 5.28f.
13. 1 Tim. 2.4.
14. Prayer in the Burial Service (Book of Common Prayer).

CHAPTER 22

The Doctrine of the Trinity

WE have already remarked that neither the Apostles' Creed nor the Nicene presents us with anything that can be called a doctrine of the Trinity. The Apostles' Creed uses the word "God" only of the Father: the Nicene Creed strongly asserts the Godhead of the Son, and by implication ascribes Godhead also to the Holy Spirit, "who with the Father and the Son together is worshipped and glorified"—though without explicitly naming the Spirit as God. Only in the Athanasian Creed do we find a full statement of the doctrine that in the one substance of Godhead there are three Persons; and the Athanasian Creed cannot claim the ecumenical authority of the Nicene.

It might therefore be argued that the doctrine of the Trinity as there set forth is not an essential part of the Christian faith, but a theological construction from the data of that faith, which may or may not be justifiable in itself, but is of importance only to those whose business it is to think clearly about theology, and in any case can claim no final validity. The tendency at the present time, however, is rather to see in this doctrine the central tenet of Christianity, the doctrine of God on which everything else depends: so that Christian theology in order to be true to itself ought always to grow out of and be consciously related to the specific belief about the nature of God which this doctrine is designed to safeguard and convey.

It would certainly be foolish to maintain that the Christian life of the ordinary man or woman will be injured or impeded by a defective intellectual grasp of Trinitarian doctrine. It is more difficult still to hold with the Athanasian Creed that correct thinking about the Trinity is necessary or even of primary importance for everyone who seeks salvation. But if this is really the least inadequate form in which to express our faith that God has given himself to men in Jesus Christ, then we ought to do what we can to make the doctrine meaningful to any Christian who desires to understand that which he has believed.

Accordingly, we shall bring our commentary on the Creed to an end by considering, first, whether we may rightly claim that the "orthodox" doctrine of the Trinity has its roots in the New Testament, and that the process of development which led to its dogmatic formulation in the fourth century was in fact governed by a true sense of what is vital to the Christian faith; and by passing in the second place from what the Catholic doctrine asserts to the different ways in which theologians both ancient and modern have attempted to illustrate and elucidate that doctrine, or to draw out its implications.

1. *The Faith of the New Testament*

It can hardly be doubted that in the faith of the New Testament the confession that "Jesus is Lord" is central, common to all the varying types of teaching to be found in Epistle, Gospel, or Apocalypse. Nor will it be disputed that every writer of the New Testament believes himself to speak from within the faith of the Old, to be an Israelite indeed. For the Greek-speaking Jew, *Kurios*, Lord, was the holy Name of God: his daily profession of faith was in the words of Deuteronomy: "Hear, O Israel: the Lord thy God is one Lord."[1] And that was quite unaffected by the fact that the same word *Kurios* was used in ordinary speech as a form of respectful address. "Sir (*Kurie*), thou hast nothing to draw with", says the woman of Samaria at the well.[2] Evidently, *Kurios Iésous* did not and could not mean for the Christian convert a sheer identification of the man of Nazareth with Jehovah; but neither did it or could it mean the ascription to Jesus of a Lordship, a sovereignty, that was either independent or secondary. What it did mean was that this man, whom Pilate had crucified and whom God had raised from the dead, was the proper object of *worship*, of a religious devotion not different in kind from the reverence and trust due from every devout Israelite to the God of his fathers. The astonishing thing is that no New Testament writer appears to feel that his allegiance and devotion to Christ involves any disloyalty to the one God, any setting up of Lord beside Lord: there is no hint of rivalry between the Lord Jesus and the Lord Jehovah. The Lord God is still one Lord. Jesus is not Jehovah, but the Lordship ascribed to him is none other than the unique Lordship of the God of Israel; so that the word of God to Isaiah—"Unto me every knee shall bow"—is truly fulfilled when "every tongue confesses that Jesus is Lord".[3] For in Jesus Christ the one God has revealed himself as Lord and Saviour. Jesus bears the supreme authority of God.

What has made it possible for this revelation to be received, this authority acknowledged? St Paul's answer—and it is an answer which is not peculiarly Pauline—is that no man can say, "Jesus is Lord", but by the Holy Spirit.[4] In the Old Testament, the Spirit is the power of Jehovah present and working in chosen men. The Spirit is not something different from God, certainly not something less than God: it is God manifesting himself in a special way—the way of indwelling or (as we call it) immanence. In the New Testament, the Spirit is this same power of God immanent, present in Jesus the Messiah and imparted by him to his chosen people, to possess and unite them to himself. The difference from the Old Testament is simply that now the indwelling power of God is inseparable from the confession of Jesus as the Christ. The Spirit is not the same as the risen and exalted Jesus; but the Spirit's presence in the whole body of believers replaces the outward and visible presence of Jesus, and supplies all—indeed more than all—the guidance and strength which outward presence gave or could give. In fact, the belief that what enables us to confess Jesus as Lord and to follow him in all godliness of living is nothing less than the real presence of God within us—this belief binds up the Christian doctrine of Grace with the doctrine of the Godhead of the Holy Spirit. Christian life is wholly dependent upon the power of the Spirit, because the Spirit is the bearer of the Lordship of Jesus.

"What the doctrine of the Trinity really asserts is that it is God's very nature not only to create finite persons whom he could love, and to reveal and impart himself to them, even to the point of Incarnation (through his eternal Word), but also to extend this indwelling to those men who fail to obey him, doing in them what they could not do themselves, supplying to them the obedience which he requires them to render (through his Holy Spirit)."[5] The God in whom Christians believe is the God who gives what he commands; because the love of God which is the first and great commandment is poured out in our hearts through the Holy Spirit which is *given* to us.[6]

2. *The development of doctrine*

"So the Father is Lord, the Son Lord, and the Holy Ghost Lord: and yet there are not three Lords, but one Lord." In that sentence of the Athanasian Creed there is nothing but what can claim (in the words of Article VIII) "certain warrant of Holy Scripture". But it falls short of the doctrine of three Persons in one Substance, distinguished as Persons by their differing relations to one another. That doctrine, with its highly technical terms, emerged from the rejection of rival forms of teaching which were professedly designed to maintain the Biblical faith in the unity of God.

On one side was the Sabellian theory of a Trinity which is not eternal but temporal—no more than the manifestation of the one God in the historic order of the world, under the successive forms and by the successive actions of Christ and the Spirit. This was a theory which removed all offence to rational comprehension—as every variety of Unitarianism may claim to do. But it ran contrary to the fundamental Christian understanding of man's reconciliation to God in Christ. That reconciliation is a reality, not because God has shown us in Christ's human life of obedient sonship a pattern for our own living as children of the Father in heaven, but because the possibility for us of becoming our Father's sons is given to us by union with Christ; and union with Christ is union with one whose Sonship to God is no transient human relationship but an eternal fact of the divine nature. It is but putting the same thing in other words to say that the revelation of God in Christ is a saving revelation because it reveals God as he truly is: God in his eternal being is not *different* from God as he is made known to us in the Gospel.

Opposed to Sabellianism was the Arian theory in its various forms, more acceptable to the imperfectly Christianized mind of the Greek, because it frankly presented divinity as a matter of degree. Absolute, supreme Godhead belongs only to the changeless and eternal being of the Father: Son and Spirit are subordinate and minor deities, brought into existence to serve the Father's purpose in creation and redemption. In effect, the Arians were betraying the Biblical monotheism which they professed to defend; for the worship which they allowed to Christ was idolatry if Christ were less than very God. But they were betraying at the same time (as Athanasius clearly saw) the Biblical faith that salvation belongeth unto God. If to be saved is to have eternal life, that is a gift which cannot come to us from one who does not in his own right possess the eternal life he is to impart.[7]

3. *The Formulation*

We may conclude that the Church's rejection of both Sabellian and Arian Trinities was governed by a true appreciation of the faith of the New Testament. The final decision upon the doctrinal dispute—the dogma of the Trinity—was virtually contained in the application of the single (non-Biblical) word *homo-ousios*, "of one substance", first at Nicaea in A.D. 325 to God the Son and later at Constantinople in A.D. 381–2 to the whole Trinity. The further elaboration of the doctrine by Greek theologians (especially St Basil and the two Gregories of Nyssa and Nazianzus) was the working out of the implications of the dogma. Obviously, the emphasis of the dogma itself is upon the unity of God: what the *homo-ousios* asserts is not the distinction of the Persons but the one-ness of being. But God reveals his being in his works. The acts of God as Creator and Saviour, all that he *does*, are the expression of what he *is*: the one-ness of his being implies the one-ness of his operation. If then in each Person of the Trinity there is the fullness of God's being, there can be no act of God that is not the act of all three Persons. If we are to associate creation with the Father, redemption with the Son, and sanctification with the Spirit, it cannot be in any such way as to imply that creation, redemption, and sanctification have separate agents in the three Persons of the Godhead. Similarly, the doctrine of the Trinity cannot *mean* that God is power, wisdom, and love—or any other triad of attributes; for that would imply that in none of the three Persons is the whole Deity present. Father, Son, and Spirit are not *parts* of God.

How then are we to know that Father, Son, and Spirit are not simply three names of one and the same divine being? The answer rests upon our conviction that if God has revealed himself under these three names, the names cannot be without signification: they must disclose to us a reality and not a mere appearance. If we will begin by accepting the historic revelation, what the Fathers used to call the "economy" or dispensation of God's dealing with the world, we can be sure that we are on the way to knowing God as he really is: the "economic" Trinity, manifested in the great divine acts of Creation, Incarnation, and Pentecost, points us to the "essential" Trinity wherein the Three are gathered together in One.

Father and Son are terms of a human relationship. What marks the Sonship of the incarnate Christ according to the New Testament is a relation of absolute *dependence*. He reveals the Father by doing in all things the Father's will. His work is the work of the Father: in him the Father speaks the Word which is divine action. In him we see, as the Epistle to the Hebrews puts it, the radiance of the Father's glory and the imprint of the Father's being.[8] And this relationship of Christ incarnate to the Father who "sent" him points us back to a real distinction of relationship on the eternal plane between Original and Reproduction: the Son is *from* the Father, not the Father from the Son.

Spirit is not so plainly a term of relationship as Father and Son. But in the Bible the word Spirit keeps something of its literal meaning. Spirit is breath; and breath is the breath of life which goes forth from the living body, as well as the breath of speech which carries the word from speaker to hearer. Spirit thus connotes the source or origin from which it "proceeds"; and the divine Spirit is the outgoing and active power of the living and speaking God. So in the New Testament the Holy Spirit is never separable from his origin or independent of it; but he has this relation of dependence upon the divine Son as well as upon the divine Father. Whether we say that the Spirit proceeds from Father and Son, or from Father through Son, the relationship is different from that of the Son to the Father, because it has this double reference. The Spirit like the Son is "sent", but the sending of the Spirit presupposes the sending of the Son. The mission of the Son is to reveal the Father: the mission of the Spirit is to create in man the response to this revelation—the response of true sonship to fatherly love.

And these distinct missions of Son and Spirit cannot be accidental. They correspond in the temporal "economy" or dispensation of the one God's revealing and redeeming activity to the eternal distinction of relations within the "essential" Trinity. The differing relations in which Son and Spirit stand to the one indivisible operation of God correspond to the differing relations which belong to them in the eternal being of God. That justifies our thought, not in dividing the work of God between the Persons of the Trinity, but in associating the different aspects in which we contemplate the work of God with Father, Son, or Spirit in particular—as these aspects are presented to us in Scripture. There is an evident correspondence between the work of creation and the Person of the Father as the original fount or source of Deity; between the work of revealing or representing the Father to men, and the Person of the Son who is the Father's image or self-expression; between the work of uniting men to God by opening their hearts to receive God's gift of himself, and the Person of the Spirit in whom Father gives himself to Son and Son to Father, so that there is perfect union and communion between them.

4. *The Language of Trinitarian doctrine*

The key-word in the technical language of orthodoxy, *homo-ousios*, means then that there are not three Gods but one God; and it follows that all that God *does* to the world of which he is Maker and Saviour is the operation of this one God. "The works of the Trinity, directed outwards from itself, are undivided."[9] This is because the Trinity itself is indivisible: the Father is *in* the Son and the Spirit, the Son is *in* the Father and the Spirit, the Spirit is *in* the Father and the Son. The Greek word *perichoresis* and the Latin *circumincessio* were used in classical theology to express, by the figure of the ring or circle which returns upon itself, this perfect inter-permeation or communion of the divine Persons, alike in being and in operation. Yet, as we have just seen, because the Persons are differently related to one another in their being, they are differently related in their operation; so that we can rightly distinguish, within the one work of God, what speaks to us more especially of one or other of the Persons. This is the principle known as "appropriation", safeguarded by that of *perichoresis*, and imposed upon us by the language of Scripture and the tradition of Christian worship and devotion.

Finally, we have to remind ourselves that the word "Person" itself, indispensable as it is for our discourse about the Three-in-Oneness of God, is a technical term. When the Greek theologians looked for the least unsuitable word to use, not of the one being, essence, or substance of Godhead, but of that which alike in Father, Son, and Spirit is the bearer of the differing relations, they chose the word *hypostasis*—which means simply the permanently existing subject which "underlies" or "supports" all predicates, all that can truly be attributed to it. *Hypostasis* is not equivalent to our word "person", for it does not of itself connote a thinking and acting individual: not every *hypostasis* is a person, though every person is a *hypostasis*. The Latin *persona*, on the other hand, is more specific in meaning than *hypostasis*, and in ordinary use is only applicable to human beings; but it denotes the individual, not as the bearer of "personality" in our sense of the word, but in his relation to society, as the bearer of rights or functions. So neither the Greek nor the Latin word carried with it when applied to the divine Trinity the implication of an individual centre of conscious life and independent activity.

Now the terms "father" and "son" on the human level obviously do imply separate and self-conscious personality in our sense of the word. But the theologians of the ancient Church were well aware that these terms can only be used of God by way of symbol, parable, or analogy. Moreover, the fact that the Son himself bears in Scripture the title of Word of God, and the consequent development of Christology by way of the *Logos*-doctrine, served as a check upon the personal symbolism of Father and Son. Spirit, on the other hand, is in Greek a neuter noun, and the Spirit in the New Testament is constantly described as "given" to men, while men are "filled" with the Spirit—phrases which would not naturally be used of a person. The fact is that when fourth-century theologians spoke of the *hypostaseis* or *personae* of the Godhead, they did not mean what we mean when we think (as we must) of all God's dealings with us as those of person with persons. That which justifies our thinking and speaking of God as "personal" is something that belongs to the substance or essential being of Godhead as such, and must therefore belong equally and in the same sense to Father, Son, and Spirit. When St Augustine came to consider the use of the word *persona* in the theology of the Trinity—a word which after all was no more Scriptural than *homo-ousios*—he frankly admitted that to speak of God as *una persona* would have been no less appropriate than to speak of him as *tres personae*. But some word we must have wherewith to answer the question *Quid tres?* —"What are these three?" And because of the poverty of our human language we say that the three are Persons—*non ut illud diceretur, sed ne taceretur*, "not because that was what we wanted to say, but so as not to be reduced to silence".[10] We cannot now substitute a better word, even if one were certainly available. We must continue to pray, "O holy, blessed, and glorious Trinity, three Persons and one God, have mercy upon us". And perhaps it is more important that we should think of the Holy Spirit dwelling within us as a "person"—a person who can be "grieved"[11] by our faithlessness—than that we should be over-careful to insist that the language we use does not mean what it says.

REFERENCES

1. Deut. 6.4.
2. John 4.11.
3. Phil. 2.10f.
4. 1 Cor. 12.3; cf. Mark 13.11; John 15.26f.
5. D. M. Baillie, *God was in Christ*, p. 122.
6. Rom. 5.5.
7. The substance and most of the wording of the preceding two sections are taken from my article "Bible and Dogma" which appeared in *The Church Quarterly Review* for April–July 1958.
8. Heb. 1.3.
9. *Opera Trinitatis ad extra indivisa sunt* was the ancient rule, put by the Schoolmen in the form *omnia in divinis sunt unum, ubi non obviat relationis oppositio*.
10. Augustine, *De Trinitate*, VII. 11; V. 10.
11. Eph. 4.30; Isa. 63.10

CHAPTER 23

Trinitarian Theology

G REGORY of Nyssa began the handbook of Christian instruction, which he wrote for the use of catechists towards the end of the fourth century, by observing that the Christian doctrine of God proceeds by a *via media* between the Jewish belief in a God whose personal being is unitary or single and the Greek belief in Gods many.[1] He implies that Greek religion did in fact prepare men's minds for the conception of plurality in unity. We are not accustomed nowadays to see any such virtue in polytheism. But the early history of Trinitarian theology is still sometimes presented as a wavering passage between the apparent contradictions of one-ness and three-ness, inclining at one time to maintain the divine unity at the expense of the real distinction of Father, Son, and Spirit, and at another to distinguish the existences of the three divine Persons at the expense of their real unity: the final result being a sort of irrational compromise between Unitarianism and Tritheism.

All modern theology takes the Biblical revelation as its starting-point; but instead of arguing, as the Fathers did, from particular selected texts of Scripture, it endeavours rather to determine the significance of the revelation as it was received and reflected in Christian experience and Christian devotion. Yet it is perhaps inevitable that the same diverging tendencies should still show themselves, and that some should take the one-ness of God for granted and make their approach thence to the mystery of the three-ness, while others begin with the three-ness as the primary and distinctive datum of Christian faith and life, and thence proceed to consider how we may best conceive the mystery of the one-ness. A notable contemporary example of the latter tendency is to be found in Professor Leonard Hodgson's Croall Lectures on *The Doctrine of the Trinity*: the former is represented by the first volume of Karl Barth's *Church Dogmatics*, and the work of various writers who have followed his lead.

1. *The Classical Theologies*

Hodgson claimed support for his way of thinking in the classical representatives of Patristic, Medieval, and Reformed doctrine.[2] But it can hardly be denied that both St Thomas Aquinas and Calvin were in this matter as in so many others followers of St Augustine; and it should be fairly clear that the aim of Augustine's Trinitarian speculation was to understand not how three Persons could be one God but how the one God could be three Persons. What Augustine assumes as starting point in Catholic doctrine is (in his own words) that "Father, Son, and Holy Spirit *mean* a divine unity in an inseparable equality of one and the same substance, and therefore are not three Gods but one God: *though* the Father has begotten the Son, and therefore he who is Father is not Son; the Son is begotten from the Father, and therefore he who is Son is not Father; the Holy Spirit is neither Father nor Son, but only Spirit of Father and of Son, himself co-equal with both and belonging to the unity of the Trinity".[3] When therefore Augustine devotes the second part of his great treatise on the Trinity to an endeavour to understand that faith of the Church which he has set out in the first part, he looks in the created world *not* for some plurality in which unity can be discerned—such as human society or the Christian Church —but for an evident and acknowledged unity in which there is nevertheless a really distinguishable plurality.

But he was not content with mere analogies, with "footprints" (*vestigia*) of the Trinity: he believed that if the invisible things of God (as St Paul says) are to be perceived through the things that are made, we must expect to see God's likeness most clearly in the highest of created things—the mind or reasonable soul of the man who is made in the image of God. The human spirit is an evident unity; yet it is not a bare or simple unity. And Augustine thinks it possible to trace in the self-conscious life of man a human trinity which even in its fallen condition preserves a likeness of the divine. A series of extremely acute psychological analyses leads him eventually to the threefold unity which he calls memory, understanding, and will.[4] We are aware of ourselves as existing, thinking, and willing. Since our existence is an existence in time, the being of the self is never a static object but always a continuously developing subject, whose character at any one moment is the product of its history. The experience of the living and growing human subject stores itself in the mind; and though the whole of it is never present to consciousness simultaneously, it forms the material of personality, in virtue of which I am the same person as I was yesterday or years ago. This enduring principle of self-identity is what Augustine calls the "memory of self"; and his account of it has striking resemblances to the modern notion of the unconscious or subconscious self. It is the necessary basis or ground of the second element in the life of the soul—the act of mental self-awareness which he calls "understanding" or apprehension—by which in this or that moment we realize our identity, become conscious of ourselves as being what we are, know ourselves as John Smith or William Jones in this particular situation. But, once more, this mental act can neither take place nor be maintained unless there is an *interest* in its object to bring attention to bear upon it. We are naturally and inevitably interested in ourselves, and this self-concern involves both feeling and willing: it is in fact a "love" of self, a self-affirmation, which is proper to humanity and in no way evil.

But the inter-connection of self-memory, self-apprehension, and self-willing is not that of three separable members of an organism. Each of the three is simply the Ego acting in a particular relation to itself. The reasonable soul is not a compound of faculties, but a single subject; and it is impossible to subordinate the act of knowing to the act of willing, the act of willing to the act of knowing, or either to the act of continuing existence in which the past is taken up by "memory" into the present. In the living unity of the personal being there are neither higher nor lower elements: the complexity of the human Ego is (in theological language) consubstantial. "Memory" is an image of the Father as being the fount or source of all self-knowledge; "understanding" is an image of the Son as the mental "word" or expression of the self, entirely correspondent to its source; "will" or "love" (synonymous terms for Augustine) is an image of the Spirit as the unifying dynamic which binds "memory" and "understanding" together.

Augustine is careful to note the points of difference between the image and its divine original. The human trinity can only reflect the divine in the measure possible for a creature, and it will do that only when under the working of grace its consciousness is centred not upon itself but upon God its Creator, when it knows itself and wills itself only *as* the image of God who made it.[5] Still, Augustine does not doubt that his leading thought is securely grounded in the Scriptural revelation: the elements of knowing and willing in the act of self-consciousness do really represent to us, albeit "obscurely, as in a mirror",[6] the eternal generation of the Son from the Father and the eternal procession of the Spirit from both Father and Son.

To be fair to St Augustine, it is necessary to remember that he had good reason for his deliberate attempt to think of the triune being of God "in himself", apart from all relation to the created world, and correspondingly of the soul "in itself", in an impossible isolation from its human environment. For he had himself become a Christian at the moment when the Church had just emerged from half a century of struggle between two rival theologies, both of which would have represented the Trinity in its Second and Third Persons as belonging not to the eternal reality of God, but to the dealings of the one God with his temporal creation. In fact, Augustine begins his *De Trinitate* with the data of the historic revelation as contained in Scripture; and only when he has sufficiently established the grounding of the Church's dogma in the story of creation and redemption, and dealt at length with the misconceptions of heresy, does he proceed to look for a way in which Reason may seek to understand what Authority has justified us in believing.

St Thomas's long treatise on the Trinity in the *Summa Theologica* is frankly modelled on Augustine, to whom he gives many more references than to Scripture—although of course the doctrine of the Trinity is for St Thomas *par excellence* a revealed doctrine.[7] He starts from the accepted principle that the Persons of the Trinity are distinguished by their relations of origin or derivation; and he proceeds at once to declare that these derivations or "processions" in the Godhead (he uses the word "procession" in a general as well as in a special sense) are two: one after the manner of knowing or understanding, and the other after the manner of will or love.[8] He discusses at length the applicability of our notions of relation and person to the divine being, and his conclusion is that the Persons of the Trinity are to be understood as "subsistent relations".[9] Fatherhood in God *is* God the Father, sonship *is* God the Son, "spiration" *is* God the Holy Spirit. The fact that he finds it necessary for theology to substitute an idea so difficult to conceive for the natural meaning of the word "person" is sufficient evidence that St Thomas is no less aware than Augustine that this natural meaning is unsatisfactory even as an analogy.

As for Calvin, whose treatment of the doctrine is very brief, he follows Augustine's statement of the Catholic dogma, but thinks it wiser not to make use of the psychological analogies drawn from the image of God in man. Yet he too is conscious of the inadequacy of the word "person", which he defends as having served like the *homo-ousios* to refute heresy. What he himself understands by "Person" in its theological reference is "a subsistence within the essential being of God, which as related to others is distinguished by an incommunicable property", i.e. a property peculiar to itself.[10] The definition is slightly different from St Thomas's, but there is not much in it to suggest the meaning which we attach to the word "person".

2. *"One in Three"*

Needless to say, Karl Barth's treatise on the Trinity is very different from St Augustine's or St Thomas's. He adheres closely to the orthodox formulation of the dogma as we have already described it. But he maintains that the doctrine is *grounded* in the very idea of Revelation itself—which for Barth is of course the saving revelation of God to man in Jesus Christ. For if God in Christ has revealed himself as the Lord, there must be a revealer, there must be a form in which the revelation is conveyed, and there must be an effect of the revelation in those to whom it has been given.[12] Here Barth is saying in his own way something which was very lucidly put fifty years before him by an Anglican theologian of the *Lux Mundi* school. R. C. Moberly, in the book *Atonement and Personality*, which well deserves its wide recognition as a classic, had suggested, in an important chapter on the doctrine of the Holy Spirit, an analogy for the triune nature of God in our own knowledge of personal life. A person exists in three ways: (1) as he really is in himself, invisible and inaccessible, but the ultimate source and spring of all that can be ascribed to him; (2) in his self-expression or utterance, his bodily presence, speech and action, through which he becomes directly known to his neighbours and friends; (3) in his working or operation, the total effect of him as seen in the *response* of his environment to his impact upon it, his way of dealing with it. None of these three "ways of being" can be excluded from a complete picture of what the person really *is*.[13] So Karl Barth says that Revelation requires its source in the "hidden God", its content in the incarnate Person, and the response which it effects in its human recipients. In Creation, Incarnation, and Pentecost, "God is God three times in a different way".[14] Barth thinks that though we can hardly now abandon the use of the traditional phrase "Persons of the Trinity", theology will do well to substitute the phrase "modes

of being"—though of course the "modes" are not temporary appearances as in Sabellian theory.[15] For the rest, Barth expounds his
doctrine of the "essential" Trinity in accordance with the principle
already set forth: namely, that God "in himself", in his eternal
being, can be no other than God as he has revealed himself. God is
revealed as our Maker, Lord, and Father; as the Son come to meet
us, the Word spoken to us in our estrangement from God; as the
Spirit who makes us free to accept and to return the love of God—
because each of these "ways of being God" corresponds to that
which God *is* "antecedently in himself", to his essential and eternal
being.

3. *"Three in One"*

Professor Hodgson too grounds the doctrine of the Trinity upon
the revelation given to us in the history of which the Bible is the
record. But he takes the essence of that revelation to be a way of life
—the life of Jesus Christ, seeking, finding, and doing the will of his
Father in the power of the Spirit by whom he was "led" or
"possessed".[16] We are called and enabled by union with Christ
and possession by his Spirit to share in that life, which is itself an
image or analogue of the eternal being of God. Hodgson finds that
the New Testament and the long experience of Christian devotion
both require us to think of each Person in the divine Trinity as
being "fully personal in the modern sense of the term".[17] Now of
course if personality in the modern sense of the term is the right
category for our human thought of God, each Person in the Godhead must be "personal" because each Person is God. But Hodgson
means, not that Father, Son, and Spirit are Persons because each
is God, but that each is personal because each severally is *a* person.
And this is certainly a departure from classical theology. Christian
doctrine and Christian devotion have always been at one in using
of each Person the personal pronouns "he" and "thou". But when
Hodgson says that "each is a he, none is an it",[18] this introduction
of the indefinite article marks the difference between his view and
that of the main Christian tradition, which has instinctively avoided
speaking of the Trinity by the plural pronoun "they", even when a
plural verb is inevitable. The original Latin of the Athanasian
Creed manages very skilfully to avoid the use even of a plural verb!

How then are we to conceive the divine unity? Hodgson argues
that the perplexities of historical Trinitarianism were caused by the

attempt to maintain the mathematical notion of unity in a sphere to which it is inappropriate.[19] Platonism had mathematics for its matriculation examination, and the mystical philosophy of the Neo-platonists found its God in the absolute One from which all differentiation, every hint of multiplicity, is excluded. But in the world of our experience it is just the pure undifferentiated unit of the mathematician which we nowhere discover. Alike in physics, biology, and art, all the unities of which we are able to speak are complex. And modern psychology confirms Augustine in his treatment of the human *psyche* as a complex unity. Human personality is one, in so far as its differing capacities or functions are integrated, made into a living whole in organized activity. So a properly revised conception of unity should enable us to think of the one-ness of God as (in Hodgson's words) "a dynamic unity actively unifying in the one Divine life the lives of the three Divine persons".[20]

4. *The Trinity of Love*

Now, in describing St Augustine's study of the human trinity, we used the phrase "unifying dynamic" in connection with his treatment of the element of will or love as that which unites the act of self-awareness to its source in the unconscious memory of self, and corresponds to the place of the Spirit in the divine Trinity. The Church of the New Testament found the power of the Spirit active above all in the creation of *koinonia*, fellowship—the unity of brotherly love which was the law of the New Covenant. Because there is one body and one Spirit, Christians must strive to keep the unity of the Spirit in the bond of peace:[21] they must clothe themselves above all things with the love which is the bond of perfectness, wholeness.[22] Augustine was not the first to suggest that the unifying power of the Spirit in the Church reflects the eternal relation of the Spirit in the Godhead to Father and Son, as the bond of their union in love. Already in the first part of his *De Trinitate* he applies to the Trinity itself the text of the Epistle to the Ephesians just quoted: the Spirit is the mutual gift of Father and Son by which they are joined together—"one loving that other who is from him, one loving that other from whom he is, and love itself". The Holy Spirit as Spirit of both Father and Son is "a kind of ineffable communion of Father and Son".[23]

We have previously taken the conception of "unifying power" as key to that doctrine of the Holy Spirit which may reasonably be derived from Scripture and Christian experience. The thought of the Spirit as the "bond of love" in God himself is familiar to us from Coffin's hymn:

> O Holy Spirit, Lord of grace,
>   Eternal fount of love,
> Inflame, we pray, our inmost hearts
>   With fire from heaven above.
> As thou in bond of love dost join
>   The Father and the Son,
> So fill us all with mutual love,
>   And knit our hearts in one.

St Augustine felt himself bound by the Scriptural revelation to hold that love belongs to the essence or "substance" of Godhead. He was only able, therefore, to identify love with the Spirit by way of "appropriation"[24]—in the same way that the Son is called in Scripture the Wisdom of God, though wisdom also must be accounted an essential attribute of Deity as such. He did indeed observe, in the course of his search for psychological trinities, that love as we know it requires the threefold existence of a loving subject (*amans*), a beloved object (*amatum*), and the relation of love (*amor*) between them; but he did not attempt to develop the argument that if God is love *eternally*, "in himself", and not only as Creator or Redeemer, the very being of God *must* be a Trinity. But this is an argument which has often been used in modern defence of Trinitarian doctrine. It goes back, in fact, to one of the most remarkable of early medieval writers on the Trinity— Richard of St Victor, a contemporary of St Bernard.[25]

Richard maintained that the plurality of Persons in the Godhead is a necessary implication of the divine nature as self-giving love. For the love which gives itself demands an other to whom it may be given and by whom it may be returned. But why should it demand a third? Richard has two answers to this question. First, the perfection of love will mean that the one to whom it is given must seek for another who will share its happiness; for the bliss of perfect love in the receiver of it cannot be selfish. Secondly, beside the love that is all giving and the love that is all responsive returning, there is also a love that both gives and responds. Now, according to the accepted doctrine of "relations of origin" within the Trinity, the Father is "from none", the Son is "from the Father alone", and the Spirit is "from the Father and the Son".[26]

We may therefore ascribe to the Father the love that is all gift, to the Son the love that is both gift and response (response to the Father, gift to the Spirit), and to the Spirit the love that is all response—in the divine being as in the human heart. Thus both the forms of love which we know on our human level—both the outflowing *Agapé* which gives itself, and the returning *Eros* which is evoked by the knowledge that "he first loved us"—find their place in Richard's Trinity of divine love.

Richard has taken up a hint in Augustine, and used it to construct a Trinitarian theology quite different from Augustine's. His analogy of love is clearly drawn from the social life and inter-communion of human persons. And this social analogy, though it can claim no support in the classical tradition, has commended itself to many theologians since the end of the nineteenth century. Its Scriptural ground is in the great prayer of Christ in the seventeenth chapter of St John's Gospel: "thou lovedst me before the foundation of the world . . . that the love wherewith thou hast loved me may be in them". Its attractiveness lies in the support it lends to our belief that the doctrine of the Trinity is no superfluous piece of theologizing, but an expression of what is most fundamental in the revelation of God in Christ. If love means a personal relationship, and if love is the very being of God, we cannot think of God as existing in unrelated loneliness, realizing himself only in the acts of creation and redemption. The glory of the love of God is a glory that belongs to the Father and to the Son and to the Holy Ghost: as it was in the beginning, is now, and ever shall be, world without end.

REFERENCES

1. Gregory of Nyssa, *Oratio Catechetica*, 3.
2. L. Hodgson, *The Doctrine of the Trinity*, Lecture VI.
3. Augustine, *De Trinitate*, I. 7.
4. Ibid., X, 17f., XIV. 11ff.
5. Ibid., XIV. 15ff.
6. Ibid., XVI. 14ff.; 1 Cor. 13.12.
7. *Summa Theologica*, I, q.27–43.
8. Ibid., q.27, a.5.
9. Ibid., q.29, a.3 and 4.
10. Calvin, *Instit.* I, 13.6.
11. Cf. p. 200f.

12. K. Barth, *Church Dogmatics*, I, 1 (E.T. *The Doctrine of the Word of God*), pp. 339–383.
13. R. C. Moberly, *Atonement and Personality*, c. viii, pp. 173ff.
14. K. Barth, op. cit., p. 353.
15. Ibid., pp. 407ff.
16. L. Hodgson, op. cit., pp. 41–55.
17. Ibid. pp. 155, 143.
18. Ibid., p. 140.
19. Ibid., pp. 89–103.
20. Ibid., pp. 95, 102.
21. Eph. 4.3f.
22. Col. 3.14.
23. Augustine, *De Trinitate*, VI. 7; V. 12.
24. Cf. p. 202.
25. His works are in Migne, *Patrologia Latina*, Vol. 196.
26. See the Athanasian Creed.

Index of References

OLD TESTAMENT

OTHER REFERENCES